"Why can't we have a normal relationship?"

"I hate this game-playing and deception. Nothing's fun anymore," Iris said, shaking her head.

"The difference between us and other couples," Grant said, "is that they're the ones playing games with each other. We're not doing that. All the games are being played around us. I actually think we're pretty lucky."

"You do?" The growing love Iris felt for Grant was pulsing in her heart. "But we've hardly had any time together."

"Don't you realize how important you've become to me?" His voice caught from the welling passion that clamored for expression. Part of him said to tell her right here and now that he loved her. Another inner voice said to wait for the proper, special moment. Several times he had been tempted to blurt out the truth of his feelings. "I wish all of this were behind us so that we could get on with our lives and start a proper romance of our own."

He reached up and crushed a tress of her hair in his hand. "Don't you realize that you're my Cinderella?"

ABOUT THE AUTHOR

Carolyn Thornton is no armchair traveler. In her work as a free-lance writer, she has visited all over the world, from Costa Rica to Germany to Hong Kong. She has even taken flying lessons in an attempt to transport herself to the exotic locations she loves. When she's not traveling, Carolyn makes her home in Hattiesburg, Mississippi.

Books by Carolyn Thornton

HARLEQUIN AMERICAN ROMANCE

144–A CLASS ABOVE
204–TO ASK AGAIN, YES

The Search for Mr. Perfect

Carolyn Thornton

Harlequin Books

TORONTO • NEW YORK • LONDON
AMSTERDAM • PARIS • SYDNEY • HAMBURG
STOCKHOLM • ATHENS • TOKYO • MILAN

Published May 1988

First printing March 1988

ISBN 0-373-16248-0

Printed in U.S.A.

Prologue

The phone was ringing as Iris Janus shouldered her way through the glass doors of *New Age Woman* magazine while unfastening her dripping rain poncho.

The receptionist held her hand over the receiver and said, "Mr. South and Maggie want to see you in the conference room. Right away." With her free hand, she held out the mail to Iris and added, "I'm sure it's about Maggie's interview on TV...last night. *New Age Woman*. May I help you?"

The clock on the receptionist's desk indicated that Iris had made it to the office a few minutes earlier than usual, in spite of having overslept. Iris rarely worried about being late since her boss, Maggie, was never on time, and her Uncle Edward was head of South Publications. She had intended watching Maggie's interview on the late-night talk show *American Scene*, but as usual had gotten engrossed in a book and had stayed up until 3:00 a.m. to finish reading.

Iris hurried through the maze of hallways that led to the editorial department to reach her desk in a recess outside of Maggie's corner office. Since she had been offered the job at South Publications because of her uncle, Iris had never complained about not having a real office. But what she did envy were staff members who had bylines with their real names.

Iris had bylines—three of them, in fact. Because she was a voracious reader, Maggie let her write a book review column under the name of Gwendolyn Greene. Because Iris liked to dine in fine restaurants, Maggie let her write reviews under the name of Epicurious. And because Maggie never had the time, Iris was allowed to write the letter from the editor under Maggie's name. Iris had been challenged by each new writing task, since she had no formal training in journalism.

Hanging her soggy poncho in the closet near her alcove, Iris checked her appearance in the glass reflection of the framed first issue of *New Age Woman*. The spring rain had made her long, wiry, auburn hair frizzy. Quickly she brushed it away from her oval face and placed her reading glasses on top of her head to hold the mass of hair back. She picked up a notebook and pen, which made her look officious, and headed for the conference room.

Edward South had launched *New Age Woman* magazine three years earlier with Maggie Maxwell as editor in chief. Maggie had been the protégée of Sheila Croft, publisher of *Trendsetter*, the first magazine designed with the career woman in mind. When she first started there, Maggie wrote a popular column for single women, but when her philosophies on love and romance had clashed with Sheila's ultra-realistic vision, Maggie had been fired. South had quickly taken advantage of the situation and hired Maggie to put out a rival magazine.

At the conference room door, Iris straightened her fashionably rumpled khaki skirt and tucked in the matching blouse, then knocked firmly.

"Come in," South's gravelly voice commanded.

Iris's uncle was standing at the window, thoughtfully tweaking the end of his graying handlebar mustache. His springy salt-and-pepper hair was perfectly groomed as always, but the worry lines around his eyes seemed deeper behind gold-rimmed glasses. Edward's jacket was off, revealing his broad shoulders and expanding waistline.

Maggie was seated at the conference table. Her soft shoulder-length blond hair, brushed loosely away from her face, revealed diamond stud earrings. Her lips appeared pale, but her slender, ski-tip nose was pink and shiny. Her spiky lashes looked damp, and her almond-shaped gray eyes seemed darker than usual.

"Maggie?" Iris shut the door and approached the conference table. "What's wrong?"

"Don't you know?" Maggie said, her voice deeply nasal, as if she had caught a cold.

"No," she said. "I just got here and was told you both wanted to see me."

South took two broad steps that carried him to the conference table. He was a big man with a cold, hard look, who rarely smiled. His prestigious and powerful position had always made him seem larger than life to Iris. Although he protected and indulged her like his own daughter, Iris had never felt fully relaxed around him.

He slid a magazine across the surface of the table toward Iris. Thinking it was the latest issue of *New Age Woman*, Iris picked it up. Instead, she saw Maggie on the cover of *Trendsetter* magazine. Emblazoned across her photograph was the headline, "Is This Woman an Old Maid?"

"Sheila Croft had that with her last night on *American Scene*," Maggie said, pausing long enough to blow her nose. "She made a fool of me in front of half the people in America."

"What was she doing on the show?" Iris said. "I thought it was just going to be you and—"

"And someone else from the magazine publishing industry," South finished her sentence. "When Maggie was invited on the show to promote her new book and talk about men, women and romance, we had no idea Croft had been invited also. Obviously, you didn't see the show."

"No, no, I meant to, but I..." Her voice trailed off as she realized it didn't matter whether she had seen it or not. Maggie and South weren't listening to her. Iris sank slowly into the chair next to Maggie.

"Croft hogged the camera when she pointed out that Maggie's new book, *Romancing a Man*, was a fake, just like her magazine," South explained.

"What?" Iris said. "How can she say that?"

"We taped the show," South said, crossing to the VCR unit at one end of the room. "Here. We'll show you." He turned the unit on and held down the Fast Forward button until the tape came to the point in the show where the host, Martin Langley, held up the advance copy of *Trendsetter*.

On the screen, Iris saw the dark-haired Sheila Croft, who wore a flashy black dress and patterned black stockings. A red scarf, draped around her neck and pinned to her left shoulder, completed the image of a black widow spider. She was ten years older than Maggie, but at fifty-three, still an extremely striking woman. Iris had learned from Maggie that Croft didn't always play by the rules. No doubt she still resented Maggie for being successful.

As the tape continued playing Croft said, "The article in *Trendsetter* concerns the man shortage and certainly doesn't imply that Maggie Maxwell is the only woman with no man in her life. Demographically speaking, unmarried women over forty have less than a three percent chance of marrying. We just used Maggie Maxwell on the cover because she considers herself a prototype of today's woman."

The camera cut to a medium shot revealing Maggie's finely chiseled features and loose blond hair. She was tall, athletic and proud of it. But on the tape, her glacé perfection looked stale, as if she were ready to faint.

"Here you are," Sheila continued, "the so-called expert on romance, telling women all over the world how to meet and marry Mr. Perfect, yet *you* haven't been able to follow your own advice." As Maggie tried to protest, Croft cut her off. "Your romanticized fantasies about men are setting women up to refuse to compromise. If it's so easy to meet a man, why hasn't your advice worked for you?" Before Maggie could reply, Croft added, "Even your longtime escort, Bradley Winchester, has recently broken up with you. The fact is, you don't have *any* man in your life."

"But I do have a man in my life right now," Maggie retorted. "A very, very special man."

Iris turned from watching the interview to look questioningly at her uncle and Maggie. On tape, Maggie was expounding on her Mr. Perfect. "He travels internationally and speaks several languages. Even though he's younger than I am, he runs his own business." Maggie's voice grew stronger, sounding like a cross between Scarlett O'Hara and Eva Perón. "He's sensuous, supportive, spontaneous, intelligent, well-read—"

In the conference room, South stopped the tape. "And then Maggie and Sheila agreed to return to the show at a later date with their respective Mr. Perfects, which is easy for Sheila, since she's married."

Bewildered, Iris looked at her boss and asked, "Maggie, is there a new man in your life we don't know about?"

"No." She took a deep breath and added, "But he sounded so good on TV, didn't he? And the audience loved it, especially when I said he was younger. I just couldn't let Sheila get to me like that."

South strode agitatedly up and down the room. "Your being labeled a fraud could hurt the concept that has made *New Age Woman* so successful," he barked. "When I offered you the position at the magazine you were constantly in the news with an intelligent and handsome man on your arm. The readers loved it because you showed them it was all possible. But now, commitment is the big issue, long-term relationships are in. With the Winchester breakup, you're out of a man, Maggie, and at the worst possible time."

"Don't you think you're making too much of this?" Iris said. She kept thinking of Croft's well-publicized temper and how she liked to be the center of attention. "Next week Sheila will pick on someone else."

South ran a hand through his carefully combed salt-and-pepper hair. "Sheila Croft knows how vulnerable we are on this. Maggie's personal crisis could quickly became a major financial problem for the entire magazine if we don't do something about it."

"Edward's right," Maggie said, lifting her chin high. "Sheila won't let this die." There was a long stretch of silence, then Maggie said, "But there are many men here in New York. I've never had trouble finding them before. I can do it again."

"You're already supposed to have someone, Maggie," South reminded. "You can't be seen around town looking for a man."

"And anyway, when are you going to have time?" Iris asked. "You'll be on the road for the next two weeks with the book tour."

"Everyone will want to see you with your new man on *American Scene*," South said harshly. "And Sheila Croft, not to mention the society press, will expect to see your mystery man at the New York Charity Ball the end of this month."

"It's simple," Maggie said as she faced Iris. "We'll just have to show Ms Sheila Croft that I can get a man, and not just any male, but a most spectacular one."

"How?" South demanded.

"While I'm on this publicity tour," Maggie said calmly, looking squarely at her personal secretary, "Iris is going to find my Mr. Perfect for me."

Chapter One

"It's a couples' world," Iris said as she and Tina Powers, the beauty editor of *New Age Woman*, stood at the edge of a crowded, smoke-filled singles' bar a few days before Maggie was due to return from her book tour. Ignoring her protestations, South had elected Iris the coordinator of the search for Mr. Perfect. Maggie had encouraged this setup by insisting that Iris was sure to find a man somewhere within her upper-crust circle of friends. If he was there, Iris couldn't find him. With time running out, Iris and Tina had resorted to the oldest way to meet men—the singles' bar.

"I know. It's disgusting," Tina said. Her hand kept flying to her mousy hair, which had just been cut in a lopsided style in her latest effort to anticipate trends. Unfortunately, most of Tina's personal beauty choices never caught on, but they did make her stand out in a crowd. Iris had hoped bringing Tina with her this evening might increase the odds on finding Mr. Perfect for Maggie. So far, it hadn't.

"Just look at this place," Iris complained. "Every table is occupied by beautiful people matched together like passengers on Noah's ark. I feel like an old maid in a deck set for blackjack."

In the search for a man, Iris had tried everything, starting with the advice listed in the pages of *New Age Woman*. She had chosen an informal "hang-out" type restaurant in Maggie's neighborhood in order to meet some eligible males. She had been to the polo matches. She had been to fund-raising events for politicians. At parties, instead of handing out her card, she had picked up the card of every single man she met. And she had even pushed an empty cart around a crowded grocery store for two hours on a "Shopping for Singles" night. Iris had never been lucky about meeting men. In fact, the few dates she had gone on since her divorce had been arranged by her uncle. Of all the single women on the staff at the magazine, Iris was probably the least experienced in meeting men. Even when she noticed an interesting man, she rarely got up the courage to speak to him. As a last-ditch effort, Iris had asked Tina to go with her as they scouted the singles' bars.

"I hate to say it," Tina said, "but I don't think we're going to find Mr. Perfect anywhere. Maggie's asking for the impossible."

Iris silently agreed as she surveyed the single men who stood grouped together on the edge of the room. They appeared too old, too balding, too inappropriate for the kind of man Maggie had described on national TV. Before leaving on her book tour, Maggie had called in her staff of women editors to come up with a composite of characteristics for her ideal mate. Maggie and South had decided he not only had to fit the description Maggie had given on TV, but also the ideals touted by the magazine each month.

The perfect man for Maggie Maxwell had to be intelligent, cosmopolitan, single and never married. He had to be wealthier than Maggie, which ruled out a lot of men. As the most important quality, and to refute the demographics of Croft's argument, he had to be younger than Maggie.

Maggie's list also included season tickets to Broadway openings, because her ex-boyfriend Bradley Winchester had spoiled her in that area. Mr. Perfect needed to have a sloop at least five feet longer than Bradley Winchester's yacht, and speak at least one more foreign language than Winchester, which meant two.

And then there were the negative characteristics: violent temper, heavy drinker, smoker, unsophisticated, balding, sports nut. While Mr. Perfect had to look like a playboy, he couldn't act like one. Once he was found, Maggie had assured Iris that she would "knock his socks off" with her feminine charms.

As if I know how to find the perfect man for myself, Iris thought, as an image of her ex-husband, Mitch, flashed through her mind. On the surface, Mitch had been the perfect man, but he was really a little boy to whom life was one long fraternity party. Since Mitch, she had taken an emotional vacation from men. Searching for a man for Maggie had reopened all the wounds she had thought had healed from her divorce. She was feeling vulnerable again, getting that mushy, lonesome ache whenever she looked at couples.

With Maggie on the book tour, Iris had complained to her uncle that he had given her an impossible task to accomplish, hoping he would see reason and stop the hunt. But he was obsessed with the image of the magazine and wouldn't listen to Iris. He had even given her a deadline to find someone before the annual New York Charity Ball. And he had been so persuasive, offering her a promotion and her own byline on a column if she pulled this off for Maggie. Even though they had never discussed it, her uncle had known this would motivate Iris in finding a solution to Maggie's problem.

As the only child of a bank vice president, Richard Janus, and Wilhemina South, Edward's sister, Iris had been pampered in a luxurious life-style from birth. Nothing had prepared her for the shock of the real world until her parents died in an auto accident a year after college graduation. Unprepared to cope on her own, and still caught up in her grief, Iris had married Mitch Phillips, the son of a friend of her Uncle Edward.

Everyone had told Iris that Mitch was the ideal man. He was a handsome, debonair jet-setter who came from a similar moneyed background and social standing as Iris. Although he had a prominent position on the New York Stock Exchange, it didn't take Iris long after the honeymoon to realize he could barely take care of himself, much less her. Mitch's public carousing finally became an embarrassment to Edward, and he quietly arranged a divorce for her.

Iris had been so excited when her uncle had found a place for her at the magazine. It wasn't that she needed the money—she had a substantial trust income from her parents' estate—but she did need some career to build her life around. She was too young to settle into a routine of organizing charity balls, as her mother had done, and she wasn't interested in Manhattan's trendy clubs, which Mitch had thrived on. A publishing career would give her a chance to do something with her life.

"Let's go stand by the bar," Tina suggested now, interrupting Iris's thoughts. "Someone may be leaving soon."

"Yeah, like me," Iris said dejectedly, "when Maggie finds out I've failed." After nearly two solid weeks of searching for a man, Iris was ready to admit defeat.

"Cheer up. Your uncle won't fire you. You still have a couple of days before Maggie gets back, and another week before the charity ball. Besides, the girls at the office are looking, too."

Tina led the way to the bar where they found one empty bar stool. Iris told Tina to take it. She wanted to stand where she could watch the people in the room in case a miraculously perfect male turned up unattached. But she got nervous just thinking about brashly approaching anyone, much less checking him out for Maggie.

"Relax," Tina said, fingering the short end of her uneven haircut. "Someone will turn up. And anyway, it's not your fault if Maggie let Bradley Winchester slip through her fingers." She tried to get the bartender's attention to order a drink. "If anyone was perfect for her, it was him. What happened between them, anyway?"

Bradley was head of Winchester and Ames, one of the most prestigious Broadway talent agencies in New York. "He's fallen in love with some twenty-five-year-old orange-haired bimbo."

"Oh, no."

"Oh, yes."

"What does she do?"

"According to Mary, Winchester's secretary, who filled me in on the details when Maggie refused to talk about it, the woman calls herself an 'artistic set designer.' But Mary doesn't think she's too good at painting, judging by the way her lipstick is always askew."

"Men and their middle age crises. They have no heart," Tina said, getting the bartender to notice her. Tina had always been good at attracting attention. The bartender signaled that he would be right with her.

"That's exactly what I think it is," Iris agreed. "I wish there was some way to get them back together, but he's got it so bad he can't see straight right now. Mary says he's even planning to take her to the ball where she's going to stick out like Bozo the Clown. But try telling him that."

Tina ordered a drink and asked Iris what she wanted. "A whiskey sour," she said, adding, "heavy on the sour."

As Tina paid for the drinks, the man next to her struck up a conversation with her. Iris tried to signal that he didn't look appropriate for Maggie before she realized Tina might be interested in the man for herself. Noticing Iris, Tina's new friend smiled and offered her his stool.

"Thanks," she said, taking his place. He winked at Iris and moved to stand next to Tina, boxing her in with one hand on the bar and the other near her bottom, grasping the stool. With her elbow resting on the bar, Iris propped her head in her palm and stared at Tina. Maybe Maggie had just asked the wrong person to find a man for her. Tina seemed to have no problem making contacts.

The mirrored walls of the bar allowed Iris to watch people all over the room from her seat. She was always nervous she would run into Mitch in a bar and didn't want to stir up old emotions, both good and bad.

Mitch had thrived on partying, which had been fun for Iris, too, when they were dating. But Iris had envisioned married life as cuddling up and reading a book together by the fire. Mitch, on the other hand, liked to prowl the streets of Manhattan until dawn. In the final months of their marriage, she would frequently meet him just coming home as she was going out for her morning jog. Finally, Mitch quit coming home at all, and their marriage ended quietly. A shiver ran down her spine and she forced Mitch out of her mind. She would much prefer being at home reading a book about romance instead of trying to produce one for Maggie out of thin air.

Maggie didn't understand the unrealistic task she had set for Iris in asking her to find such a perfect man. Like the magazine she edited, life for Maggie was always a bowl of Bing cherries, sans pits. Maggie dreamed incredible romantic scenarios that the readers desperately wanted to believe could come true for themselves. She believed lovers made mad, passionate love in waterfalls. Men with blond hair and stomachs that rippled with muscles seduced women with alabaster skin, firm breasts and bottoms. Maggie's fantasies were illustrated in beautiful four-color photo spreads every month with details in Nikon-sharp focus. And then there were the true-to-life success stories of women who had found Prince Charming suddenly sitting next to them on the subway or living next door.

Iris's thoughts darkened. She suddenly realized her uncle's concern for the magazine. It was not just Maggie's belief in her own fantasies that was at stake. If the readers found out that Maggie's dreams couldn't come true for her, how could they believe they could come true for them? Iris wiped the tiny beads of sweat from the palms of her hands with a napkin, as her eyes slowly scanned the mirrored walls.

A pretty blond woman with a spray of flowers in her hair was sitting alone at one of the tiny cocktail tables, playing nervously with the fruit in her glass. Iris studied her, wondering how long she would be alone. She was too pretty to be overlooked, but she was going about it all wrong if she was trying to pick up a man. Iris should know. She had mentally been rehearsing her encounter techniques for a couple of weeks now, but hadn't found the courage to use them.

Just as Iris was thinking the woman could probably learn a few things from reading *New Age Woman*, a dark-haired man in his early thirties and wearing a French-cut suit with a bright silk handkerchief in the pocket walked up to the woman. *Of all the dumb, blind luck,* Iris thought. *She doesn't even have to establish eye contact to get noticed.*

Iris watched enviously as the man with a slow, sure smile handed the woman a bunch of flowers he had been hiding behind his back. He had the look of success and self-confidence, yet when his lips parted to reveal an open-mouthed smile, a boyish quality appeared fleetingly on his face. Mentally, Iris removed the blond and seated herself in front of him.

She liked the way his eyes centered on the woman, giving her his full attention. As he sat down next to her, hugging the blond, Iris realized they knew each other. The woman had obviously been waiting for him. She sighed and let her eyes drift away, searching the room for someone else.

In spite of herself, Iris's eyes homed back to the attractive couple. He was the most interesting-looking man in the place. She tried to figure out why. Perhaps it was the set of his shoulders, which gave him a relaxed yet authoritative air. Whatever it was that he did, Iris was certain he would be good at it.

He was very attentive, pulling his chair closer to the blond's so that they could obviously tell each other secrets in the midst of the noisy room, lighting her cigarette, getting the waiter to bring a refill of her drink. Iris suddenly felt deep, emotional longings, which she had so successfully suppressed since her divorce.

As if he sensed her watching him, the man with the blond glanced across the room and caught Iris's eye. She felt herself flush and looked away quickly, pretending interest in the ceiling fans. While she couldn't be sure, she felt as if he were mentally undressing her. She crossed her left arm across her breasts self-consciously.

When she dared to look at him again, he was engrossed in conversation with the woman. She felt cheated. Perhaps he hadn't really noticed her. Perhaps he wasn't seducing her in his mind. She sat up straighter and thrust her shoulders back, looking at herself in the bar's mirrored walls. Another furtive glance told her the man's attention was totally focused on the other woman. Iris felt safe enough to indulge herself in her fantasy. Mentally, her hands adjusted his silk tie and ran over the solid muscles she imagined were under his linen shirt. She thought ties looked sexy on men, especially when it came time for removing them. It had been a long time since she had been intimate enough with a man to touch him—shirt or no shirt—the way she imagined caressing the man with the sexy smile.

The bartender shattered her sexual reverie as he slid a drink in front of her. Embarrassed, Iris quickly slumped forward and fumbled with her purse, removing a bill to pay for the drink. As she settled back with her whiskey sour, she gave in again to her fantasies about the mystery man. It was like watching someone on TV who was safely out of reach and who would never guess the heat of her thoughts.

If she was sitting next to him, Iris would be cuddling much closer than the blond with the flowers. She would be running her hand down his arm, or along his thigh, encouraging him to hold her close. Whatever they would be talking about, *she* would have the power to make his eyes light up with amusement and interest. And no matter what they would be discussing, they would really be thinking about being alone together, making love.

She thought of the color proofs she had seen of next month's centerspread in *New Age Woman*. The female model wore a white, see-through, gauze dress, which she held up around her middle to keep from getting wet in the surf that surged around her knees. Only the gathered folds of the dress hid her nakedness from full view. The male model had on striped white cotton pants that were barely held up by a loosely tied drawstring. His pant legs, wet from the surf, clung to his body like spray paint. The couple was wrapped in full embrace with their lips firmly planted together. In her imagination, Iris could feel the heat from the man as he embraced her and they slowly tumbled over into the warm surf. They laughed and she slowly rose from the ocean knowing that her body was fully revealed to him through the wet gauze.

The sexy man in the bar threw his head back, laughing at something the blond said, and he briefly intercepted Iris's gaze again. Her heart skipped a beat from the friendly look he gave her.

Flushing guiltily, Iris gave him a half smile and was about to look away when he smiled, at *her*. The blond picked up on the distraction and turned, too. Iris buried her nose in her drink and turned her back. It wasn't like her to boldly assess some other woman's man, much less mentally make love to him. After a minute, when she felt it was safe, she let her gaze stray to the mirrored walls that reflected the entire room. She would have picked him out in the crowd, even if he hadn't suddenly stood up as another man approached their table, shook hands with him and kissed the blond, who threw her arms around the second man's neck and clung to him.

Iris raised her eyebrows and turned a quarter turn on the stool where she could keep an eye on the table with the threesome. Maybe the man with the flowers had just been keeping the blond company until her real date turned up. Beside her, Tina was oblivious to everyone but the man who had given Iris his place at the bar.

Iris looked in the mirror and noticed that the pretty blond was leaving with the second man. Iris took a sip of her drink, playing with the ice and straw. When she looked up at the mirror again, her fantasy man had left the table, too. She frantically scanned the bar, but he was nowhere to be seen. She sighed, smiling to herself at the pleasant thoughts he had evoked and took a deeper sip of her whiskey sour.

Beside her, someone began speaking in deep, guttural tones. Iris couldn't understand a word the man was saying, but she liked the tone and gentleness of his voice, which sounded compelling, almost seductive. She sipped her drink and eavesdropped, pretending she understood the language.

Turning slightly to get a glimpse of the speaker, Iris found herself staring into deep brown eyes framed by long, dark lashes. The man she had been watching was now standing close to her. He seemed tall, especially from her position on the bar stool, and slim with a strong physique that looked as if he worked out. And he was definitely smiling at *her*.

"I—I'm sorry," Iris stammered, flustered by the knowing look he was giving her, as if her illicit thoughts had been picked up by him. She put her hand to her chest, suddenly feeling shy, "Were you speaking to me?"

"Yes," he answered with a show of surprise, his voice as soft and rich as homemade ice cream. "You'll have to excuse me. I thought you might be European. You have such a classic beauty about you."

"I do?" she said, looking down and away, anywhere but at him. Flirting with a man who was with another woman was safe. Making love to a man in your mind was safe. But now, here he was in real life and alone.

"Yes," he said. "Very aristocratic, as if you come from a long line of royalty. Your hair looks as if it should be crowned with a tiara."

"Thank you," she said, but couldn't prevent the skeptical look from creeping into her expression. She allowed herself a quick glance up at him, liking the tousled, dark hair that tumbled over his forehead. His deep tan made him look like a man who probably made love to women in warm oceans in real life.

He smiled again. It was a pleasant smile that seemed to start in his eyes and gave the impression he was very pleased with what he saw.

Iris was glad she had taken extra care with her make-up that evening, darkening her lashes and artfully blending shadows to give her eyes a smoky look. A hint of blusher accented her high cheekbones. She hoped her nose wasn't shiny. It looked like a button on her face when it was. At least the bar was dim, but she wished she had her glasses on so that she could see him more sharply up close. "What language were you speaking?"

"German," he said. "I didn't think you were French because of the way you're wearing your hair so long and loose. Austrian, perhaps, or Swiss. Have you ever been to Vienna?"

"No." She shook her head, lowering her chin to let the loose curls of her auburn hair partially hide her face. His frank yet friendly gaze unnerved her. "What was it you were saying in German?"

"What?" he asked, as if the intensity of his glance had made him forget what they were talking about. "Oh, I was asking if you would mind if I talked with you a little while. You have such an arresting face, open and inquisitive. You look like the kind of person who embraces life."

"Thank you," she said again. "But what about your friends?"

He looked over his shoulder as if they were still sitting at the table he had left. "Mark and Sally have a theater date tonight. We just came from a friend's wedding."

"I see," Iris said. The surprise of finding him next to her made her forget everything except how devastatingly beautiful he looked. *Beautiful* was an unusual word to use to describe a man, but Iris had that same sense of awe she felt in the presence of a strikingly beautiful woman.

"If you'd rather be alone, I'll understand," he said. "But I'm at loose ends tonight, just passing time until I catch a plane."

"No, I don't mind." She lowered her lashes, concentrating on the rim of her glass. If she didn't do something quickly he might lose interest in her. She almost wanted to stand up and kiss him, long and hard on the lips, to make him understand the emotions he had caused to come alive in her again. She pushed her hair out of her eyes, "Then you're from out of town?"

He signaled the bartender to order a drink. "I live in New York," he said, adding, "off and on." The bartender nodded to him as if they were old friends, and didn't bother to ask what kind of drink he wanted. "But I have some business to attend to in Europe."

Iris waited until the bartender had set a drink in front of him before asking, "What kind of business are you in?"

"I do a lot of investment counseling and placement for foreign businessmen." He lifted his glass to clink it with hers. Iris noticed he wasn't wearing a wedding ring. "But I can't talk about it," he said, knocking back half of his milky drink with a single swallow.

"I promise I won't give away any secrets," Iris challenged, braced for some glowing yarn, but secretly hoping it was the truth. She had heard it all before from other men when she had occasionally accompanied Mitch on his all-night bar crawls. The wedding band on her finger had not deterred some men from hitting on her. Regardless of the charisma she felt radiating from the man beside her, Iris felt the same dubious sensations she always experienced in singles' bars.

"Another drink?" he asked, signaling the bartender.

"No, really," she protested as the bartender took his order. "I don't want to feel obligated."

Gently he placed his hand over hers where it rested on the top of the bar. His touch was warm and friendly. "Don't think I'm trying to press you into anything because I ordered a drink for you. It comes with no strings."

Out of the corner of her eye, Iris glanced at Tina who was still deeply engrossed in conversation. She seemed to have forgotten Iris. Iris looked down at the man's hand on hers. It was a strong hand, very masculine, with dark hairs across the back. His nails were well kept. Beneath the dark jacket sleeve and cream shirt cuff, she glimpsed an expensive-looking watch. "You're very nice, but I can pay for my own drinks. Thanks anyway."

"I'm not offering anything," he said clearly, with those sincere brown eyes on a level with her own, "except another drink." As the bartender set another whiskey sour in front of Iris, the man beside her pulled out his wallet to pay. "Damn," he muttered. "It looks as if you're going to get your way, after all."

"What?"

He pulled out the edge of a bill in a denomination of five hundred. "I'm out of U.S. currency. All I have are Austrian schillings until the banks open."

Iris caught her mouth widening and quickly tried to hide her surprise. The sight of the foreign money seemed to confirm the truth about his travels. "That's okay," she said, softening as she began to take him at face value. "I told you I could pay for my own drink, and yours, as well."

"I feel badly about this," he said, letting her pay the bar tab. Clinking his glass with her new one, he said, "Cheers." He smiled. "At least I was right about you."

"Oh? In what way."

"Not only are you an interesting-looking lady, but you're nice, too. I had a feeling you'd be friendly."

Iris smiled and sipped her drink. "What's your name?"

"Grant Peters," he answered, and reached into the breast pocket of his jacket. "Here, let me give you one of my cards."

Iris took it. Above his name, a coat of arms depicted two keys with a flag between them on a blue background. "The address is in Vienna," she said.

"That's where my European office is," he said. "What's your name?"

"Elizabeth Howell." She made up a name off the top of her head and hoped she remembered it for the remainder of the time they talked.

"I'm delighted to meet you," he said. "And what is it that you do?"

"I'm just a secretary," she said, giving the sparse details she always gave men she didn't really know. "For the IRS," she added, watching his reaction. It usually halted further questioning, as it did in this case. She stirred the ice in her glass with her finger.

"We're sort of in the same business," Grant said.

"How so?" Her eyes flitted to his briefly.

"We're both in the money business. I'm in the business of making it and you're in the business of taking it."

Iris laughed, liking his sense of humor. She looked down at her shoes resting on the rung of the bar stool. "So how does one make money in Vienna?"

"Surely, you jest. Think about what's in Vienna," he said, lowering his voice and moving closer to her.

Iris was very aware of him standing so near, watching her slightest move. "All I can think of are sausages."

"No," he said, his eyes sparkling with interest. "OPEC is headquartered in Vienna."

"Oh? So you're with OPEC." She avoided looking directly at him, because now that he was standing so close to her, she had trouble thinking of anything but what he would look like without the formally tailored suit. She felt the warm surf lapping at her knees.

"Not really. Can you keep a secret?"

Iris leaned closer to him, feeling the warmth of his body as she inclined her ear. The ocean was now roaring in her ears.

"You know the World Trade Center?" She nodded. "I'm negotiating to buy it on behalf of a Saudi prince." He reached in his pocket and took out a silver package of paco rabanne cigarettes and offered, "Cigarette?"

"No, thanks. I don't smoke," she said.

"Mind if I do?"

Iris shrugged noncommittally. She hated the smell of smoke, but never knew how to say no when anyone asked to light up a cigarette in front of her.

He struck a match from the packet he picked up from the bar. As his face lighted up from the flare of the match, Iris really looked at him, holding his gaze, liking him even more now that he was standing so close. His jaw was square and dark. She guessed he probably had to shave twice a day. And unlike other men she had met in bars, he looked directly at her, as if no one else in the room interested him. Maybe that was what had attracted her across the crowded bar. He had singled her out of the crowd.

She ran her finger up and down the beads of moisture collecting on the glass. He suddenly seemed very familiar, and that made her nervous.

He placed his hand on his hip on the inside of his jacket and leaned against the bar. "You have the most arresting green eyes," he said, setting down his drink. A slow grin spread across his face as he noticed a blush heighten the color in her cheeks. "Did the IRS move you to New York, or did you come on your own?"

"What? Oh, I came on my own." She rolled her drink between her hands uncomfortably, caught in her own web of lies. "I've always lived here."

"What exactly do you do for the IRS?"

"I don't want to talk about it," Iris said, and to deflect his questions added, "I'd much rather talk about you. Making money sounds much more interesting than taking it away, as you termed it."

He chuckled and stubbed out his cigarette. "As they say, after you reach six figures money's just a way of keeping score."

"I suppose you're now in the keeping-score stage?"

"The last person I would tell is a pretty lady from the IRS," he said with a laugh. "Let's just say I'm very comfortable." He changed the subject. "I have to admit you're the most pleasant company I've met in a long time. Business has kept me too busy to have a few minutes to myself. But I guess that's good, because it can get awfully lonely traveling around the world the way I do."

"You're not married, then?"

"No, but I'd like to be if I could find a woman who would like to travel with me." His eyes held hers briefly.

"Having money without someone to share it takes all the fun out of making it. I think it bothers me most on nights like tonight when I come into a place like this and most of the people are couples. Especially after you've just come from a wedding."

"I guess so," Iris said, turning with him to look at the room behind them, feeling a sense of pride that he had chosen to stand next to her. How many other women in the bar were jealous of her now? How many were creating fantasies of themselves and the beautiful Mr. Grant Peters?

He turned his engaging eyes in her direction and added, "Maybe that's why I felt so compelled to talk to you, because I sensed that we were kindred spirits. Are you here alone?"

Iris softened toward him. He seemed sincere and very secure. She liked men who had their own money. They were not afraid of accidentally stepping out of line and getting fired the way the men her uncle had introduced her to had been. "I came with my girlfriend, Tina." She gestured to the couple still talking heatedly beside her.

"It looks like your friend has become part of a couple," he observed. "Why don't we?"

Iris gazed into his sensitive brown eyes and gave her thoughts free rein with his suggestion. It would be so easy to say yes to him, listening to his seductive voice, giving in to the desire that was rising like steam after a summer rain. She liked talking with him. "Why don't we...what?" she asked hesitantly, knowing very well what he meant.

He turned to rest his back against the bar. "Get out of this smoke-filled room, go somewhere quieter where we can—talk." He lowered his voice and said, "I'm only going to be here a short while longer, and I hate the thought of losing you so soon after finding you."

Iris caught her breath, wanting to give in to the desire hammering in her veins. She still couldn't believe this handsome adventurer had singled her out at the bar. He must have known she was considering saying yes, she decided, because he added, "We could go to your place and have some champagne and listen to some soft music. I bet you look wonderful in candlelight."

Iris could feel the heat from a million candles burning inside her. The waves were thundering against the rocks in her ears. She imagined him looking up at her from the foaming surf, his eyes slowly moving over her every curve. Then with an impish grin, she thought of him rising from the white, churning foam, totally naked, the cotton pants lost in the surf.

"Excuse me," Tina interrupted Iris, and then caught herself as she noticed the tall, good-looking man, "but don't you think we'd better call it a night?"

Remembering where she was, Iris felt herself blushing and looked down at her shoes. She was tempted to invite Mr. Grant Peters home with her to quench the fires he had started within her, but she quickly talked herself out of it, grateful that Tina's intrusion on her thoughts had brought her back to reality. "Yes, we'd better," Iris agreed, slipping her purse from the bar and standing unsteadily. He gently caught her by the arm to steady her. His hands felt warm and dry. "Tomorrow's going to be a big day at the tax office."

"Tax...?" Tina mumbled in confusion, then caught the drift of Iris's protective deception and quickly changed her question to, "Taxis run in the Village this late, don't they?"

"I believe they do," Grant replied. "Would you like me to get one for you?"

"That's nice of you, but we can manage," Iris responded crisply. "It's been fun." She held out her hand and watched in enchantment as he brought it to his lips and kissed it. "Look me up if you ever get audited."

"But I don't know how to reach you," he said, retaining her hand and holding her gaze.

Iris had the feeling he wouldn't let go until she told him something. And he had been nice. She gave the address of the magazine's subscription department.

He jotted it down on a cocktail napkin. "Maybe I'll see you in here again some night. My business trip will only keep me in Vienna a couple of days," he suggested. "I come here sometimes when I'm in New York."

"Perhaps," she said hurriedly before she could change her mind. "Good night." She followed Tina through the bar to the street outside, relishing the feel of the cool night air. "What was going on with you and that guy at the bar?" Iris asked.

"The usual," Tina answered. "He wasn't very original, told me I had a nice tan." She held out her white arms. "I mean, *me*, who never gets out of the office!" She faced her friend as they walked rapidly to a cross street where they would each take a cab home. "But what about you and that hunk? Is he as good as he looks?"

"I don't know," Iris said. "He is the nicest man I've ever met in a bar, but he was so incredible, he was almost unreal."

"How so?" Tina asked.

Iris explained what little she knew about Grant Peters and his mysterious work for OPEC and Saudi princes.

"He certainly dresses well and looks the part," Tina mused.

"I didn't believe it when he started speaking German to me, either."

"He speaks a foreign language?" Tina stopped walking. "Iris, he sounds perfect."

"I'm not so sure," Iris hedged, thinking how tempting it had been to spend more time with him. "You know how I am about proper introductions."

"I'm not talking about for *you*," Tina said. "This guy sounds, looks and from what I could tell, acts like the perfect man for Maggie."

Chapter Two

Stopping short in the middle of the sidewalk, Iris nearly caused several people to run into her. "Perfect for Maggie! It never occurred to me."

A rush of feelings assailed her: anger, regret, joy, jealousy. She had been so entranced by the thought of a romantic evening with Grant Peters that it didn't seem fair for Maggie to benefit from her fantasy. But he could be the answer to her problem. "You're right," she told Tina. "He's just the sort of man Maggie described." She turned back toward the bar. "We've got to catch him before he leaves." She started running.

The bar seemed more crowded than before. Iris and Tina scanned the room for a tall man with curly dark hair. He was no longer at the bar. "You take the right side of the room," Tina suggested, "and I'll take the left."

Iris nodded and set off in search of him. By the time she had scoured her side of the room with no result, she had lost sight of Tina. She stood on tiptoe at the far side of the bar, searching faces for the man from Vienna. All the dark-eyed, curly haired men who caught her looking at them were the wrong ones. Leaving the crowded, smoke-filled bar, Iris waited hopefully for Tina.

A few minutes later Tina stumbled out of the bar with a did-you-find-him look on her face. Spying Iris, who held the same look of expectation, her expression turned to dejection.

"Now what are we going to do?" Iris asked.

"Wait a minute," Tina said. "Why are we worrying about this guy? You said his office is in Vienna. That won't do us any good for the charity ball."

"It's just a business trip. He'll be back in a few days."

Tina looked at her wristwatch. "Then you'll just have to go out to the airport tomorrow to find him."

"Kennedy is a zoo," Iris said. "I don't even know what airline he's flying or what time he's leaving. There are a million flights from New York that could connect to Vienna from anywhere in Europe. He could even be leaving tonight for all I know." Iris tried to recall every detail he had given her. "The bartender!" she cried.

"No, he won't do. Maggie would never go for a guy with a ponytail."

"Not for Maggie," Iris said in exasperation. "He might be able to tell us how to find our guy." Like a zoom lens, her mind zeroed in on each exchange he had had with the bartender. They seemed to have known each other. The bartender hadn't even asked what kind of drink Grant wanted. "I have to go back."

"Iris, it's late," Tina pleaded.

"We're running out of time," Iris reminded. "Maggie will feel like the emperor with no clothes if I don't find her a man. But I can handle this alone. Why don't you go home?"

"Sure?" Tina asked, torn between loyalty and exhaustion.

"I wouldn't be able to sleep, anyway, without knowing I at least tried. I'll see you at the office."

Tina gave her a quick hug and went on her way.

Odd, Iris thought as she watched Tina disappear into the stream of other night people in the Village, that Grant Peters should be heading for Europe at the end of a week. She shrugged. He probably had to conduct business on European time schedules. That was his problem. Hers was to contact him in time for the New York Charity Ball.

As Iris squeezed back into the bar, she prayed she'd find out some information about him. "Hi," Iris said when she finally sidled next to the bar and got the bartender's attention. "Remember me?"

"What'll it be?" He wiped down the bar as he waited for her order.

"I had the whiskey sour," she reminded.

"One whiskey sour coming up." He spun around.

"No! Wait."

"Change your mind?"

"I don't want a whiskey sour. That's what I had last time, remember?"

"If you say so." He strummed his fingers impatiently on the counter of the bar.

Iris clutched her purse tightly to still her frazzled nerves and said, "Do you recall the man with dark hair from Vienna? He stood next to me while I sat at the bar. He tried to pay with Austrian schillings—"

"Oh, yeah, sure. You want a White Russian like he had." The bartender gave her a wide-gapped grin.

"That's right!" Iris said with relief.

"Coming up."

"No! Wait. I don't want a White Russian. I want a dark Austrian!"

The bartender leaned across the bar and said, "Hey, babe, I don't mean to make life difficult for you, but I haven't ever heard of a dark Austrian. If you tell me what's in it I'll try to fix it."

"I want that man, not the drink he was having," she clarified.

The bartender whistled between his teeth and moved back from the bar, shaking his head. "That figures."

"You do know the man who was here with me a while ago, don't you?" She crossed her fingers beneath the bar hoping he would say yes.

"He comes in here every now and then," he answered warily. "Hey, look, I got customers. You want something to drink or not?"

"I have to get in touch with your friend from Vienna."

"Who said he was my friend?" The bartender spread his hands. "I just work here. A lot of people come in and go out. Some I remember. Most I forget." He wiped up a spill on the countertop.

"You know the man I'm talking about," Iris persisted. "You remembered the drink he had."

"That's my job, to remember drinks. If I was a dentist, I would remember teeth. Lady, I don't run a dating service here."

"I don't need him for a date. I need him for my job," she said in frustration.

"Look, the guy comes in here all the time. Whatever your problem is take it up with him. I don't have anything to do with his little acts."

"That's the problem. I don't know how to reach him."

"Try the café around the corner, Eve's Garden. I've seen him there. They might know something."

"Is that all you know about him?" Her spirits sank.

"That and he drinks White Russians. You want a drink now?"

IRIS DIDN'T SLEEP at all that night trying to figure out what connection Grant Peters might have with a New York restaurant. She also tried to figure out a way to explain herself to Grant. *Hello, I think you are an absolutely beautiful man, and you also just happen to meet all of the specifications for a lover given to me by my boss, Maggie Maxwell. No, I am not here because I wish with all my heart you would ask me out, I am here because I want my own byline. Therefore, would you agree to meet Maggie so that the female bombshell knocks your socks off and saves the magazine and my budding career?* After mentally rehearsing a million times what she could say, she decided to just try to get Grant's New York address where Maggie could find him and take over. But there was no Grant Peters listed in the phone book, so she decided to go to Eve's Garden.

The next morning she went to the restaurant as soon as it opened. A string of cowbells jangled as Iris entered. It was a small eatery with only six tables. A food counter stretched the length of the narrow room. The cook's stove was in the picture window facing the sidewalk. A woman stood at the cash register talking with the proprietor. Both looked up when Iris entered the restaurant. The proprietor, who was in his early forties and had a short, military-style haircut, nodded in her direction. Iris waited until the woman paid her bill and left before she walked up to the man and said, "I was hoping you could help me."

He returned her friendly smile. "If I can."

"I'm trying to find Grant Peters—tall, curly dark hair—"

"I know Grant. But he doesn't come in until around ten-thirty. He keeps late nights."

Iris's heart pounded with relief. Whatever his business, it seemed he belonged to this address. Perhaps he supplied the restaurant with Viennese pastries.

"He's our short-order cook," the man said. "...Come back after lunch. Then the rush will be over."

Iris's spirits sank. She was chasing wild geese with a very slim lead. Either she was very tired or very desperate. Grasping the edge of the counter to steady herself, she said, "I must have made a mistake. That doesn't sound like the man I'm looking for. I'm sorry I bothered you." She turned to leave.

The owner kept staring curiously at her, with a look that said he had met women like her before. "Do you want me to tell Grant you were looking for him?"

"No, thanks," she said, feeling uncomfortable from the restaurateur's speculative gaze. "It couldn't be the same man. This Grant is in his early thirties. I met him in a bar last night." She reached for the doorknob.

"Dream On."

Iris turned back. Her eyes widened. "That's the bar. How did you know?"

"Grant's my wife's brother. He spends a lot of evenings there, improvising."

"I don't understand." He talked as if Grant Peters were an entertainer. "He told me he was rich and had an office in Vienna. It can't be the same man."

Shaking his head, the restaurateur picked up a stack of receipts and said, "Judge for yourself. Here he comes now."

As the door opened with a jangle from the cowbells, Iris turned. Grant Peters walked into the restaurant.

Grant recognized Iris the instant he saw her. He stopped short, feeling like a caged ferret, but quickly rebounded like a tennis player recovering from a bad volley. "Well, hello," he said. "Do you have lunch here, too?" Grant had always prided himself on his improvisation and rapid return. But from the incredulous look in her eyes he guessed that what had worked so well with her the previous evening wouldn't get results this morning. She had obviously been talking to his brother-in-law, Bob Perleman, who had never thought much of Grant's acting.

Grant's cheeks were dark and unshaven, his hair loose and curly in an all-American way. If Iris hadn't caught the glint of recognition in his eyes, she might almost have thought he was a different man in the faded jeans and T-shirt with the Eve's Garden logo on it. "I don't eat here any more than you do," Iris answered icily. "You lied to me last night."

"Hey, now, wait a minute," he said, stepping into the cooking area behind the counter as if it would protect him from her. "I can understand how you'd get that impression. But I can explain." He mentally ran through his repertoire of roles, wondering if a different approach would help.

"Grant, you haven't been telling your Irish Sweepstakes winner stories again, have you?" Bob asked. He frowned to show his disapproval.

Iris looked from the stout restaurateur to Grant Peters. "So this isn't the first time you've done this," she accused. She clenched her fists, hanging on to her anger to keep her embarrassment at bay. She felt like a fool for being taken in by his line, no matter how original it had been. "You're nothing but a—a fake."

"I'm an actor," he insisted, giving his brother-in-law an annoyed glance. Bob wanted him to settle down in the restaurant business, but Grant still had the wanderlust of acting in his blood. "Last night I was just testing out a role."

"A perpetually out-of-work actor," his brother-in-law pointed out. Then seeing that no one cared what he thought, Bob shrugged and went to set the tables.

"I'll bet your kind of plays fold after a one-night stand, don't they?" Iris said with venom dripping from every vowel.

Inwardly Grant winced. She didn't even know him and she could tell that. It made him all the more determined to continue the role of starving artist on the verge of stardom. "Last night I merely acted out a role I created for your entertainment. And you did enjoy it. Tell me I wasn't good."

"I only believed what you told me because you didn't let me know which rules you were playing by. If you weren't standing behind that counter, I'd—I'd hit you."

Grant stepped out from around the counter and advanced close enough for her to carry out her threat. When she didn't say or do anything, he said, "Look, I can tell that you are a very sophisticated lady. If I had told you I was a short-order cook, would you have given me two minutes of your time?"

The effect of him standing in front of her was just as heady as the previous night when she had met him in the bar. Angry at herself because she had been taken in by his male sensuality, she whacked him with her palm, hurting her hand, she was sure, more than she could ever hurt that solid male chest. "Chauvinist," she spat, and stalked out of the restaurant.

Grant watched her saucy walk as she disappeared into the crowd on the sidewalk. With regret, he relived the previous evening and the thought of how he had planned to turn up at Dream On again to look for her. He had even rehearsed how he would tell her the truth about himself, and ask if they could start over without any games between them. Something about her had drawn him to her, causing him to single her out from that roomful of unattached women. He had woken up this morning with her on his mind. And he had thought of all the things he *should* have told her about himself instead of the lies he had made up as he went along. He wanted to watch that soft, mesmerized look come to her eyes again and know that it was because of *him*, not some stupid image enhanced by a few drinks. But he didn't think he'd get a third chance to set the story straight after this.

"Now that's a real classy lady," Bob commented, holding out a white butcher's apron to Grant. "Too bad you blew it right at the start. But pretending to be something you aren't has always been your downfall."

IRIS FUMED all the way to the office, too angry and disillusioned to concern herself with the fact that soon she might not have a job to return to, never mind her dreams of a byline. Maybe she didn't need the prestige of being a writer as much as she thought she did, especially if it required such public humiliations. "The nerve of that man," she muttered to herself as she stormed past the receptionist's desk and ran into her uncle in the hallway.

Always one to be concerned with appearances and not exhibiting one's emotions in public, Edward South grabbed her wrist, halting her. He pulled her aside and in a deep voice asked, "What are you raving about?"

"A fool I met last night in a bar."

"Still no luck?" he asked.

Iris sighed. "I'm just no good at finding perfect men, Uncle Edward. I swear I think I attract slime like a sewer pipe. The one guy who appears he might even come close to meeting Maggie's specifications turns out to be a con artist," she said, and explained how taken she had been with the fictional man from Vienna.

South listened attentively and kept asking her questions about the evening. Still angry, Iris told him all about it. "This guy sounds perfect," her uncle said, an amused expression on his face. With his thumb and index finger he played with his mustache, lost in thought.

"That's right, *sounds* perfect, but that's all. He made everything up. He's nothing but a short-order cook who fancies himself to be an actor. Can you believe he takes on different roles every night in that bar just to pick up women?"

"What an act. He sounds too good to be true."

Iris glared at her uncle. It was just like him to side with Grant Peters simply because he was a man. "And I believed everything he said, just like an idiot." Iris still felt like screaming, but remembering where she was and who she was with, she restrained herself. "I'm so mad I could eat nails."

South clamped a hand on her shoulder. Iris winced from the firmness of his grip. "Hold on a minute. Let's think this through." Tweaking his mustache, he stared off into space. His eyes held a gleam of power. "Do you know what we have here?"

"We have nothing."

South lowered his voice and spoke slowly. "This man was able to fool you, maybe he could fool Maggie, too. I mean, if he had been who he pretended to be, he would be Maggie's Mr. Perfect." He paused, rapidly thinking through his own suggestion. His face folded into its well-worn frown lines, and his eyes narrowed. "Yes," he said, nodding to himself.

"I don't know," Iris argued. "How could you deal with a man who is so unethical?"

"This isn't a question of ethics," Edward stated, lowering his voice further as he glanced up and down the hall to be certain no one was paying attention to their conversation. "I have a business to think of. This magazine staffs more than fifty employees and many free-lancers and pressmen. Where are the ethics in letting those people down?" His eyes bore down on her. "It's not just your new position you should think of, but every job that could be saved by this man if you can recruit him to our cause."

"Has it really come to this?"

"This is the best thing you've come up with so far," South said, speaking rapidly. "Let's hire this guy to play the same role he did for you, at least long enough for Maggie to get off the hook with Sheila Croft for the charity ball and the TV interview. We could follow him and Maggie around for a series of photo features on the ideal romance, the way Hugh Hefner used to take readers on his dream dates. Think of it. The publicity will be wonderful, just like the old times, before Maggie started letting her heart get in the way of her head."

Iris put her hands on her hips. "The guy is a chameleon. Maggie's perfect man just doesn't exist."

"Maybe not, but it's crucial to the magazine that we keep Maggie's fantasies intact." When Iris didn't answer, Edward South began laying plans. "You find this actor and hire him to play the same role he did for you. I'll get our legal people to draw up a contract that no one could refuse."

"But—"

"It'll be no different than paying models to act out Maggie's fantasies in the magazine's photographs. And Maggie will simply assume we've come up with a blind date for her." He spoke more rapidly, making a Machiavellian list of things to do. "I'll arrange a meeting of the key staff members at our photographer's studio later this afternoon to meet this guy. If he's as good as you say he is, we might be able to make him over completely to fit Maggie's description."

"But that seems so deceptive."

Behind gold-rimmed glasses, South's dark brown eyes defied Iris to contradict him. "No, it's a last, desperate roll of the dice. Do it Iris. Time has run out on real romance for Maggie and all of us."

GRANT PETERS WAS JUGGLING seven hamburgers at once when Iris returned to the restaurant. Awkwardly she stood and watched him from the sidewalk, trying to get up enough courage to go inside. When he noticed her standing at the picture window, he motioned to her and she went in.

"One for lunch?" he asked her, when after several minutes she still hadn't said anything. *She's back!* he rejoiced, feeling a flutter in his chest like a flock of wild birds taking flight. He had to be careful not to blow things this time. Something in her expression made him feel chance was in his favor. She looked as if she wanted to ask him something.

She shook her head. "One for an apology," she said humbly. "And a proposition."

Surprised that she wanted to apologize to him, Grant smiled cockily. Maybe he hadn't lost his touch, after all. "Didn't you imply last night you weren't interested?"

"Not *that* kind of proposition," she answered hastily, lowering her voice and glancing around her. The room was small and crowded with lunchtime workers. A woman with long, straight hair was running back and forth to the counter, keeping the tables serviced. The owner was working the cash register. Fortunately no one seemed to pay much attention to her. Those who were looking in their direction were more interested in Grant's antics at the grill. "At least not for me. And not in the way you mean."

He flipped a hamburger high in the air and caught it upended on the spatula. A small crowd had gathered outside the window to watch his exhibitionist-style cooking. "Maybe you'd better explain the way *you* mean." He removed a burger from the grill and hastily assembled a sandwich with lettuce, tomato, onion and a dab of mayonnaise spread with a wide plastic spatula. He set it down on a paper plate and scooped out a mound of potato salad from a bin, added a pickle slice, then shoved the plate along the counter to the waitress.

Longing for the pickle, Iris asked, "Do you make up these games very often?"

Reading the next order slip, Grant said, "As I said, they're more like acting roles." He picked up another bun, spread on mayonnaise and began piling up slices of roast beef. "They keep me sharp, just in case a role materializes."

Iris glanced at the owner who was ringing up a customer's order. "I'd like to offer you the role of a lifetime,'' she said, hoping she could make the proposition sound so good he wouldn't be able to say no. She hesitated, wanting to choose her words carefully. ''It would help a lot of people. And you'd be paid.'' She detected the barest flicker of interest in his eyes as he filled another sandwich order. ''Exceptionally well,'' she added, trying to quickly close the sale.

''I'm real busy right now. I've got a lot of irons in the fire,'' he said coolly. A professional wouldn't commit before hearing what kind of deal was being offered. A professional would not offer to pay *them* to let him act.

''Too busy to play the role of leading man opposite one of America's most famous leading ladies?'' she asked. Like Maggie Maxwell, he lived in a world of make-believe. They *would* be perfect for each other. ''Your role wouldn't be much different from what you did for me last night.''

''That was easy,'' he said, giving her a look that reminded her how desirous he had made her feel the previous evening. He slapped another hamburger on the grill. It sizzled in the silence between them. ''Are you an agent or a producer? Did you see one of the tapes or résumés I've left with the talent agencies around town?'' In spite of follow-up phone calls and visits, the tapes and résumés had been out so long without response that he'd lost hope of hearing from anyone. He kept telling himself it was time to give up the ghost of acting, but he found it hard to let go of his dream. He cut his eyes in her direction and poked at the hamburger with the spatula. Grease spattered and popped.

''No, nothing like that. I just want to hire you. As you said, you totally took me in last night. I'm convinced that you are an excellent actor.''

He nodded speculatively and lied, "I'm a member of Actor's Equity, and I don't work for any less than scale."

"I don't know what scale is," she admitted, "but..." She named the figure her uncle had suggested to hire him as an escort for Maggie. "Plus, I have a contract with me stipulating that you will receive that figure for a minimum of ninety days, with expenses, the full use of a Fifth Avenue penthouse, plus twenty-four-hour limousine service at your beck and call."

The hamburger he flipped landed with a splat on the floor. "Just how *real* are we talking with this role? I don't do murderers or drug dealers."

"It's nothing like that," Iris assured him. She turned to see if anyone was paying attention to them. The couple at the table nearest her were listening as if their conversation were part of a live soap opera. "Can't we go somewhere and talk about this in private?"

Grant liked the way she bit her lower lip when she was under pressure. He knew he was going to say yes if for no other reason than to see her again. "As I recall, you said no to that last night when I suggested it." His voice was heady with seduction.

"Look, are you interested or not?" she said, her green eyes flashing with impatience. Realizing she was right back to square one if he wasn't, and she would be faced with explaining her failure to her uncle, she softened, adding, "Please?"

He thought about it a minute. A change would be nice, plus this woman was offering to pay him as much for a ninety-day job as he made in a year. As much as he loved his sister, Eve, and enjoyed cooking, he really hadn't planned on making a career of it. Besides, he was frustrated working with Bob, who had his own ideas about how the restaurant should be run. Deciding he'd kept her guessing long enough, Grant said, "Okay. Elizabeth Howell, you've got yourself an actor."

"Huh?" she said, startled, wondering who he was talking to. She glanced behind her at the couple observing them.

"Short of murder, I agree, Elizabeth," he repeated. He tossed a fresh hamburger on the grill. "This is my last hamburger."

"Oh," she said, remembering the name she had given him the previous evening. "Elizabeth isn't my name."

"It isn't?" His eyes told her he had regained the upper hand. "You mean you lied to me last night, misrepresenting who *you* really were? I thought only men did that."

"That was different," she said. "I was only protecting my identity, not pretending to be someone fake, as you were doing."

"I see," he said calmly, flipping the fresh hamburger. "Then this role you're hiring me to play has something to do with your job at the IRS."

Iris clenched her hands. "I don't work for the IRS, either," she said through gritted teeth. "But I will be happy to turn you in anonymously for an audit." Switching to a crisp, businesslike voice, she pleaded, "If we could just go somewhere private, I will be happy to explain, which is more than you offered to do last night or today."

He flashed that devilish grin, which reminded her she needed him whether he understood why or not. "The worst of the lunch crowd will be out of here in another thirty minutes. We can talk then. Meanwhile, can I offer you some crow?"

"A hamburger will be fine," she responded, adding, "dressed."

When Grant was finished with the lunch crowd orders and Iris had eaten her hamburger, his brother-in-law, Bob, called Grant aside. "You going ahead with this idiotic deal?" he asked. He had overhead Iris's offer and had sent Grant several warning glances that had been ignored.

"The money's good and it's a chance to do some real acting for a change," Grant replied.

Bob shook his head and said, "When are you going to grow up and forget this business of being an actor? Nothing good has ever come of it for you. You upset your father, lost your wife, you couldn't get a job acting in L.A. or New York. As good as you are as a chef, it's a downright crime for you to waste your life chasing two-bit roles in some catsup commercial."

Even though they disagreed about everything from how much salt to put in the soup to how to arrange the chairs in the restaurant, Grant was grateful to his brother-in-law for bailing him out when he was down on his luck. Bob wanted him to become a full partner in the restaurant, but Grant thought it would make him feel as if he were taking handouts from his family forever. Sure he was a good cook, and he didn't mind the work, but something was missing in his life. He had always dreamed of filling that void with acting. "This will be my last hurrah," Grant replied. He wanted some time away from Eve's Garden to get some perspective on his life. "I promise. Then I'll settle down, and we'll make some of those changes you've been talking about for the restaurant. C'mon Bob, you heard the pay. This is my chance to get solvent for once in my life."

"Yeah, I heard the pay, and that bothers me the most. You better listen long and hard to exactly what this role is before you sign that contract, or do you still believe in the tooth fairy, too?"

"Hey, this is show business. Anything's possible."

IRIS WASN'T CERTAIN she felt any better about her part in the dating deception later that afternoon when she brought Grant Peters with her to the photographer's studio for South Publications. There wasn't an hour or a day to be lost in their preparation for his meeting with Maggie. Key staff members, recruited by her uncle, were waiting on them, ready to examine Iris's "find."

Without so much as a handshake in greeting, Edward South looked Grant Peters up and down, turned to Tina, who Grant recognized from the night before, and said, "He looks a little rough around the edges. See if you can't buff him up a bit. Be sure he understands he doesn't get the ninety-day contract until he passes Maggie's approval. Until then it's strictly per diem pay."

Dawn Collins, the managing editor, led him into the studio. She was in her late-thirties, overweight and wore her bleached blond hair pulled back in a severe bun. Her earrings jangled as she walked. Inside, the photographer's lights played on a seamless backdrop where they had placed a stool for Grant to sit. "If looks are his only problem, we can handle that," Dawn announced. "He'll need a complete wardrobe, and a decent haircut will help a lot. He'll have to shave more often."

Tina Powers agreed, "He looked pretty good last night. I think we can work with him."

"Okay then, ladies, do your best," South said, unable to meet Grant's eyes. Iris wondered if he felt uncomfortable over what was about to take place. "The magazine's counting on you girls." Edward checked his watch, announced another appointment, and quickly left the studio.

How like him to just disappear and let others do all the dirty work, Iris thought ungratefully, wishing her uncle had been the one to discover Grant. She felt an emptiness in the pit of her stomach.

"Sit right here," Dawn said, inviting Grant to take the stool spotlighted by the lights.

Grant sat where she pointed and pleasantly faced the women in front of him. They circled him, contemplating the man as if he were a free-standing art object they were considering buying. Grant kept Iris in his peripheral vision, hoping the attention from all these women would get a rise from her. Iris stepped back, pulled her glasses from the crown of her hair, and sat in a chair outside of the spotlight, feeling as much on trial as Grant was.

"He has a few gray hairs," Tina pointed out. She put her hand on her wafer-thin hip and turned to Iris. "He looks so different today. Are you sure he's younger than Maggie?"

"I'm thirty-one," Grant supplied, smiling pleasantly at the other women and deciding none were half as attractive as Iris. There was something about her that went beyond mere physical appearance to make her stand out.

"We'll have to give him a rinse along with the haircut," Tina decided.

"Make a note of that," Dawn said, crossing one arm under her ample breasts to brace her other arm upright against it. Her assistant took out a notebook and jotted a reminder on the page. Dawn rested her chin against her hand and paced around Grant.

Iris nervously crossed her legs and bit her fingernails. She pushed her glasses up the bridge of her nose and watched Grant closely, braced for an accusing glance from him. Instead, he appeared to ignore her completely and sat as relaxed as if he weren't on exhibit. He reached in his pocket for his cigarettes.

"No cigarettes," Allison, the art director, stated. "Maggie can't stand men who smoke."

Grant shrugged, slipped the cigarettes back in his pocket, crossed his legs and laced his fingers around his knee. Their poking and prying annoyed him, but he had long ago learned in acting class how to disguise his true emotions.

Tina grabbed him by the chin and studied him. "You have to cut out late nights. It's showing in your face."

Dawn patted his stomach. "Looks like you better cut out the beer, too."

Grant sucked in his stomach and glanced surreptitiously at Iris, wondering if she was as critical as the others. The photographic lights were making him hot.

Iris looked away from Grant, afraid that he would hate her for getting him into this. He was stoically accepting the women's criticisms as they made suggestions for changes in Grant's appearance. The overweight, rail-thin and mousy-haired women in front of him were anything but the perfect-model image the magazine's cover displayed each month. Like Maggie, these women were so caught up in their work, they rarely heeded their own advice.

"Make a muscle," Allison said, bending her arm upward to demonstrate. She had freckles and wore her hair in a braid to keep it out of her way when she worked out.

Grant complied, enjoying the chance to show off in front of Iris.

Allison poked and prodded the muscle of his upper arm. "Hmmm. A bit flabby. Better sign him up on a crash course at a health club with a personal trainer, otherwise Maggie will leave him at the bus stop with her fanaticism over fitness."

"I like a man with a firm rear end," commented the assistant, who was making note of all the changes. "Would you mind standing up and turning around Mr. Peters?"

"Isn't this getting a bit personal?" Iris demanded, feeling more uncomfortable than Grant appeared to be. She felt sorry for him. Everyone was ogling him as if he were the star attraction in a private peep show.

Everyone, including Grant, looked at her as if they had forgotten she was there. Secretly, Grant was pleased to know she had been every bit as aware of him as he was of her. He wondered how he could arrange to get her alone.

"We have to get personal if we're going to make this work," Dawn pointed out.

"That's right, it's just business," Tina agreed, looking at Iris over her shoulder, then studying Grant critically again. "He's getting paid for this. And if we don't make sure he's perfect, Maggie won't approve of him."

"It's okay," Grant assured Iris, as if she were the one on display. "I'm a professional. It's just part of the job. Now which of you ladies wants to see if my behind passes muster." None of the women volunteered. He gave Iris a friendly wink, and thought how much more arousing this make-over business could be if he was alone with her.

Iris settled back uncomfortably, feeling as if she were an intruder. She was the only one who didn't seem to be enjoying herself.

"We have a few questions we want to ask you," Dawn said, taking a seat in one of the chairs that had been positioned to face Grant's stool.

"Sure," Grant said agreeably, turning his eyes to Dawn, but keeping his heated thoughts on Iris.

"What kind of underwear do you wear?" Dawn asked.

"Fruit of the Loom," Grant answered.

"That won't do," Tina decided. "We'll have to get you some designer briefs."

"The briefer the better," Allison, the art director agreed. "If he works in Europe the majority of the year, he should have a tan, all over, European-style."

"Oh, yes, firm brown buns. I'd like that," said Dawn's assistant, adding another note to the list. "But, no need to check your tan lines, Mr. Peters," she added quickly.

Grant let the embarrassing questions roll over him and trained his mesmerized attention on Iris, knowing he'd like to leave her without a doubt as to his qualifications for *her*.

"Do you have hair on your shoulders?" Allison asked. "I hate men with hair on their shoulders."

"I like hairy men," Dawn argued, facing her editors as if they were alone and having this discussion about men.

"I'll introduce you to the gorilla I went out with Saturday night," Allison told Dawn. She looked squarely at Grant. "How often do you bathe? Do you sleep in the nude? Do you understand a *woman's* meaning of the word *foreplay*?"

"For crying out loud, Allison, we're supposed to be prepping him for the New York Charity Ball," Iris reminded the editor, "not an orgy."

A few of the editors looked uncomfortable in their seats. Tina coughed and looked apologetic. "Those are the sort of questions every woman who reads *New Age Woman* wants to ask," Allison said defensively. "And Maggie's the one who thinks up those questions. We need him prepared for every eventuality."

"It's okay," Grant assured Iris, smiling. He admired her spunk and liked an emotional woman. "I'm a damned good actor, and I take my roles seriously, even if they are for an audience of one."

Dawn sat forward on the edge of her chair and crossed her arms into *The Thinker* position again. "Maggie may be the prime focus of your performance, *if* she passes final approval on you," Dawn pointed out. "But that's just the first step. You're going to also have to fool Sheila Croft, and she doesn't miss a thing."

"I'm your man," Grant said cockily, folding his arms across his chest, smiling pleasantly.

Iris tried to relax, but she couldn't help tensing for the next questions directed at Grant.

"Are you affectionate in public?"

"Do you hold hands?"

"Open doors?"

"Walk on the traffic side of the sidewalk?"

"How do you kiss? Maggie will expect you to kiss her good-night."

"Shall I demonstrate?" Grant asked, grateful that the inquisition had finally given him an opportunity to draw Iris into the action.

Before anyone could say yes or no or Iris could guess his intentions, he stood and crossed the room to where she sat with her arms folded, and took full advantage of the situation. With his hands on her upper arms, he pulled her out of the chair and gently toward him.

As she realized what he was doing, Iris went limp, refusing to give in to his macho demonstration for the benefit of a roomful of women. But by relaxing, she unwittingly gave in to his plan. His hands soothed and caressed the muscles in her upper arms. It was a gesture of half massage and half lovemaking. His lips teased hers, not pressing for an advantage, but tempting in their nearness. His warm breath was like a whisper, hinting of many more delights in store.

Grant had set out to kiss her like Clark Gable in *Gone With the Wind*, but the minute his lips touched hers he found himself lost in her soft caress. For what seemed like long, luscious minutes, but could only have been mere seconds, he thought only of her in his arms. Someone coughed, intruding on the embrace the way a director calls "cut!" to end a love scene. Remembering where they were and the role he had been hired to play, he gradually drew away from her and composed his face as if nothing had happened while he took his place in the spotlight again.

It's only make-believe, Iris drilled herself. But when Grant eased back, for the briefest second, the look in his eyes was serious, as if he, too, needed to remember the kiss had no real intentions behind it.

"That'll do," Dawn called out, fanning herself with her notebook. She cleared her throat and fussed with the notes in front of her. "You seem to be pretty good with kissing, but do you know how many member countries there are in OPEC? Their names? The world price of a barrel of oil today? The U.S. dollar rate of exchange for the English pound, German mark, Austrian schilling?"

Grant shifted in his chair. "No, I don't know," he answered, looking bewildered, unable to concentrate on the questions as he tried to calm his racing pulse.

"Do you know anything about horses?"

"Wines?"

"Yachts?"

The editors fired question after question from Maggie's list for the ideal man.

Grant's lack of sophistication showed once the questions turned to economics and current events. Iris watched as the women's probing soon revealed that his highly polished coolness was an extremely thin layer of chrome over blue-collar steel.

"What do all these questions have to do with being an escort for Maggie Maxwell?" Iris demanded.

"He'll need to know something about the world economic situation for dinner conversation," Dawn responded. She flipped through the notes in front of her that the editors had compiled at Maggie's request and said, "He has to speak two foreign languages. Speak some German for us, Grant."

"Haben Sie genug Gemüse?" Grant responded in the same words he had used with Iris the evening before. *"Achtung, fertig, los!"* He lifted his shoulders and added, *"Ja, kommen, wir schauen zum Fenster hinaus!"*

Allison, who spoke German, started laughing as she translated, "Do you have enough vegetables? Attention, ready, free! And yes, come on, we'll look out of the window. What's all that supposed to mean?"

"It's the lines from a play I tried out for once," Grant answered. "Sorry, but that's all I know. I didn't get the part."

Iris's jaw dropped. Unless she was mistaken, he had used those same phrases with her the previous evening. As if sensing she had made the connection, Grant slanted his eyes in her direction and shrugged in apology.

"It'll have to do," the art director said, running a pencil down the list in front of her. "Thank God he doesn't speak French."

"Why not?" Grant asked.

"Maggie does."

"This business card," Dawn said. "What's this coat of arms stand for?"

"I found a picture of it in a book," Grant explained. "It's from a monastery in Melk, Austria."

Iris groaned as the deceptions piled up. The role of Mr. Perfect had mushroomed out of her control.

"This is going to be quite a script you'll have to memorize," Dawn said as she reviewed the notes her assistant had taken during the get-acquainted session.

"Don't worry," Grant assured her. "That's what I'm good at."

"Yeah, one-night stands," Iris muttered as she listened to each woman add her own particular requirements to the composite for the perfect man, who Grant Peters would become.

By the end of the three-hour session, the staff had enough notes to fill an issue of the magazine, and had set up haircut, tanning, exercise and tailoring appointments for Grant before the gala ball. Dawn, Allison and the other editors left the photographer's studio pleased with their plans for the make-over. Grant, who left agreeably with Tina for a haircut appointment that afternoon, seemed to take it all in stride. He even winked at Iris as they left the studio. He was getting paid, Iris reminded herself. So why did she feel like Judas Iscariot?

Chapter Three

Iris slammed the back door of the cab and reluctantly handed the driver his fare through the window. In this unfamiliar neighborhood where she had asked to be driven, she felt as if he were abandoning her, like the first time her parents had dropped her off at summer camp. It didn't help at all to hear the click of the door locks on the taxi before the driver revved the engine and left her standing alone in the middle of the street.

She looked up at the drab, gray buildings then down at the cracked, uneven sidewalks. So this was where Grant Peters lived. She took a deep breath, skirted the abandoned car sitting on its wheel hubs and hurried to the entrance of his building.

She knew the entire staff had been working with him for several days, but since that day in the photographer's studio, she hadn't seen him, although he had been heavily on her mind. She had felt unsettled, guilty, and wanted to apologize for getting him into this, but at the same time she told herself she wanted to be sure he could play the role well. If all went according to plan when Grant met Maggie for lunch the next day, Edward South would move him into the penthouse apartment that belonged to a friend of his. Iris felt for the key in her skirt pocket and wished now that someone else had been given the honor of showing Grant his new home if Maggie approved of him.

A row of mailboxes in front of the stairs indicated that Grant's apartment was on the third floor. Iris stepped around the staircase looking for an elevator, realized there wasn't one, and started up the steps, conscious of every hollow echo of her low heels against the tread. From the sound, she expected everyone in each apartment to poke their heads out of the doorways to see who was coming. She hoped no one would recognize her, then reminded herself this was not the kind of place her friends were likely to be found dead in. The walls were thin, and she heard crying babies and family disputes as she climbed to the third-floor landing.

At Grant's door, she heard low voices coming from his apartment and thought he must have company. She hesitated, and almost changed her mind about staying until she heard the sounds of a scuffle. Instinctively Iris knocked on the door. "Grant!" she shouted. "Grant, are you in there?"

Suddenly everything became quiet. Iris realized the foolishness of her move. What if Grant was being murdered? What if she would be the next victim?

When the door opened, she cringed in alarm, then quickly tried to regain her composure as Grant stood in front of her wearing a sleeveless undershirt and jeans. He held an open bag of Corn Doodles in his hand.

"Is something wrong?" he asked, eyes alight as he realized who the visitor was. His ego shot as high as the World Trade towers. He must have made an impression on her the other day if she had come here of her own volition, especially when they were scheduled to meet again tomorrow morning.

"Oh . . . I . . . no . . ." she stammered out of confusion over the voices she had heard. She peered into the apartment behind him. "I heard people shouting. It sounded like you were having a fight." As well as she could tell, he was alone in the apartment.

Grant laughed, and held the door wider to invite her inside. "That was just the VCR. I was playing one of my old movies. What brings you here?"

"Oh, I came to get you," she said as she refocused her attention on him now that she realized he was alone. "My uncle wanted you to know where you'll be living, if Maggie approves of you tomorrow. You don't have a phone," she finished lamely as she looked beyond him into the cramped and cluttered apartment. "So, I came to get you to show you the other place."

"Your uncle goes all out, doesn't he?" Grant said, holding the door wide. "I thought the new suit for tomorrow's meeting was pretty extravagant, on top of my salary and all. Come on in. I'll just throw on a shirt and we'll go."

As she stepped through the doorway, Iris, dressed in a comfortable sweater over a chambray skirt, felt as big as Tinkerbell and as out of place as a Dresden china statue in a bull-pen. His apartment was a two-room efficiency. There were two director's chairs, a wooden trunk that served as a table, a Murphy bed that had been left down and unmade. There was an exercise bike with a broken chain, a set of weights with dust an inch thick on top and a bicycle with a flat tire. A bank of books, records and cassettes were lined up along one wall, while the opposite one was mirrored. Next to the single window, which overlooked the fire escape, was a television set, VCR and sophisticated stereo equipment. A narrow bookcase was filled with cassette tapes. A cactus plant stood on top of the bookcase. An ashtray filled with cigarette butts sat on the floor beside the bed. "I think you'd better put a suit on," she suggested politely. "I don't believe anyone even owns a pair of jeans in the building where we're going."

"Sure thing," he said agreeably, and went to the closet, removing the suit he had worn the night they had met in Dream On.

Iris smiled wanly and stepped over a pile of magazines that were strewn across the floor, *Show Business*, *Backstage* and *Variety* lay on top of current issues of *Time*, *Forbes* and *Town & Country*. "I wasn't sure you would be home," Iris said as he went into the bathroom to change.

"Where would I be?" he asked, shutting the door.

Iris felt claustrophobic. The room smelled of stale smoke. She stood by the window. "I thought you might be at Dream On, practicing roles again."

"I only do that when I don't have a role to work on," he answered.

Iris was glad he was in the other room so she could hide her embarrassment at the sight of his apartment. With a three-story brownstone to herself, she couldn't imagine living in such cramped quarters. And the dust made her realize how much she took maids for granted. She sat in the canvas director's chair that looked the cleanest, and waited for him. She crossed her legs, then uncrossed them, wiggling farther back in the chair in an effort to look casual.

When he returned he looked like a different person, and Iris couldn't help thinking how clothes made the image of a man. She relaxed at the sight of him and kept on telling herself that Maggie would never see him in his true colors, living in this ancient building that had somehow escaped the wrecking ball.

Her eyes strayed to the unmade bed between them and her imagination filled with the thought of both their bodies sprawled there, together. Grant was the kind of man who could make you forget the surroundings, so that all that mattered was the two of you. She shifted in the director's chair, not certain if that thought made her feel more at ease about the meeting with Maggie, or uneasy about what might take place once the two of them were alone.

"Look, this really isn't fair, your showing up unannounced and all. I mean, I'm afraid you are seeing me at my worst," Grant said, sensing her discomfort with his apartment. He still couldn't believe she was here, whatever the excuse. It made him nervous because his apartment was such a dump, and she was the kind of woman who looked as if there were castles in her background. But he couldn't tell her how much he hated this place and how he spent so much time with Bob and Eve just to avoid being alone in what he termed "This Property Condemned." "Shall we go?" he asked.

She stood, not wanting to spend any longer than necessary there. "What would you have done the other night if I had suggested we go to your place?" she asked as they went down the stairs together, their bodies brushing accidentally in the confined space. "Surely you couldn't have afforded a hotel room." She felt herself growing hot the longer she entertained the thought of them making love. She could imagine his solid, tanned muscles glistening with sweat and how secure and sensuous he could make her feel if he held her in his arms.

"Don't let this place fool you," Grant said. "I make a good living as a chef." Grant smiled, rubbing his hand against his dark, unshaven cheek. "But if you had said yes, I would have had a plane to catch." They reached the street and Grant set about hailing a cab.

"What?" she said, slightly confused and somewhat disappointed.

"I like to make women feel good about themselves, so I tell them the things they want to hear that most men don't take the time to say. But women get so emotionally involved when you take them to bed that I draw the line there. I don't want to hurt anyone."

His reply made her feel as if she had just been rudely awakened from a warm, sensual dream. "So, what's in it for you?" Iris asked as she sighted a cab.

Grant stepped out into the street to flag it down. He held the door for her and waited until she had told the driver where they were going before he said, "I just like to play different roles to test my acting skills." Grant didn't want to admit they were the only kinds of roles he was ever likely to play again if he kept his promise to his sister and brother-in-law. "Singles' bars epitomize the life of an actor—you have to get noticed, you have to get the lines down, put on the costume, subject yourself to constant rejection. And you have three minutes to sell yourself to the producer, or woman in the case of the bar, because there are a thousand other guys trying out with you."

"So," she began, reminding herself that they were working together now for Maggie's sake. There was no place in their association for sentimentality or a show of emotion. "You just picked me out of that roomful of people, like I was the lucky sweepstakes winner or something. I suppose I should be relieved that you weren't really attracted to me. I never liked men who came on to me in bars."

He didn't reply immediately. When she looked at him, she found his eyes absorbing the sight of her. Grant was remembering every detail of the first time he saw Iris in Dream On. The room had been hazy with smoke. She had been sitting at the bar where a light behind her gave her lush hair an astral look. In spite of the noise and the crowd in the room, she had stood out, as if she were a queen sitting on her throne. There was something very different about this woman. Bob had called it "class." "I wouldn't have singled you out in the first place," he said carefully, waiting until she looked at him, then holding her eyes, "if I hadn't been attracted to you." He paused. "But it wouldn't have gone any further unless we had known each other better, and maybe not even then."

And now? she felt herself wondering, and surprisingly heard herself asking, "So what do you think of me now that I've gotten you an audition for this role as Maggie's ideal man?"

"I'm grateful," he said, lowering his voice in case the cab driver was paying more attention to his fares than the reggae music playing on the radio. Sadly his eyes rested on her. He wanted to make things right between them, be honest with her. "But it does put a strain on *us*, since I'll have to be Maggie's perfect gentleman for a while."

The way he spoke made her uncomfortable. He was assuming that they were part of a relationship. Just a few days ago she had been sealed in her nice, emotion-free cocoon. She looked out the window and remained silent until they reached the building, which fronted Central Park. Grant paid the fare, with money supplied from her uncle she was sure. Then Iris led the way past the doorman to the elevator that would take them to the penthouse.

She opened the door, and Grant stepped inside as if he were entering a museum and stood in awe of the view of Central Park. The apartment had been designed with the location in mind. The living room, master bedroom and kitchen had floor-to-ceiling windows. The study, guest bedrooms and maid's room also had beautiful views of the park. The master bath and dressing area were larger than Grant's entire living room. A skylight was over the Jacuzzi, which was big enough to hold twelve people. The terrace, with full-grown fruit trees, reminded him of a tropical island.

The minute he had stepped through the door, Grant seemed to have taken on the character of another person. Iris couldn't help thinking how well the apartment suited him. "Maggie has the final say over whether or not you'll work out," she reminded.

"Yes, I know," he said, strutting like a rooster in a henhouse. The overstuffed leather furniture made him feel as if he had entered the Playboy mansion. "Lunch tomorrow is like a go-see or an audition. Don't worry. I'll get the part of her attentive lover."

"I would think that's a role that would come naturally to you." She almost wished her uncle's scheme would fail, although she couldn't put her feelings into words.

He stood in front of the windows, as if all of Central Park were nothing more than a model layout belonging entirely to him. It was a long time before he answered, and only when Iris looked at him did he say, "Only with a woman I love."

Iris couldn't meet his eyes. She was remembering how deep and penetrating they had looked to her that night in the bar. "Have you ever really been in love," she asked, "or only pretended to be?"

Grant laughed and sat on the couch. "I was in love once," he said. "That's why I was so generous with the furniture in the divorce settlement before I moved here from L.A., not that we ever had much."

"Why New York?"

He stared toward the window. "There are more options here. In Hollywood there's only TV and movies," he said, remembering how high his hopes had been before the move. At the time acting had been his sole consideration. "Here there are commercials, soap operas, Broadway, Off Broadway, Off Off Broadway." He grinned. "Besides, most of the casting directors for out-of-town productions start looking here. It may not be any easier to achieve stardom here, but you're more likely to make a living."

"Oh," Iris said quietly, thinking of her own position at *New Age Woman*. She wished she could be so sure of herself when it came to a career. Grant relied on his wits and talent. Iris depended on her family connections. Without Uncle Edward, she probably wouldn't have a job at all.

"But the truth of the matter is," he said, clearing his throat as if that would make it easier to say, "my brother-in-law, Bob, offered me a job." After being out of work in L.A. for ten months, Grant hadn't been able to refuse. And he didn't have one successful audition in New York to show for his so-called acting career. He had told Bob and Eve often enough that he had given up his dreams of acting, but Grant couldn't convince himself as easily.

"Did you have any children?"

He shook his head. "How about you?"

"I told you the other night I wasn't married," she reminded him.

"You also told me you worked for the IRS."

"Don't remind me," she said with a laugh. "I tell that to every man I meet in a bar, unless they really annoy me, and then I say I'm a policewoman on a stakeout and they'd better get lost."

Grant laughed with her. "You see, we all have our little deceptions."

Iris didn't like being caught in her own lies. Thinking of Grant's acting role reminded her why they were in the penthouse. "The person who owns this place is going to be in Europe for the next six months. Uncle Edward has arranged for you to apartment-sit. Sheila Croft is bound to have you followed, the way she's always nosing for news. And you might have to entertain Maggie from time to time."

"Your uncle's surely pulling out all the stops." First a new wardrobe, a complete make-over with hair and facial treatments, and now a penthouse apartment to live in. Wait until he told Eve and Bob about the perks of this acting job.

Money was always Uncle Edward's answer to problems, even when it came to helping Iris get what she wanted. "That's my uncle's style," she said.

THE RUSSIAN TEA ROOM was crowded when Iris and Maggie arrived for lunch. Usually, Iris liked to settle back with a drink and count how many rich and famous people she knew on a personal basis, no matter how tenuous the connection. Anticipating Maggie's reaction to Grant Peters made Iris too nervous to bother looking for notable patrons. She trained her eyes on the entrance as she slid into the booth beside Maggie.

Maggie checked her watch, and Iris did too. They were a few minutes early. She had warned Grant that Maggie couldn't stand waiting on anyone.

Maggie ordered a Perrier. Iris asked for the same. With her gaze riveted on the entrance, Iris asked about Maggie's book tour, but only half listened to her response. She watched elegant couples stroll into the restaurant and be seated by the maître d'. Each time a single man appeared, she sat straighter, thinking it might be Grant. When he did appear, at first she didn't recognize him. His hair was slicked back in a European wastrel style. He wore a smoky-gray suit, expertly tailored to make his shoulders seem broader and his stomach nonexistent. His shirt was pale blue and his tie, a dusty-rose color, matched the handkerchief in his jacket pocket. She felt butterflies in her stomach and thought she had never seen a more striking man. "There he is," Iris said, interrupting Maggie's monologue.

"Where?" Maggie asked as her hand flew automatically to straighten her shoulder-length hair. She ran her palms down her skirt.

"He's walking straight toward us," Iris said, noticing that Grant was precisely on time. *So far, so good,* she thought. She smiled and waved to make certain he had noticed where they were sitting. His expression registered recognition, and his deep brown eyes seemed to bear down on her, increasing the flutter in her stomach. Iris glanced away self-consciously, wishing he was here to meet her instead of Maggie. "Oh, no," she groaned.

"What's the matter?" Maggie asked, smiling politely as Grant approached their table.

"Sheila Croft is here," Iris whispered. The publisher was just getting up from a table with a reporter Iris recognized from one of the gossip tabloids. "No, don't look," she said, hastily thrusting one of the menus toward Maggie and opening the other to hide her face. She peeped over the edge. Iris wanted to flag down a waiter for a double Scotch, wishing Grant would go away and come back in fifteen minutes or so. Oblivious to her silent plea to go away, he kept heading their way. She readjusted the menu-shield to see if Sheila Croft had left yet and nearly jumped to find the woman standing beside their table.

"Looks like you're without an escort, as usual," Croft said, her quick glance dismissing Iris as someone unimportant.

What if Sheila decided to stay, Iris worried? What if Grant didn't measure up to Maggie's standards? What if he made a fool of all of them? He wasn't expected to give a fully polished performance until the charity ball on Saturday night. Her eyes flashed a warning to Grant who kept smiling and kept getting closer.

Maggie set the menu down. "Not for long," Maggie responded, shifting nervously.

"I should hope not, if you plan to save face," Sheila said. "The New York Charity Ball is this weekend. And no one has had the first glimpse of your mystery man." Her satisfied smile told Iris she had done her homework where Maggie's man was concerned. "The mystery is why he isn't here with you now, or anywhere else, for that matter."

"He's been in Vienna," Iris said, her voice coming out in a croak, since Maggie was sitting with a stunned expression on her face. "That's where his company is headquartered. He wanted to get his business out of the way while Maggie was on her book tour."

Sheila's glance flickered over Iris's face while Maggie smiled politely. "I have the best detectives in the business, Maggie," she said carefully, "and no one has so much as picked up a line about you with anyone other than Bradley Winchester, who we all know is old news."

Iris pushed her glasses on top of her head. "I'm going to get the waiter to bring us a drink," she said, preparing to slide out of the booth and intercept Grant before he got to their table.

Blocking Iris's exit, Sheila pulled out her compact to repair her lipstick just as Grant approached. He stepped up to the table, offering his hand toward Maggie as he started to introduce himself.

Maggie suddenly snapped out of her daze and jumped up. "Oh, you're *here*!" She hugged him quickly and said, "Darling, I missed you so much."

Startled by her exuberant greeting, Grant looked questioningly over Maggie's shoulder at Iris, who realized she had stopped breathing. She took a deep breath and said, "We were just visiting with *Sheila Croft*."

Smoothly recovering from Maggie's enthusiastic welcome, Grant said, "Hello. Am I late?"

Astonished by his sudden appearance, Sheila glanced from Iris to Grant to Maggie. Iris realized there was no chance for her to properly introduce them to each other. She felt as if she were turning blue from the suspense.

"So, this is the mystery man," Sheila said, stepping back to study him from head to toe. Her surprised expression quickly turned to one of annoyance. "Aren't you going to introduce me, Maggie?"

From Maggie's bewildered expression, Iris realized her boss didn't remember his name. Iris started coughing as a distraction.

"I don't believe we've met," Grant said smoothly to Sheila Croft. "I'm Grant Peters."

"This is Sheila Croft, Grant," Maggie said, recovering from her bewildered stupor.

Sheila extended her left hand, which was weighted down with diamonds. "Hello."

"A pleasure," Grant said to the dark-haired woman, bowing graciously. "Sorry if I'm late, darling," he added to Maggie, kissing her on the cheek. "I got tied up with an international business call, to Vienna."

Iris held her breath and hoped Maggie and Sheila didn't realize that with the time change it was after working hours in Vienna.

"Well," Sheila said to Maggie while studying Grant openly, "he certainly is a surprise. Tell me something about him."

"Oh, well, he—and I—um—" Maggie stumbled, not knowing the first thing about the man who had picked up her hand and was now stroking the back of it.

Grant chuckled and confided to Sheila, "I have such a confusing schedule that Maggie sometimes doesn't know where to begin explaining. I'm an international financier," he explained, elaborating on the role he had played for Iris in the bar. "My work is negotiating everything from timber deals in Georgia to Caribbean resort-hotel purchases for my clients from the Middle East."

"I thought you said he was from Vienna," Sheila said to Maggie.

Grant gave Maggie a loving look and answered, "My office is in Vienna because that's where OPEC is headquartered. I have quite a few clients within the member nations."

Iris started to relax, but hoped Sheila wouldn't ask him to speak German.

"I see," Sheila said. "Just how did you two meet?"

Again, Maggie looked flustered, while Grant just smiled wider in Iris's direction. No one had coached him on the loving couple's fictional past history. "That's one of *my* favorite stories," Iris improvised. "You don't mind if I tell it, do you?"

"Oh, no, please—why not?" Maggie and Grant practically answered in unison. And Grant added, "If you two ladies will excuse us for a moment, I need to talk to Maggie alone. I'm afraid I won't be able to stay for lunch. I'd like to explain." He pulled her aside, away from Sheila Croft's hawkish eyes. Maggie trotted willingly after him.

"They met here, in the Russian Tea Room," Iris said, when Sheila remained expectantly in front of her. She tried to figure out how they would have met if there had been no one to introduce them.

"Yes, go on," Sheila said with a glance over her shoulder at the loving couple who stood just out of hearing range. She snapped her compact shut and replaced it in her clutch.

"Grant thought Maggie was Candice Bergen and asked for her autograph. And Maggie was so flattered that she pretended she was. Grant, who's a big movie buff, knew something was wrong when Maggie didn't know the names of any of the movies she was supposed to have been in. When Grant found out the truth, and that Maggie wasn't married, he invited her to lunch. They've been together ever since, just like you see them here now."

"Very touching," Sheila said, placing a ruby-red fingernail to the tip of her ruby-red lips. "Especially since Maggie's always been good at making things up." She glanced at her watch.

Smiling, Grant and Maggie returned to the table.

"Well," Sheila said, "this time I have to admit I'm impressed, Maggie."

"Me, too," Maggie said, looking at Grant who still held her hand.

Sheila hovered at the table. "I'll be interested in finding out more about you, Grant Peters, when we meet again on Saturday. Is your company listed with the New York Stock Exchange?"

Grant smiled at Maggie as if the rest of the world didn't exist and ignored Sheila's question. "I'm afraid I have to dash to catch that plane. Can you live without me this evening?"

"If I have to, darling," Maggie answered, entranced by his dark brown eyes.

"Don't worry," Grant said, patting Maggie's hand as he continued to ignore Sheila Croft, "I'll be back in plenty of time to escort you to the New York Charity Ball. I know how important that event is to you and how much you're counting on my being there."

"We're all counting on you being there," Sheila said, reminding them of her presence. "We'll have more to discuss then," she promised Grant and Maggie. "I'll see you both on Saturday." She turned and stalked away with a final backward glance at Maggie and Grant.

Perfect or not, Iris knew that Maggie had to accept Grant as her mystery man now that Sheila had met him. Once Croft was out of sight, Iris felt her hands shake and her knees weaken. Grateful to be sitting, she picked up her glass, noticed it was empty and turned to Maggie. Grant was covertly appraising Maggie's blond, beautiful appearance. His look reminded Iris of the night they had met. *It's all a big act,* she told herself. *You should be happy, since you're in on it this time.* She upended her glass, searching for a final trace of liquid.

"Well, Mr. Peters," Maggie said, facing Grant as they both sat down, "after that performance I have to assume Iris filled you in on my particular situation."

Grant's eyes darted to Iris, as if asking how much Maggie had been told about his "performance." Iris answered him with a blank look, nervously rolling her glass between her palms. Relieved, Grant winked at Iris over their shared secret. He picked up Maggie's hand again to stroke it as he had done earlier for Sheila's benefit and said, "Under the circumstances, don't you think you should call me Grant, Maggie?"

Maggie looked down at his hand on hers as a scientist would observe microbes wedged between glass slides. "You're quite right," she said, judging him safe and shifting so that she could sit closer. She put her hand on his arm and ran it down the sleeve of his newly purchased Austin Reed jacket. She lowered her voice to add, "Grant."

Iris felt like an uninvited voyeur as a rush of feelings again overwhelmed her. It wasn't fair. She hadn't had a date in more than six months. Now that she finally had found an interesting man, she had to turn him over to Maggie. It was like buying an expensive car and only getting a test drive. He was probably all hands and no brain, she consoled herself as she watched his long, tapered fingers play with the upturned collar of Maggie's pink cotton-twill jacket. He has probably never had a thought of his own, she decided. That would explain why he was an actor. He would be lost if someone didn't prompt him with his lines.

"I'm sorry about our, uh, rather awkward way of being introduced," Maggie said, watching the play of Grant's hands as carefully as one watches a bee about to light.

"I'm honored just to meet the famous and very beautiful Maggie Maxwell," he returned, charming her with his smile. He took his hand from her collar and rested his arm along the back of the booth behind her. "You're practically a legend in your own time."

Maggie brushed a hand through her hair, which fell loosely around her face and tumbled becomingly to her shoulders. She tugged down the hem of her skirt. "That's where you have the advantage over me, Grant. You can read about me in the magazine every month, but I don't know anything about you."

"Why don't we order an appetizer?" Grant said, checking his watch and signaling the waiter. "I think I have time for something quick before my flight." He unbuttoned his jacket and adjusted his tie.

"Good idea," Iris said, reminding them of her presence. "I'm starving."

No one looked at her as the waiter approached the table to take their order. Grant casually remarked, "I wonder if they have stuffed artichoke bottoms on the menu. Those are your favorite, aren't they, Maggie?"

Mouth agape, Maggie drew back and asked, "How did you know that?"

Grant's eyes were on Iris as he said, "I've always been a fan of yours. I've read every single article that has been published about you."

Iris propped her chin in her hand, trying to be objective about Grant's meeting with Maggie. After all, they both wanted this: Grant for the money and the recognition, Iris in order to get her own byline. So why was she upset?

"This looks good," Grant said, indicating a new addition to the menu. "Shall we try it?"

Maggie sat with her menu unopened, staring dreamily at Grant and answered, "Yes, very good."

Iris looked away, feeling like leftover hamburger smothered in onions. When the waiter came to take her order, she said, "I'll have whatever they're having."

By the time they had finished the appetizer, Iris knew Maggie was as convinced of Grant's act as she herself had been that night in Dream On. Iris watched Maggie's luscious peach lips close around the fork Grant held for her. As hungry as Iris had been, she had barely eaten anything. Throughout the meal, Grant's conspiratorial glances in her direction had kept her on edge. She wasn't sure if his flirtatious glances were directed at her or to pique Maggie's attention.

His actions seemed casual, as if every subtle, sensual move came naturally to him. But Iris knew now that everything about him was cleverly contrived, for he had managed to keep the conversation and questions directed on Maggie in a most flattering manner. Maggie knew very little more about him than when he had first sat down beside her. What irritated Iris most was that Maggie didn't seem to care. She was too taken with his illusion of international entrepreneurship.

"How am I doing?" he asked Iris when Maggie excused herself to repair her makeup in the ladies' room.

"I'm sure your inflated ego can answer that far better than I can," she said, placing her palm against her chest and looking at the empty glasses in front of her adding, "since I am little more than a potted plant decorating this table."

He laughed, regarding her with his sexy brown eyes. "Isn't that what you wanted?"

"Basically yes," she said, glancing over her shoulder to make certain Maggie wasn't on her way back to the table yet. She lowered her voice, "But don't you think you're carrying things a bit too far on the first meeting? I noticed you resting your hand on Maggie's knee."

"You did?" he said with a devilish grin. He had hoped it would get Iris's attention. "That's funny. Maggie didn't seem to notice."

"Maggie noticed," Iris said through gritted teeth, and felt herself flushing from the implied sexuality of that move.

"We are supposed to be on familiar terms with each other," he reminded Iris. He glanced casually around the restaurant as if he belonged there the way he did at Eve's Garden. "I told you before, I take my roles seriously."

"Just who are you playing this role for, Maggie or me?"

He shrugged nonchalantly and flicked a speck of lint from his jacket. "Just because I'm an actor doesn't mean I can't read and think. I like to really get into a role, researching it as much as possible before a performance. For example, I found the chapter on seduction in Maggie's new book particularly enlightening."

"Well, you'd better keep up your research," she said testily, wishing he wasn't so self-righteous, and so damned good at it, "and hope Sheila Croft isn't better than you at it."

"Anything you say, sweetheart," he crooned.

"I'm not your sweetheart," Iris said with annoyance, reminding both of them, "Maggie is."

Chapter Four

Iris left the Russian Tea Room with a list of a million little errands to run for Maggie. Playing "wife" wouldn't last much longer, she consoled herself, now that Maggie approved of Grant and Iris would be promoted.

The minute Grant had left "to catch a plane," Maggie had grilled Iris. "Where did you meet him? Did he like me? Isn't he a bit young? I thought you'd find someone closer to forty."

Iris had scrambled to make up answers as close to the truth as possible, starting with how she had met him in a nightclub. "He had just come from a wedding and we started talking," Iris had said.

"He wasn't the groom, was he?" Maggie worried. "I forgot to look for a wedding ring."

Iris had assured her that Grant was *very* single, so single and good-looking and downright interesting that she hated to give up all claim to him herself. It just wasn't fair. Handing Grant over to Maggie was like spending hours making a rich, sinful dessert just for yourself, then finding a troop of Boy Scouts at your door asking for a taste. Only in this case she couldn't even share Grant, since he had to *appear* to be Maggie's perfect man.

After finishing the tasks for Maggie, Iris picked up her dry cleaning and ran a few errands of her own. She told herself that she didn't want Grant, anyway. What Maggie was impressed with was all fluff. The perfect man truly didn't exist. Besides, what would Iris's society friends think if she started hanging out with a short-order cook?

Sour grapes, sour grapes, she chanted to herself, wearily trudging home after the cab dropped her at the cross street near her East Side town house. Grant seemed like a nice guy. Money or not, he certainly had gotten her off the hook with Maggie, not to mention her Uncle Edward. But the whole charisma about Grant was merely an act. And she'd better remember that, because she knew she could fall hard for him if she, too, started believing his role. *Remember the dusty apartment,* she thought, a symbol of how much at odds their life-styles were.

Someone was sitting on her stoop. Some man. Iris slowed her pace as she drew nearer, wondering if she should just keep on walking. She wasn't expecting anyone.

"Do you always get home this late?" Grant called out to her. He had changed clothes and wore khaki slacks, a navy-and-blue striped pullover and dark brown leather sandals. Iris wondered if he was wearing his familiar Fruit of the Looms or the bikini briefs the staff had suggested during the make-over session. His hair was all loose curls again, and his cheeks were shadowed by the growth of his heavy beard.

"What are you doing here?" she asked as she went up the steps and stopped in front of him. She rearranged the dry cleaning in her arms to get out her key.

"Playing tiddledywinks with manhole covers," he answered, then grinned. He stubbed out his cigarette and flicked it toward the narrow patch of garden beside her building. "Waiting for you, what do you think?"

"I mean, why here?" she asked, when what she wanted to know was *why me*? A breezy gust of wind ruffled her hair. A cherry tree blossom fluttered down from the branch near the front window. She heard a bee buzzing among the daffodils.

"It's where you live, isn't it?" he asked, rising and stepping aside, eager for her to open the door and let him inside. "After living in Los Angeles, I can't get used to this damp, chill weather so late into the spring," he said with a shiver. "Your friend, Tina, from the magazine, told me you lived here. Did I get the part?"

Iris inserted the key into the lock of the teakwood-and-beveled-glass door, biding for time. Why should she be upset that Maggie had approved of Grant one hundred percent? "Yes, you got the part," she said, opening the door and holding it wide as an invitation to him. "It was very clever of you to audition with Sheila Croft looking on. How could you not have gotten the role under those circumstances?" She hooked the dry cleaning on the antique hat rack.

"A true stroke of luck," he said, walking into her home and unabashedly looking at everything. He whistled through his teeth. "This is some place. Do you live here alone?"

Wondering at the implications behind his question, Iris ignored it and busied herself closing and relocking the front door.

He seemed not to have noticed that she didn't answer him as he walked deeper into the living room. Hardwood floors were covered with a thick, wheat-colored South American rug. Blue couches facing each other picked up the blue from the Peruvian design in the rug. Primitive Mayan, Peruvian and Aztec pottery stood on little pedestals and on the glass-topped tables. Potted plants, almost as tall as the ceiling, added to the tropical, south-of-the-border decor. "Very nice," he commented, looking through the wide doorway into the dining room where her dark wood Mexican table and leather-backed chairs stood.

"Would you like a drink?" she asked, pushing her thick hair back from her face. "We might as well celebrate your new job."

"Sure, that'd be great," he said, sprawling elegantly on the couch nearest the white-brick fireplace. He gave it the once-over. "Does this thing work?"

Iris nodded, deciding she might as well open a bottle of champagne. After all, it was something to celebrate—having a man in her house again, even if he was supposed to belong to someone else.

"I'll get a fire going while you get the drinks," Grant said, rubbing his hands together in anticipation of chasing the chill he felt from sitting on her cold steps. He reached in his shirt pocket for his lighter and removed his pack of cigarettes.

Iris wanted to protest. Building a fire was like those rich desserts she made just for herself, on those nights when she felt the need to be pampered but had no one to indulge her. Having Grant take over was infringing on her privacy, but she didn't know how to explain without sounding like a fool. Instead she said, "Would you mind not smoking? I don't like it any better than Maggie does." She turned her back on him and the room and went to the kitchen pantry to find a bottle of champagne.

The fire was crackling merrily behind the brass peacock grate when Iris returned with two fluted glasses and a bottle of Moet. "Will this do?" she asked, holding up the bottle.

After reading the label, Grant gave a low whistle and looked up at Iris. "You don't save any pennies with this stuff, do you?"

"It's not exactly Dom Perignon," she defended.

"It's not in a wino's price range, either," he said, holding the bottle between his hands and, like a surgeon, gently but firmly opening the sparkling wine without sending the stopper flying with a pop.

Impressed at his skill in properly uncorking the bottle, Iris held the two glasses toward him. "Is this knowledge of wine and spirits something you've learned for Maggie's benefit?" she asked as he poured. "Or did you pick it up from some play you were in?"

Setting the bottle down on a crystal coaster, Grant took one of the glasses from her. "It comes with the package," he said with a grin as big as a sport fisherman's who had just caught a record-size marlin. "I happen to like good food and knowing about good wines goes along with that. Knowing the exchange value of the dollar and the current price of oil doesn't." He tipped his glass to hers. "To us, and the beginning of a long and successful relationship."

Iris watched him over the rim of her glass as she sipped the sparkling wine. The bubbles tickled her throat. "Don't you ever stop?"

"Stop what?"

"Practicing your role and what you're going to say when you're with Maggie."

"I wasn't even thinking of Maggie. I meant that, for us."

She wished she had her glasses on now or that he wasn't standing quite so close. It made it harder to read the truth in his eyes. *He's an actor,* she reminded herself. And if he wasn't one, he'd still be a short-order cook. "Oh," she said contritely, realizing her snobishness was showing. "Well then, thank you."

"But speaking of Maggie, let's sit down," he invited, as if *she* were the guest. "And you can tell me what she said about me after I left."

Iris would have sat elsewhere if he hadn't had his hand on her shoulder, steering her to the couch nearest the fireplace and sitting next to her. She needed some distance from this man, not only to sharpen her farsighted vision without her glasses, but to get some objectivity about the things he was saying. Sitting this close reminded her of the night they had met when he had stood so near and had entranced her with little more than lies. "Maggie was satisfied."

"And?"

Emptying her glass, she held the fluted vessel out for him to refill. When he got up to get the bottle, she scooted down the couch so that he wouldn't box her in so snugly when he sat down again. "Maggie thought you were the perfect man. She wanted to know where I found you and what you thought of her. Thank you," she said as he stopped pouring.

After Grant had departed, Maggie had acted like a teenager worrying over a prom date. She had even remarked, "Grant Peters will certainly give Bradley Winchester a run for his money at the charity ball." Iris knew her boss was still hurting from her lover's rejection.

"And, what did you tell her?" Grant prodded, his eyes moving around her face in rapt attention.

Iris refocused on Grant as well as she could without her glasses. The room felt hot, and it had nothing to do with the heat from the fireplace. "It wasn't easy coming up with answers." His gaze made her nervous, so she turned her face toward the fire. "Even staying as close to the truth as possible." She took a deep breath, hoping to relax. "I told her I'd met you in a nightclub and we'd started talking about her and that you'd said you'd always wanted to meet her. I made that up since you'd said you were her biggest fan."

"After you," he said in that gentle, melodic voice.

Iris gave him a skeptical glance and continued. "I made it sound like arranging something of a blind date. She was very impressed with your calm during the Sheila Croft ambush. I told her you had picked up on their feud from reading about her. Fortunately she didn't question the 'hows' or the 'whys' of your agreeing to take her to the charity ball." Maggie was like that, just skimming the surface of life, always with her head in the clouds. Iris really couldn't blame Bradley Winchester for leaving Maggie in the lurch, as flighty as she sometimes was. Iris felt angry, but couldn't reason why. Grant was happy to be working in this role. She would be getting her byline. Maggie had her perfect man. Edward South was gearing up for a round of good publicity. Where was the problem? "You certainly lived up to Maggie's expectations."

"I'm much more interested in what *you* think of me," Grant said. He waited until she looked at him before he added, "If a man was going to Mr. Perfect for Iris, what sort of man would he be?"

She squinted into his deep brown eyes. In spite of her reservations not to get emotionally involved, his eyes had the power to make her smile. She felt herself softening. Maybe it was the drink. Maybe she was just tired. But she decided to be swayed by the sincerity in his eyes. "I'm not going to tell you," she said, "because I don't want you to conjure up some incredible being who only exists whenever there's an audience."

"But I'd like to audition for the role," he coaxed.

"Then just be yourself, if you can figure out who that really is."

Grant laughed nervously and looked away. What was it about this woman? Was she psychic, or was he such a bad actor that she saw through his confusion over who he really was and what he was meant to be in life? Ever since he had moved to New York he had known he needed direction in his life. For a long time he had convinced himself he was doing just that by working for Bob and Eve. But deep inside he had known it was their decision, not his own he was following. He had just been drifting, working at the restaurant and going to Dream On at nights, delaying any decision-making about his future. Bob wanted him to buy into the restaurant as a full partner, but Grant had been afraid to fully commit himself to anything, even though he loved cooking. Now, here he was chasing rainbows again, playing this role for Maggie. "I'll work on it," he promised and got up to poke at the fire.

"That's all anyone can ask," she answered to keep the conversation rolling while she admired his slim physique. He pushed up the sleeves of his pullover to reveal the sinews and muscles in his arms. His hands were slim, but strong. She couldn't help but speculate that he must be firm and muscular all over.

What *did* she want in a man? She slouched into a more comfortable position so that she could rest her head on the back of the couch and speculate aloud. "I fell in love with the perfect man once before. But he was only ideal on the surface. So trying out a repertoire of various performances won't work on me as easily as it did on Maggie."

"I knew right away that Maggie isn't anything like you," he said over his shoulder. A log fell in a shower of sparks. Grant rearranged the wood with the poker.

"How are we different?" Iris challenged. They came from the same social background, which was one of the reasons Maggie got on so well with Iris. They both had inherited money. They even had many of the same social acquaintances.

"She's too old, for one thing," Grant said, then added, "at least for me. I'd like to have children one day with the woman I settle down with."

"A lot of women are having their first babies over forty these days," Iris said.

"Maybe her age wouldn't be a deterrent, then," Grant conceded. He replaced the fireplace grill and rejoined Iris on the couch. "But her attitude would. Unless I miss my guess, Maggie is the epitome of the career woman. The only way she'd have babies is if someone else did it for her. There's nothing wrong with that. It's just not the kind of future I see for myself."

Iris ran her fingers around the rim of her glass. In such a short time, Grant had certainly understood a lot about Maggie. Considering all of the errands Iris had run for her that afternoon, she had to agree. "I'm sure she'd add childbirth to my list of things to do if the opportunity arose."

Grant emptied the bottle between their two glasses. "Just what do you do, Iris Janus?"

"What do you mean?" She looked bewildered in her effort to focus on him. He was sitting close enough for Iris to feel his body heat.

"Look at this place," he said, gesturing with his hand, his eyes never leaving hers. "You can't tell me your salary as a secretary, for the IRS or otherwise, is enough to afford living here. That one-room matchbox I live in is five hundred a month."

"My father was a banker."

"Was?"

"Yes." She fixed her eyes on the weeping fig tree across the room. Several of the leaves were brown and withered, ready to fall off the supple branches. "He and my mother died in an auto accident not long after I graduated from college."

"I'm sorry."

"It's okay. It's been more than five years. I've been able to supplement my life-style from my inheritance, which was considerable." She ran her finger up and down the stem of the glass. "My mother was Edward South's sister. He was generous enough to offer me a job when I decided I wanted to be a writer." Iris wondered if he would be surprised at that, the way some of her girlfriends had been when she had told them. They didn't seem to think Iris should work, or understand why she would want to.

Grant looked around the room as if seeing it for the first time. His brother-in-law, Bob, had been right in the split second he had sized up Iris. She had class. That's what made her different from all the other woman he had met in the past. She came from a world cushioned with greenbacks. She didn't have to work or ask herself what she wanted to be when she grew up. "Why would you want to be a writer?"

Iris laid her cheek against the cushion of the couch and looked up at him. The material felt smooth and comforting against her skin. "Why do you want to be an actor?"

He didn't want to answer that for himself, much less voice his thoughts to anyone else. It was a dream that looked as far away as a child's wishing star. Playing the perfect man for Maggie Maxwell could very well be the final role of his acting career. He finished his drink to avoid speaking.

Iris looked up at the ceiling, feeling the need to unburden herself. It had been so long since anyone had asked about *her*, even longer since she had felt like opening up about her private life. "I also came out well, financially, in my divorce settlement."

Grant shifted his gaze to Iris again. Her thick auburn hair looked soft and bushy as she rested her head against the cushions. He felt the urge to dive his fingers into the billowy mass and cradle her face in his hands. Her face looked smooth and innocent, her lips devoid of makeup, her light brown eyebrows enhancing her half-closed green eyes. He wanted to be Sir Lancelot to her Guinevere, picking her up and carrying her to bed. But she didn't want roles. He'd have to win her on a more earthly level. "What about emotionally?" he asked softly, referring to the effects of her divorce.

"Emotionally, I'm over it," she said, sitting up and setting her empty glass on the coffee table. "But it wasn't easy." She rested her chin on her shoulder as she gazed back at him and said, "I'm hungry. Why don't I see what I can find in the refrigerator?"

"Did you love him?" Grant asked.

"My ex-husband?" When he nodded, she lifted her shoulders and said, "At the time I thought I did, and I really tried to make the marriage work. But if the circumstances had been different, getting over the shock of my parents dying and being on my own for the first time, I don't think I ever would have married him." She thought about it a minute more and decided there was no point in rehashing the past or trying to explain how she had wanted to please her uncle. She stood up. "Are you game to accept potluck?"

Grant smiled, wanting to reach out and soothe the hurt he saw lurking in her eyes. But he sensed a reserve within her, as if she were holding out both arms so that he couldn't get too close. "Mind if I come with you?" he asked. "I can work wonders with leftovers. It's my job, remember?"

"THAT IS DELICIOUS," Iris raved, biting into the sampling of chicken Grant had speared on a fork for her. She couldn't help remembering how intimately he had fed Maggie in the same fashion that afternoon at the Russian Tea Room. "Better than anything I've ever tasted at Lutèce. And that's my favorite restaurant."

"I haven't ever eaten there," Grant said, sprinkling a tad more soy sauce over the chicken-and-broccoli concoction he had stir-fried with almonds. "But there's a great, inexpensive sushi bar not far from it."

When they had gone into the kitchen, Iris had put her glasses on. Now, she pushed them to the top of her head and stepped back with her hands on her hips. "I'm still amazed at what you've cooked." He had found things she hadn't even known existed in the back of her cupboards and had prepared a meal to rival any she had paid for in some of New York's finer restaurants. "And all without a cookbook."

Removing the skillet from the fire, he said, "You have a well-stocked kitchen."

Iris pinched another morsel from the skillet and knew there was more to it than that. "Before I started working for Maggie, I loved to cook very elaborate, classic French dishes. But everything I do takes all day, and I can't boil water without detailed instructions in front of me."

He transferred the chicken and vegetables to plates and said, "I'd like it if you cooked something for me one day."

They had opened a second bottle of Moet while they worked together in her kitchen, where the walls were brick and the ceiling had exposed beams. Copper pots hung near the stove. She picked up her glass and swirled it as she imagined impressing him with quenelles de brochette mousselines. "Do you like pike?"

"Sure," he said, handing her one of the plates. He tucked the wine bottle under his arm and led the way to the dining room where Iris had set the table for two.

Iris brought the salad. "How did you learn to cook so well?"

Grant spread the napkin over his lap and picked up his fork. "My mother died when I was fourteen. My dad's idea of cooking was potted meat and crackers, with peanut butter and ice cream for dessert. It was either learn to cook or starve. Fortunately, our next-door neighbor was a caterer who taught me a few tricks. And I had my little sister, Eve, to look after."

"Were you and she the only children?" Iris tasted a spear of broccoli and closed her eyes in appreciation of the heavenly flavor.

"Um-hmm. How about you? Any sisters or brothers?"

Iris shook her head. "Not even any cousins. Uncle Edward never married, and Dad was an only child, too." She took another bite of chicken and couldn't help herself from speaking with her mouth full. "This is so *good*."

"You think so?" Grant said proudly. He'd prefer to have that reaction from her because of his lovemaking rather than his culinary skills. But at the moment he'd settle for whatever he could get. "Maybe I'll speak to Bob and Eve about adding this to the restaurant's menu. We're always trying to offer variety in the luncheon specials to keep the customers coming back."

"I should definitely let you raid my refrigerator more often."

"I wouldn't mind that privilege," he said.

Iris felt warm from his look and changed the subject. "Tell me about your childhood. Where were you born?"

"We lived in Pittsburgh," he answered. "My father's still a professor there at a junior college. I'm afraid I was a disappointment to him when I dropped out of school to become an actor and moved out to California."

"Didn't he approve?"

"No," Grant said, continuing with his narrative. He didn't want to admit that his father's fears had been correct. Grant had some talent... when it came to little theater productions in Pittsburgh. But being one of many talented actors in L.A., Grant didn't stand out. He had only managed to get a few bit parts, and all few and far between. "While I was waiting tables between auditions, I fell in love with a California surfer girl. I guess she's the reason I stayed out there as long as I did."

"Would you still be out there now if you hadn't gotten divorced?"

"I don't know," he answered. Mari had helped foster the dream of stardom. She had worked for a film-making studio as a prop girl. For a long time, Grant had thought her connections would help things click for him. But they hadn't. He had gotten a few more screen tests because of her, but he had never been good enough to get the kind of parts that would bring him recognition. The director always wanted someone shorter, taller, older, younger, or someone other than he. It was almost a relief when Mari left him for a wealthier, more muscular tennis player. It allowed Grant to use the excuse of a broken heart to head back to New York to work in his sister's restaurant. That way he didn't have to admit he had been a failure in acting as well as in marriage.

Iris went to the kitchen for seconds, asking if she could bring anything for Grant. When she returned, she asked, "Do you miss her?"

"Mari? No." He attacked his food with gusto. "And I don't miss Los Angeles, either. Dad was right about that. It wasn't the life for me. But when you're nineteen, you don't listen to anyone. Anyway, when Eve offered me the job at Eve's Garden, I saw it as an opportunity to leave L.A. and try my luck in New York."

He didn't tell her about Bob's reservations in hiring him as a cook in the family business, or how Grant had jumped at the chance for a steady income again. At the time, he didn't tell Bob and Eve he was ready to give up his dreams of being an actor. Instead, he had kept up the charade and the ever-waning hope of someday making it big as a star. The week he arrived in New York, he had sent out his résumé and videotape to numerous agencies, and begun auditioning for roles in plays and TV. He didn't want his little sister to think of him as anything less than a hero. And he didn't want to give his brother-in-law the satisfaction of saying "I told you so" as his father did every time he went home to Pittsburgh. "I guess the only way you grow up is by making mistakes," Grant said now.

Iris nodded solemnly. "I think I'm still growing."

He grinned. "What kind of mistakes could you possibly make? Look at this place. You have everything." An Oriental theme from Andreas Vollenweider's "White Wings" played softly in the background. Original artwork hung from the walls in the dining room. Her kitchen was filled with gadgets, some he had never seen before.

"I have things, but things can't keep you warm at night. Things can't make you feel fulfilled. You're lucky. You know what you want, and you've always gone after it."

"I haven't achieved anything," he said. "I'm still nothing but a cook."

"Maybe, but no one ever taught me to strive for anything in my life. All I ever had to do was follow—what my parents wanted for me to do, what my husband wanted. Working on the magazine is the first step

I've taken in doing what I want. As it is, my uncle had to get me the job because I wasn't qualified."

"I'm sure that's not true," Grant said, laying his knife and fork across the plate as he finished eating. "You went to college. That says a lot, at least in my father's book."

"Oh, sure," Iris replied. "It says I can read recipes in French. I went to a fancy girls' school where I learned all the proper social graces. No one cared if I was prepared for a career or not because it was understood I'd be like my mother."

"What was she like?"

Iris smiled as she thought fondly of her mother. They had gone everywhere and done everything together, like sisters. "She was a very good mother and absolutely devoted to my father. She knew how to give good parties and organize charity drives. But she never could have made it in the real world on her own."

Grant shoved his plate forward so that he could lay his folded arms on the edge of the table. "That doesn't sound so bad."

"It's not," Iris defended. "But after my divorce, I realized it wasn't enough for me. I need to prove, to myself if no one else, that I can be somebody without my money."

"We're not so different," Grant said, "except that I don't have the money. Believe me, it's a lot harder going after those goals without the green stuff."

Iris shoved her plate aside, too, even though there was still some food left. She suddenly felt exposed. What she had just told Grant surprised her, because she had never tried to put her thoughts into words. For the first time she realized why getting her own byline was so important to her. She wanted desperately to know she could be someone other than Miss High Society. She wanted to be liked for who she was, not who she knew. "I'm sorry. I don't know why I told you all of that. Forgive me for rambling."

"It didn't sound like rambling to me," Grant said. He smiled, then placed his hand on top of hers. "I'd like to think it creates a kind of bond between us. We both long for recognition on the basis of our talents." As he thought of how much more clearly defined hers were than his, he added, "Such as they are." Grant was tempted to open up to her and tell her the truth about his less than sparkling acting abilities. But he still wanted to impress her. And at the moment it was the only way he knew how, by being a star in this role she had created for him with Maggie.

Iris slipped her hand away from his. She had had too much to drink and had forgotten herself. She shouldn't be getting so friendly with the man who was supposed to belong to Maggie. She pulled her glasses from the crown of her hair and settled them over the bridge of her nose, striving to create some distance between them. "You'd make better use of your time concentrating on the bond you're supposed to have with Maggie. Everyone will have their antennae tuned toward the two of you at the charity ball Saturday night."

"Yes," he said. "I was just thinking that." Later, when he knew her better, he would tell her the demons he was struggling with. Right now all he had to offer a woman from such an esteemed social position and background was his determination to succeed at *something*. At the moment, that something was this job as Maggie's man, a position that Iris and everyone else at the magazine was depending on him to master. "Don't worry. I'm planning to live up to your expectations for the perfect man."

Iris looked down at her plate. Now that she had her glasses on she could tell from the look in his eyes that he wasn't talking about Maggie.

Chapter Five

Arriving at the Helmsley Palace on the arm of her Uncle Edward, Iris was immediately recognized as the daughter of Wilhemina, who was fondly remembered as one of the annual charity ball's most ardent fund-raisers. Iris promised to speak with her mother's friends later, and allowed her uncle to steer her through the lobby to the coat check room. The evening was seasonably cool, but the charity ball was a hot enough affair to warrant wearing a fur. South wanted to get to the ballroom early to make certain they sat at the same table with Maggie and Grant.

While her uncle was getting the claim check, Iris draped the handkerchief-cut Bruges lace shawl she carried over her bare shoulders, and knotting the ends, adjusted it over her right shoulder to complement her strapless royal-blue satin gown. Her mother's antique pearl choker and a matching clutch were her only accessories. She wore her hair up with soft tendrils cascading over her ears.

In the ballroom, the crystal-and-brass chandeliers had been dimmed to enhance the romantic effect of candlelight flickering from crystal candelabras at the center of each table. Throughout the room, the sparkle of diamond jewelry and glittering gowns was only slightly less obvious than the sight of showy mink furs and wraps. One could almost smell the money in the mingling scents of sickly sweet designer perfumes.

"I knew we should have left earlier," South complained as they stood just inside the ballroom. "Grant and Maggie are already here. Damn. Why does she always have to be so punctual?"

The band was softly playing "Lara's Theme" from Dr. Zhivago as patrons found their tables and stood talking in groups. "Where are they?" Iris asked, scanning faces in the room, feeling her heartbeat speed up at the anticipation of seeing Grant again. Before she spotted him, Sheila Croft stepped nattily around her. Iris tensed and clamped her hand on her uncle's arm.

"Come on," Edward said, tucking her hand into the crook of his arm.

Iris lurched at the suddenness of his move and nearly tripped over her skirt. Hastily she clutched a handful of satin above her knee to lift her hemline.

When they stopped at the table set for eight, the sight of Grant stunned her. His elegant but strong hands rested on Maggie's chair back, behind which he stood as if poised for a formal portrait. Wearing the expertly tailored black tuxedo with gray lapels, he appeared taller than ever. A royal-blue silk handkerchief accented his jacket pocket. The sight of it caused an unreasonable wave of jealousy to wash over Iris. He should have been *her* date. She was wearing blue, while Maggie, elegant as always in gold lamé, seemed to clash with Grant's colors. Iris glanced away, trying not to imagine Maggie's long, polished fingernails untying the knot of Grant's tie later, as Iris longed to do.

While she had been staring at Grant, he had been standing with squared shoulders greeting Sir Ashley Croft, Sheila's English husband. Formally shaking hands, they looked like foreign diplomats in a receiving line. Sheila was talking, staking her claim to the two seats next to Grant and Maggie, in spite of name tags that read otherwise. "Ashley, dear," she said, waving her heavily jeweled fingers at her husband the way a charwoman uses a feather duster, "change the little cards around. I'm sure no one will mind."

Ashley appeared to have been trained like a well-disciplined pet. "Of course, darling." He reminded Iris of a butler, particularly with his clipped British accent. Before leaving the table to exchange name cards, he held a chair to seat his wife.

Iris thought it was a nice gesture on Ashley's part, considering how bossy his wife could be, but Sheila frowned in annoyance as he pushed her chair closer to the table. Only as her uncle bodily maneuvered Iris into the chair next to Sheila's did Iris realize that the woman was annoyed not to be sitting directly next to Grant.

"I'll be right back," South said as he scooped up two name cards to follow Ashley's example. "Talk to Sheila while I'm gone."

Grateful that she had left her glasses at home so that Sheila was a pleasant blur beside her, Iris said pleasantly, "Hello." Sheila rolled her extremely padded shoulders and turned her bare back to Iris. Grant, on the other hand, halfway around the table, was sharply in focus to Iris. The sophisticated game of musical chairs had called his attention to her.

Iris felt cheated. She had tried to prepare herself for tonight, knowing she would only be part of the audience, even if she did have a front-row seat on this very private play. But she had also spent hours choosing something to wear, imagining what his response would be and how she would act when she saw Grant again. She wiggled impatiently in her chair, and banged her knee against the table leg.

When Ashley Croft returned with the proper name cards and took the seat between his wife and Grant, Sheila was dominating the conversation while giving Grant and Maggie interrogating glances. Iris leaned forward, letting the drape of her shawl slip enough to reveal the smooth slopes of her cleavage. That rated half a glance from Grant and caused him to lose the trend of his sentence. Iris smiled to herself. Grant *had* noticed her, and had not been unaffected. She settled more comfortably against the back of her chair, which practically hid her from Grant's view with Sheila's imposing black shoulder pads between them.

Her uncle returned with their name cards and sat on Iris's left. More people were taking their places. Iris imagined Maggie in another state and herself sitting next to Grant. It would be fun to be with him, to find out what he thought of high society. He would probably agree there were a number of starched shirts at this boring function. Sir Ashley Croft had to have the most starch of all. He acted like the wooden dummy on a ventriloquist's arm, except in this case, Sheila did all the talking. Iris would have preferred listening to his pleasant English accent.

The final two chairs next to Edward South were taken by an elderly couple just as the waiter began serving the caviar appetizer. The pungent scent of a finely chopped onion garnish brought Iris back to reality.

On Grant's right, Maggie, in a gown with a high collar and drop waist, kept glancing lovingly at Grant. Her hair had been crimped for the occasion, and it flowed around her shoulders like a golden hood designed to match her dress.

Iris took a deep breath and tried to concentrate on the background music the live ensemble was playing. She couldn't identify the tune. Picking up her water glass as a distraction, Iris whispered to her uncle, "Sheila has more questions than a TV quiz show." She sipped the water, wishing it would quench the rising anger she felt from watching Grant eyeing her.

Her uncle squeezed her hand. "It's going well, I think. Don't you? Grant seems to be answering everything with the ease of a man in his particular station."

She had to agree. Grant conversed intelligently and appeared calm. Iris set the crystal water glass down while checking to see that Sheila wasn't paying undue attention to their conversation. "But it's as if she's conducting a personal interview. Have you heard some of her questions? Where was he born? How long did he live there? Where did he go to school?"

"You always did worry too much. Just like your mother."

Iris straightened in her chair so that she could return her attention to Sheila's current round of questions. If her uncle wasn't worried, why should she be? Thank goodness Sheila hadn't asked Grant to reply in German.

From the appetizer to the main course of prime rib, Iris was forced to watch the slightest caress Grant made for Maggie and Sheila's benefit. Whenever he wasn't patting Maggie's shoulder or holding her hand, he was watching Iris, making her too nervous to eat.

Next to her, Sheila's black, silky dress clung to her ample curves and drew together in a design centered at the waist. Mentally, Iris pinned a big red patch there to match her lipstick and complete her black-widow-spider ensemble. Whenever there was a lull in the conversation, Iris could feel Sheila checking her reserves of venom for the next round of questions, skillfully trying to lure Grant into her web. Iris hoped dessert would be served quickly. By then the dance music would start and Grant might be able to escape with Maggie on the dance floor.

"You say your office is in Vienna?" Sheila said, delicately touching the edge of her napkin to the corners of her lips. "What street?"

Iris held her breath. Someone nearby was toe tapping to the beat of the music. China clattered as tables were cleared for the dessert. She smelled the aroma of freshly brewed coffee.

"On Wiedner Hauptstrasse. It's on the tramcar line," he answered. Eve and Bob's scrapbooks from his military tour of duty in Europe had armed Grant with images, names and countless bits of trivia about Austria. He had several amusing stories he'd like to tell. "Have you been there?" He smiled pleasantly at Maggie as if in apology for not speaking more with her that evening, and squeezed her hand.

How did he do it, Iris wondered? Remember his research, talk to Sheila, cuddle Maggie and flirt with Iris—all at once? *He's an actor,* she remembered. *It's his job.* The question was, where did the act begin and end?

"Yes, I've been to Vienna. Ashley and I try to attend the opera at least once each season. We love to go to that pastry shop in the old town. What is its name?" Sheila pondered. Her husband Ashley started to reply, but Sheila signaled him to be quiet, lifting her chin in

Grant's direction the way a headmaster would wait on the class mischief maker to reply. "Yes, Grant, you were saying?"

"I assume you mean Demel on the Kohlmarkt," he replied. "They are the most famous, but do live up to their reputation. Speaking for myself, I'd never go anywhere else." Thank goodness he remembered that from one of Eve's pastry cookbooks. He could give Sheila a few recipes, too, if she wanted them.

Croft shifted in her chair, as if flipping through her notes to come up with another question. Maggie filled in the silence with a remark about dessert, just as the lights dimmed for the presentation of baked Alaska.

Iris resmoothed her crumpled napkin and took a breath. She felt as if she had been sitting on the edge of her chair for the past half hour, like a teacher hoping her pupil has learned all of the answers to the test questions. Dessert would keep Croft quiet a few more minutes.

Waiters carrying trays of the frothy white mounds with flaming sparklers on top, paraded around the tables before stopping at each one to serve the rich dessert. The participants at the charity ball applauded the dramatic presentation. As the sound of clapping hands drew down, Maggie engaged the elderly couple on her right in conversation, and Iris heard Sheila ask, "Grant, how did you meet Maggie?"

Grant fixed a smile on his face as his mind went blank. He had been all prepared to drop Salzburg into the conversation so that he could tell everyone about the archbishop at Schloss Hellbrunn who sprayed his guests from hidden water fountains in the seats of their chairs. What he wouldn't give to be the archbishop now with one of those chairs for Sheila.

That's easy, Iris thought, remembering her story of Grant mistaking Maggie for Candice Bergen. *But he doesn't know about that,* she realized in a panic as she heard Grant's version. Her hand strangled her napkin. Grant had been out of earshot with Maggie when Iris had made up the story about meeting at the Russian Tea Room. Iris could tell he was searching for clues, making tiny delaying gestures to allow time to think. He reached for Maggie's hand and smiled at her as she turned away from the elderly couple long enough to smile romantically back at him.

Iris's eyes darted frantically around the table. She had to do something, fast, to interrupt his story before Croft remembered the version Iris had made up.

"I came to Maggie's aid," Grant said, improvising on the archbishop's water jokes, "when a waiter accidentally spilled an entire glass of ice water down her back."

Behind Uncle Edward, the waiter was waiting for the sparklers to die out in order to slice into the dessert. Iris started coughing, as if she had swallowed crookedly. When no one noticed her unduly, she started waving her napkin in front of her face and pushed back her chair as if to get more air. The move gave her just enough room to wave her napkin in the direction of the still-fizzling baked Alaska, igniting the cloth dinner napkin.

"Oh, dear," she said, standing up and holding the napkin just long enough to kindle a healthy flame, and then she dropped it, hastily, right in front of Sheila Croft.

Sheila shrieked. Ashley jumped into action, dousing the napkin with water from his glass, soaking Sheila in the process. "Ashley!" she wailed, turning accusing eyes first on her husband, then on Iris. "How *could* you?" Her shoulders seemed to rise and set as if physically expressing an exclamation point.

"Are you all right?" Grant and Edward asked Iris almost simultaneously.

Iris calmly sat down and tugged upward on the bodice of her strapless royal-blue gown. "Yes, thank you," she said in a tiny voice. She prayed her skin wouldn't start blotching red from Sheila's deadly looks. It was bad enough knowing that the murmuring burr of voices from elsewhere in the room were all discussing Irisflambeau.

Sheila snatched her husband's napkin from him and began dabbing at her prominent breasts. "My dress will be ruined from these water stains," she complained.

"You could easily have been Joan of Arc," Maggie pointed out with an Eva Perón snap in her voice and a Scarlett O'Hara flutter of her lush lashes. She hid her lips behind her napkin, but her shaking shoulders revealed suppressed laughter.

Grant was biting his lips, too, to keep from laughing. Sir Ashley Croft was acting very proper and British. He was probably too afraid of his wife to look amused, Grant thought.

"If you will excuse me," Sheila said as formally as if she were taking her leave of the queen. "I must attend to this dripping mess." She took two steps away then said, "Ashley?" as if it were a command.

Her husband looked blankly at her a moment, then excused himself to escort his wife from the room.

Everyone at their table and several people nearby started laughing. When Grant turned his dancing eyes her way, Iris suddenly felt like a heroine. He looked proud of her for being such a good actress. But before

Sheila returned, she had to get him alone to prompt him past his error.

The waiter served the baked Alaska and departed.

Iris leaned closer to her uncle. "I have to speak to Grant."

"We're just here to observe, remember?" He patted her shoulder as if to say she should be a good girl and eat her dessert.

"He was telling Sheila the wrong story about how they met."

"What difference does it make as long as it sounds plausible?"

"It makes a big difference when *I* told her something else."

South drew back and picked up his dessert fork as if he hadn't heard what she said. But Iris could tell by the muscles pulsing in his cheek that he was grinding his teeth in consternation. They finished their desserts in silence. He crossed his arms in front of his chest, then began pinching his mustache.

After the waiter cleared the table and took orders for after-dinner liqueurs, Edward cleared his throat and said, "Grant, my boy. Would you mind if I had the first dance with Maggie? I've barely had a chance to speak with her all evening. Perhaps you could keep Iris company?" He rose and held out his arm for Maggie.

"I'd love to dance, Grant," Iris said, getting out of her chair before he could refuse.

South and Maggie led the way to the dance floor, while Grant stood poised for Iris to take his arm.

When she touched the sleeve of his tuxedo and felt the tension of his forearm, she was tempted to run her hand up and down the finely woven texture of his jacket. She squinted up at him, wishing he wasn't standing so close, longing for him to move even closer. He closed his hand over hers where it rested on his arm and slowly walked her to the dance floor. Iris's heartbeat quickened. Her breath came in shallow gasps. Having Grant at her side felt like a dream.

He was particularly handsome tonight in a white ruffled shirt that Iris imagined running her hand over...and underneath. His lean cheeks were closely shaven without the first hint of his usually heavy beard. Iris knew it would be smooth to the touch if he were to brush his cheek against hers. She didn't like the slicked-back wastrel style in which he wore his hair. It made him look too much like an imitation James Bond. But she couldn't fault anything else about his appearance.

As they reached the dance floor, he turned, holding out his hands to take her into his arms. She felt the strength of his grasp as she put one hand in his and rested her other hand on the sturdy wall of his chest, gradually inching her arm upward to his shoulder, longing to trail her fingers across his collarbone to the back of his neck and into his hair. She restrained herself from rubbing the back of her hand against the softness of his lapels.

"Do you know you've been driving me insane all evening?" he asked. His touch sent a warm current through her as his hand contacted her bare, left shoulder blade and slowly caressed its way downward to rest at the small of her back. Iris felt his hand compelling her to move closer, hip to hip, breast to breast, but she resisted, maintaining a decorous distance between them.

"Me?" Iris asked innocently, wanting to taunt him with flirtatious words, but finding herself too breathless to do more than utter a simple syllable.

"That dress makes you absolutely ravishing," he said, grateful for the excuse to hold her. "I like you with your hair up." It had been driving him mad all evening to be making small talk with Maggie and Sheila when Iris was just out of reach. Since the night he had fixed dinner at her brownstone, he had thought of little else but Iris. They had shared such an easy camaraderie together. It had been after midnight before he had noticed the time. And he had left her without even trying to kiss her. "What time are you going to be home tonight?"

"What do you mean by that?" Iris asked, drawing slightly away and squinting up at his brown eyes. "You're Maggie's date this evening, and don't forget."

"I can hardly do that," he replied, "when Sheila Croft has been giving me the inquisition for the past two hours on that subject. But I have to take Maggie home eventually. I want to be with you. You look so gorgeous."

He twirled her around on the dance floor, and the movement brought them closer together. Iris hoped no one was listening or watching them too closely, because she didn't want to move away. "I'm not the kind of woman who dates on the second shift," she said. "Forget it."

Grant smiled. "Oh, I won't, as long as you don't forget it, either." As he spun her around again, he reeled her in a little closer. Conversation with her the other evening had been as relaxing as if they had known each other for years, yet it held all the challenge and excitement of two people who had only just met. He should have done more to impress her that night. But she had asked him to be himself, and in her company he had forgotten about acting. But he should have kissed her, as he longed to do now that he finally held her in his arms.

Iris felt as if she were dancing with Grant in a 1950s movie. Their cheeks were so close together, their lips almost touching, a breath away. It was exquisite torture to wonder how, when, if he would brush his lips against hers. Or would he tantalize her so long that *she* would end the suspense and move that extra millimeter closer toward the kiss. Just as in the movies, the kiss was forbidden, yet ever so tempting. "Remember where we are," she said, forcing herself to widen the space between their lips. She wouldn't meet his eyes. Her cheeks were blushing rose at the thought that anyone watching may have already assumed the kiss had been executed. That made her want it even more. "Maggie's watching us."

"Everyone's watching us," he agreed, his mouth drifting closer to hers again. "That's what's so hellish. Normally, I love an attentive audience, but I didn't factor in the effect you'd have on me this evening. You could have at least warned me about this dress you're halfway wearing."

"Don't get personal," Iris said, feeling next to naked now that he had called attention to her décolleté. "At least not with me, tonight." She glanced briefly at him, so overwhelmed by the frustration of being in his arms but not being his date that she momentarily forgot the purpose behind the dance. She wanted to be drawn closer to him, to find his hands roaming all over her body, warming her skin the way a single glance could warm her heart. But as far as the world was concerned he belonged with Maggie.

"The other night you told me you didn't want me playing any roles with you. I'd be lying if I said you were anything but beautiful tonight. The belle of the ball for me."

Iris felt the whisper of his warm breath near her ear. She closed her eyes. Just for a minute she wanted to imprint the sensations rushing through her in her memory as she imagined Grant belonging to her. When she opened her eyes she caught their reflection in mirrors across the room. They looked like a couple in love. She missed her step and drew away from him. "Grant, we have to talk."

"I want to do much more than talk," he murmured, trying to pull her closer.

She resisted. "Grant, you don't realize the mistake you've made. You told Sheila Croft the wrong story about how you met Maggie."

"What did I say?" he asked, running the dinner talk through his mind. "What's so bad about rescuing her from a careless waiter? I was trying to think of something general."

"I told her you met Maggie at the Russian Tea Room when you mistook her for Candice Bergen."

"When did you tell her that?" As he thought through the things he had told Croft, realization dawned. "Is that what all your coughing theatrics was about earlier?" She nodded as the music ended. He didn't release her immediately. "Don't worry. I'll fix it by telling her something to connect my story to yours."

Maggie and South were returning to their table, motioning for them to follow.

"It'll be all right," Grant promised, kissing Iris's hand as he reluctantly prepared to leave her. He lowered his voice and whispered, "Just remember, I want more than another dance with you, sweetheart, whether it's tonight or some other more enchanted, and private, evening."

Iris gathered up the material of her skirt to raise the hem and returned to her seat more confused than ever. Now that Grant had made his feelings for her clear, she wasn't certain she could idly sit through the remainder of the evening watching him dancing and touching Maggie. She couldn't even talk to him unless they arranged a rendezvous behind a potted palm like clandestine lovers. It made Iris feel like the other woman.

Just as she had that thought, Iris noticed Bradley Winchester with his new girlfriend who had stolen him away from Maggie. At fifty, Bradley's muddy-brown hair was shot through with gray. His cheeks were gaunt, brows dark, and his thin upper lip unsmiling. He stood six-two, which had been perfect for Maggie's five-eight height. He was slim and rock hard from daily workouts at the New York Athletic Club. He and Maggie had shared a love for the theater, sailing and ice skating. Bradley had introduced Maggie to skeet shooting and she had introduced him to art. Now it looked as if art had been their downfall.

Mary, Winchester's personal secretary, had been right. Bradley's date, who looked as if she were half his age, did have hair with an orange cast. She wore it spiky in a punk style with a streak of white at the crown that made her look as if she had unluckily walked beneath a painter's ladder just as a can of paint tipped over. Her silver dress with fur trim looked wild and unnatural, but no more so than some of the other way-out styles Iris had observed that evening. Iris stole a glance at Grant. At least he gave the appearance of fitting into her social circles. Iris wondered if Maggie had seen her ex.

Noticing Sheila Croft returning from the ladies' lounge, Grant asked Maggie if she would like to dance. As he helped her with her chair, Grant thought how right Iris had been. Maggie did resemble Candice Bergen. It was the ski-tip nose and the pointed chin, he decided. Her eyes were beautiful, too, but not like Iris's green eyes. He loved the way Iris squinted up at him when she wasn't wearing her glasses. But he liked it best when she did wear her glasses to correct her farsightedness. Without them she was always trying to back away from him.

Grant wondered what he would talk to Maggie about now that they were alone. His performance had almost been easier with a big audience. Her eyes held a faraway look as Grant took her hand and touched her waist to dance with her. She was a beautiful woman, and quite influential, judging by the way nearly everyone they met in the Helmsley lobby had stopped to talk to her. Grant couldn't understand why dozens of men wouldn't jump at the chance to be with her, unless it was that career intensity he had glimpsed. A lot of men were still looking for "the little woman" homemaker.

Not Grant. He wouldn't mind a woman who could hold her own with any man. He wanted an equal who had outside interests so that they could each bring something unique to the relationship. Thinking of the perfect relationship reminded him of Bob and Eve. He had promised himself he would make some decisions about the partnership in the restaurant as soon as this role with Maggie ended. Meanwhile, he intended to enjoy the performance in his very own swan song.

"You're a very good dancer," Maggie complimented, intruding on his thoughts. "What else do you do as well?"

Grant chuckled cynically, biding time to invent a reply. "You might say I'm sort of a Renaissance man."

"Ah, ha," she said, her lips curving in approval, "the kind who does everything well." Dimples appeared in her cheeks when she smiled and her nose tilted enchantingly. But her eyes didn't sparkle the way Iris's did.

"Something like that," he replied. He did a lot of different things, but not anything as well as cooking. He turned with her in his arms, wishing he held Iris.

"I love this song," Maggie said, and softly began to sing along.

Listening politely, Grant watched Iris over Maggie's shoulder. He didn't recognize the song, only that it came from the fifties era. Grant didn't mind older women, but Maggie was more than ten years older than he. Iris was the ideal age for him. And in spite of what other men said, Grant had never had a weakness for blonds.

Sheila and Iris were looking their way. Grant pretended to nuzzle romantically closer to Maggie and said, "If they were playing 'Sixteen Bottles of Rum on the Wall,' I'd hum along with you."

"You're so amusing, Grant," Maggie said, but the smile didn't reach her eyes. "I love a man with a good sense of humor."

Why didn't she laugh if it was so funny? He wondered why those beautiful blue eyes looked so sad. It was as if she were playing a role tonight, too, one of happiness when her eyes seemed glazed over with a thick shield of gloom. Suddenly he watched her eyes snap to life as she caught sight of something beyond his left shoulder. Her body, which had felt like deadwood in his arms, stiffened to rock hardness.

"Grant, darling," she said as her body relaxed, like molten lead, and she moved closer, tightening her arms around his neck. "Dance a little to your left and backward." She closed her eyes and kissed him on the corner of the mouth. It reminded Grant of his childhood when fish had nibbled at his toes down at the old swimming hole.

Grant followed her instructions, hoping there wasn't some ancient dance step he should have known to accomplish the same maneuver. Now she was leading, urging him backward, dance step by step until he bumped shoulders with some other man. "Excuse me," Grant apologized, turning with Maggie, intending to dance around them.

But Maggie had locked her knees like a giraffe, exclaiming, "Why, Bradley, what a surprise to see you here."

Grant stopped trying to dance by himself and turned, keeping his hand at Maggie's waist. Maggie reeled him in closer.

"It shouldn't be a surprise," Bradley replied. "I told you a month ago I'd be here, with Liv." He pulled the young woman he was dancing with up against his side. The gesture was about as graceful as a cowboy lassoing a calf.

Grant looked at the woman with the orange-tinted hair. She had to be half the man's age—it was about as ridiculous as him being with Maggie. And then Grant understood that this man meant something to Maggie. The sight of him had brought her to life for the first time that evening. "I'm Grant Peters," he introduced himself, since Maggie was staring at the odd couple.

"Bradley Winchester." He shook hands with Grant. "And this is my date, Liv Germaine."

Grant never looked at the woman again. *This* was Bradley Winchester, *the* theatrical agent? Of all the people in New York who could make or break an actor's career, Winchester was the most renowned. Grant had tried unsuccessfully for months just to get past his watchdog secretaries. He had left his résumé and videotape. He had tried several telephone ploys to trick the secretary into putting Winchester on the line for him. But the man was either "not available at this time" or "in conference."

Now, Grant was actually shaking hands with the man, speaking face-to-face with him. But it was as Grant Peters, the entrepreneur from Vienna, not Grant Peters, starving actor. Unless he broke character, which would cost him this role and embarrass Maggie, not to mention let Iris down, he couldn't say a word to Winchester. He dropped the man's hand and smiled weakly at his orange-haired date.

"So, you work in Vienna?" Winchester said.

"Yes, that's right," Grant replied, realizing Maggie had been talking about him.

Maggie snuggled closer and beamed up at him. "We've been inseparable since we met. Grant is such fascinating company, Bradley. He knows all about international finance and how OPEC works."

"Foreign business always was your favorite topic, wasn't it?" Winchester said sarcastically. He patted Liv's arm and said, "Liv is quite an artist. I'm arranging with one of the galleries in SoHo for her to have a private show."

Grant watched Liv tapping her foot to the music. Life could be so much easier for Grant knowing Bradley Winchester. If he had wanted to have an art show, Winchester could be the key. If he wanted to be an actor, Winchester could arrange it. Out of the corner of his eye Grant noticed one of the society photographers making his way around the room, taking snapshots of various groupings of socialites.

Maggie's face was flushed and her eyes looked moist. She was trying so hard to impress Winchester with Grant, but the few details she knew about him made him sound dull. Grant interrupted her. "I hear you're auditioning for a new play. Something about single women and single men?" Grant put his hand around Maggie's shoulder and tried to read Winchester. The man's expression was stony and clearly resentful of Grant.

"That's the official word," Winchester admitted, his eyes narrowing as he paid closer attention to Grant, "but the leads are already cast. How do you know so much about my business?"

"Oh, Grant's the original Renaissance man," Maggie cut in. "He keeps up with everyone's business." She smiled and then said to Liv, "My, what interesting hair. Did a bird have an accident over you, dear?"

"Maggie!" Winchester sputtered.

Liv laughed and said in a deep voice, "At least she's original. Don't mind her, darling. She's just jealous that I have you now, all to myself."

Grant felt Maggie trembling next to him and squeezed her shoulder to show his support. He wished he understood what he was getting into, or getting her out of. "Maggie," he said gently, "Iris wants to speak to you." What he meant was he wanted Iris to speak to *her* to find out what was so upsetting. As they turned, the photographer surprised the two couples with a flash of strobe light. Grant didn't even have time to smile.

Maggie blinked and put her hand up over her eyes, letting Grant lead her back to the table. "I'm sorry, Grant," she apologized as they wound their way among the dinner tables. "Bradley is an old flame. It was a shock to see him here with that woman. I hate to see anyone make a mistake with his life like that."

He didn't think Winchester was the old flame she said he was. In his opinion the embers were still burning between both of them.

When they reached the table, Maggie excused herself to go to the ladies' room. Sheila got up to follow Maggie.

Iris had noticed what had happened on the dance floor when Grant had accidentally danced into Bradley Winchester. She could imagine how Maggie must be feeling to face a lover for the first time after the breakup. Iris had gotten the shakes the first time she had seen Mitch after the divorce. And *she* had been the one to divorce him.

Iris excused herself, hoping she could get Croft back to the table and give Maggie a few minutes to compose herself. As she entered the ladies' room and came into the vanity area, she heard Sheila asking, "Now tell me dear how you met that gorgeous Grant Peters."

Not that again, Iris thought, hoping Maggie would at least get Grant's version straight. But as Maggie started talking about a lovely party she had gone to on a yacht in Boston harbor, Iris groaned inwardly. Hadn't *anyone* but Sheila Croft been listening? Maggie had been talking to the elderly couple when Grant had been telling Sheila how they met. The story of how Grant and Maggie met was growing longer than Pinocchio's nose.

Chapter Six

In spite of Iris telling Grant not to even consider showing up at her house after he took Maggie home from the charity ball, she couldn't fall asleep until after two. She kept listening for street sounds, half expecting him to disregard what she had said. Every few minutes she checked the clock, wishing he would call. As the hour grew later, she began to wonder what was happening between them.

After following Maggie into the ladies' lounge where Iris had quickly interrupted her boss's glowing tale of how she had met her Mr. Perfect, Iris never found another opportunity to be alone with Grant. Throughout the remainder of the evening she had been forced to dance just within reach of him, but always with someone else. Friends whom Iris hadn't seen since she had begun working at *New Age Woman,* wanted to catch up on old times with her. They couldn't believe she had gotten a job, never mind that it was in her uncle's publishing empire. Working implied that she must be having financial problems.

When Iris wasn't dancing, Edward insisted that she act as court recorder to all exchanges between Sheila, Grant and Maggie. The last time she had had such an exhausting evening was when Mitch had decided they should entertain the partners in his stockbrokerage firm, then had come home drunk just as everyone was arriving. That was all behind her now. She had a future with a fulfilling career to look forward to, if Grant played his role well enough.

By ten the next morning Iris still hadn't heard from Grant. So, she decided to pay him a visit at the penthouse apartment, which her uncle had arranged for him to move into. As she dressed, changing outfits three times before selecting an oversize Egyptian-cotton shirt belted over a flower print skirt, she told herself it was part of her job to follow up on loose ends and make certain Grant had done his task.

Her knocking must have woken him, because he looked dazed when he opened the door. His cheeks were dark from the growth of his beard. His hair was back to the natural, fluffy way she liked it, although more tousled than normal. Wearing a loosely belted bathrobe and what appeared to be little else, he looked like a shipwrecked sailor.

Iris relaxed. At least he had slept in his own bed last night. But it didn't look as if he had gotten much sleep. "Did I wake you?"

He ran a hand through his hair, which made it stand out in every direction, reminding Iris of Bradley Winchester's date. Yawning, he stepped aside for her to come in.

"You look like you could use some coffee," Iris said, stepping around his slick, black dress shoes where they lay in the middle of the plushly carpeted floor. Had it not been for the jacket and pants draped over the back of the leather sofa and the crumpled, white dress shirt lying in the hallway leading to the bedroom, Iris would have found it hard to believe this was the same man she had watched romancing Maggie the previous evening.

"Help yourself," he said, waving toward the black-and-white art deco kitchen. He yawned again. "I'll be in the shower."

The kitchen cupboards were practically bare, which made it easy to find what she needed. Spying a small jar of instant coffee, she put the kettle on. She went back into the living room and started picking up his clothes as she ventured down the hallway to the master bedroom of the penthouse apartment. She could hear the water running in the shower. Iris stood in the middle of the bedroom and shouted, "I guess you're pretty pleased with yourself after last night's performance." She tossed his clothes onto the rumpled bed. Either he was a restless sleeper or a pack of circus dogs had slept with him.

"Maggie was satisfied," Grant answered as the stinging hot water started to wake him up. "And the evening did have a few shining moments." He thought of the dance with Iris.

Iris wanted more details. "It looked as if you were really loving the role you were playing."

"Acting is the only career where you're paid to pretend to be someone else," he shouted back, dousing his face with water, soaping his back. "By portraying other people's fantasies I constantly learn who I am." But after coming face-to-face with Bradley Winchester last night, he had had plenty of time to think. He realized he had also used acting to avoid finding out who he really was.

The water stopped and Grant reappeared wearing the bathrobe and toweling his hair. "And did all your fantasies come true last night?" Iris asked. She watched him walking unabashedly around the bedroom, pulling out clothes to wear and drying his hair as if she were his sister instead of an extremely eligible female.

"Last night was one of the most frustrating nights of my life," Grant admitted. "This role has done nothing to help my career." It was just as well he had decided to give up on the dream of being an actor.

When Iris realized he was planning to get dressed right in front of her, she ducked into the hallway, using the excuse of the whistling kettle to remove his sexy body from view.

"Since coming to New York," Grant said, when he followed her to the kitchen a few minutes later, "I've worked my buns off trying to meet someone as influential as Bradley Winchester, hoping he would represent me as my agent. And when I finally meet the man, I'm supposed to be an international entrepeneur—and his ex-girlfriend's lover." He walked into the kitchen, tucking his shirt into a pair of well-worn jeans.

"Oh, Grant. I'm sorry." A wave of guilt washed over her. All she had been thinking of was how much he had appeared to be in love with Maggie. It hadn't occurred to her that this role was holding him back from his acting career.

He put his hand over hers to stop her from pouring the water over the coffee crystals. Gently he turned her around to face him, backing her up against the stove. "What was worse, was being with Maggie when I wanted to be with you."

Iris had worn her glasses that morning and could tell that he wasn't pretending now. She let him move even closer as he grasped her upper arms, massaging her heated skin with his thumbs. She felt the same breathless anticipation of riding a roller coaster toward a peak, the simultaneous fear and thrill of moving closer to the edge. When he reached up and pushed her glasses onto the crown of her head, she felt the release, giving in to her increasing wish to plunge headlong into romance.

His kiss made her feel like soaring as a host of sensations played throughout her body. There was warmth and tingling currents of racing emotion, tender affection and ardent passion. She moved so that the handle of the lower oven wouldn't be butting against her leg, and in moving she unwittingly gave him an excuse to press more tightly against her.

Sighing, Iris parted her lips and disentangled her arms to put her hands behind his neck, weaving her fingers into his damp hair as she had longed to do throughout their dance the previous evening. It felt so good to feel the breadth of his chest and the solidity of his thighs pressed close to her. It was how she had wanted him to hold her last night at the dance. She wondered if she was dreaming.

Grant gathered her closer, running his hands over her shoulders and down her back, breaking the kiss to rub his rough cheek against hers and whisper into her ear, "This is what I wanted last night."

"Me, too," Iris admitted with a breathless sigh. She hadn't allowed herself to dream he could want this, too.

He drew away just enough to smile at her, then pulled her back for another luxurious hug. The insistent kettle eventually broke their contact. Holding her at arm's length, Grant said, "That kiss was an accident."

"I knew that," Iris said, and they both laughed as he picked up the kettle to fix the instant coffee.

As he poured, Grant kept glancing at Iris with a pleased expression on his face. Now this was the American dream: having a penthouse apartment in New York

City and finding himself alone there with Iris. But it really wouldn't matter where they were as long as they were together. Last night, as he had fallen asleep in that big, empty bed, he had thought of her, imagining what it would be like to find her lying next to him. Every annoyance he had felt from the previous evening had smoothed away at the memory of her pressed against him on the dance floor. He had tossed and turned all night, wondering if she was giving him the first thought. "I couldn't get you out of my mind last night," he admitted.

"I know," she said, breathless to discover he had been just as tortured by her as she had been by him. She felt her face growing red as he kept watching her, as if they had just learned a secret about each other. "I guess I was keyed up about everything that happened at the dance, because I couldn't sleep."

"Well, I couldn't sleep, either, but it was because of everything that *didn't* happen," he said, "with you." As Grant handed her one of the cups, he noticed her hand shook slightly.

Now that they were alone, he didn't know what to do with her. He knew what he *wanted* to do, but he was so afraid of rushing things and making the wrong move again. But he wanted to get closer, to know more about her. "Let's go sit in the living room," he suggested.

Iris followed him quietly, not quite believing she was here, alone with him. She sat near the end of the leather couch, hoping he would sit close to her as he had done that night at her apartment. When he did, she smiled to herself, then frowned when he immediately lit a cigarette. Iris fanned the smoke in hope that he would get the message and put out the cigarette. But all he did was exhale away from her as a concession to her disapproval. "I wish you wouldn't smoke," she said quietly.

He smiled apologetically as he took a final draw on the cigarette, then crushed it out in the oversized ashtray on the coffee table. Turning to her, he rested his arm along the back of the couch where he could touch her and pull her closer, if she would just relax a little.

"How do you like the apartment?" she asked, bringing her cup to her lips, as if it would provide an adequate barrier between them. She wanted him to kiss her again, but she didn't want him to know how badly. Resting the cup in her lap, she held it with both hands.

"It's a little lonely after my place," he said. "I find it difficult to hear through the walls."

Iris laughed. "That's because you don't have any neighbors on this side."

"I realize that," he said, running his fingers through the ends of her hair as if it were an idle distraction. "And I never thought it could be so boring without all the domestic spats that kept me entertained at the old place. It's almost like being insulated from real life up here. But don't worry," he assured her with a mischievous grin, "I'm making a true effort to adjust."

"There's probably a lot of truth in what you're saying," she agreed as she felt herself relaxing, becoming more aware of his idle touch than anything he was saying.

Grant ran his hand along her thigh and invited, "What do you say we spend the day together?"

As much as she wanted to be with him, she was wary of letting things between them progress too rapidly. "I don't know," Iris said cautiously. Love affairs that started off with a short fuse fizzled out too quickly for

Remember! To receive your free books, manicure set and mystery gift, return the postpaid card below. But don't delay!

DETACH AND MAIL CARD TODAY.

If offer card has been removed, write to: Harlequin Reader Service, 901 Fuhrmann Blvd., P.O. Box 1867, Buffalo, NY 14269-1867

MAIL THE POSTPAID CARD TODAY!

NO POSTAGE NECESSARY IF MAILED IN THE UNITED STATES

BUSINESS REPLY CARD

First Class Permit No. 717 Buffalo, NY

Postage will be paid by addressee

Harlequin Reader Service®
901 Fuhrmann Blvd.
P.O. Box 1867
Buffalo, NY 14240-9952

her taste. "I don't think it would be good for Maggie's sake if we're seen together."

He took her hand. "We'll go somewhere where no one can see us, like out of town, or to the top of the Empire State Building where all the tourists go."

"I don't know if we should take that chance." She thought again of Grant and how good he had looked last night. She only wished he had been with her.

"Listen, I'm having a late lunch with my sister and brother-in-law today. I'm sure Eve wouldn't mind if I brought a friend."

Iris protested, "What if Eve says something to someone and it eventually gets back to Maggie, or worse, Sheila Croft?"

"Think of it," he said, his eyes dancing with good humor. "It would be like having an affair."

"I am thinking," Iris said. "And someone always finds out."

"Look. They're family." He set his coffee cup on the floor and shifted on the couch so that he was again facing her and could play with her collar. "Besides, Bob, my brother-in-law, was in Eve's Garden the day you asked me to take on this role. He and Eve already know what's going on."

Iris resisted. She wanted to spend more time with him. Anything was safer than being alone with him. "It wouldn't be polite to impose without an invitation of my own." In her social circles, an unexpected guest would throw off carefully calculated seating arrangements.

"They're not the kind of people who would see it as an imposition," he argued. "But if it makes you uncomfortable, I guess we could always stay here." He kissed her cheek and began nuzzling at her neck. "This was my first choice, anyway. I wanted to see you today. Remember, I told *you* I wanted to go by your place after dropping Maggie off last night." He put his index finger over her lips to halt her reply. "I would have come knocking on your door today if you hadn't beat me to mine."

"Okay, you win," she said, laughing as his nibbling kisses tickled her. She set down her cup to keep from spilling the coffee and playfully met him kiss for nibbling kiss. "But speaking of Maggie, what *did* happen when you brought her home?"

Grant shrugged as if it were inconsequential. "She asked me in for a nightcap. Her dog almost bit a hole in my trousers. I played hard to get and told her it was late and that I'd better be on my way. Then I kissed her good night, like this." He rolled so that Iris was pinned against the back of the couch. Cradling her face between his palms, he ardently pressed his lips against hers.

If Iris still didn't have doubts that Grant was playing games with her, she would have melted from his skillful kissing techniques. But the thought of him kissing Maggie, and like this, caused her to freeze.

Reacting to her lack of response, he inched his lips far enough away from hers to ask, "What's the matter? Wasn't that good enough?"

"That was horribly forward of you for a first date, Grant," she replied haughtily. "I'm surprised Maggie stood still for such a crass demonstration of your virility."

"Unless I've miscalculated, this is our fourth date, counting the night we met."

"We're not talking about us. We're discussing Maggie."

"Oh, Maggie! I just gave her a good night peck on the cheek. Didn't I tell you? She's not my type."

"You—you—" Iris sputtered as feelings of anger dissolved into laughter. She pounded on his chest with soft, playful taps.

He caught her wrists and searched her eyes. "No games, remember? Those were your rules."

Iris smiled warmly and put both arms around his neck. "Grant Peters, I think I'm going to like you very much."

"Iris Janus, I hope so."

AS GRANT HAD PREDICTED, his sister, Eve, greeted Iris warmly, welcoming her into the apartment above the restaurant, tidying up all the loose pages of the Sunday paper as she led the way into the living area. Iris recognized her as the restaurant's waitress the afternoon that Iris had offered Grant the role. But her husband, Bob, was only icily polite.

The room reminded Iris of the attic of her parents' home. Fringed cloths covered select items of furniture to keep them looking new, in case of company, but were never removed because they had become such fixtures. A magazine rack stuffed with old periodicals was too full to hold newer editions, which were stacked in neat piles in a small bookcase. Bric-a-brac ranging from a mule harness to a cuckoo clock decorated tabletops, shelves and hung on the walls. Nothing matched, which made such an unlikely collection look as if it all belonged together.

While Iris looked at the eclectic treasures, Bob mixed drinks and Eve set an extra place at the dining table. The room smelled of pot roast and roses.

When Grant's sister returned to the living room with a gin and tonic, she said, "You're the girl from the paper. I should have recognized you immediately, but you're wearing your hair down today and you didn't have your glasses on."

"What are you talking about?" Grant asked.

"The paper this morning, in the society section," Eve said, rummaging through the stack she had just finished bundling out of sight. "They covered that ball you went to. You'll be pleased, Grant, at your picture, too."

Bob helped his wife sort through the discarded sections of the paper. "Here it is." He folded the page back and handed it over to Grant.

Iris scooted closer to him on the couch, sinking into a well-worn low spot. Looking over his shoulder, she saw her picture first. "Thank goodness we're in two separate pictures," she mumbled. She had been photographed standing next to her uncle.

"Oh, great," Grant said, thumping his finger at the page. "This is the picture of us when we were talking with Bradley Winchester and his date. The man and I look like we're engaged in a battle to decide who gets Maggie." He set the paper on the arm of the couch and picked up his drink. The ice cubes clinked against the glass.

"I thought you might want to put it in your scrapbook," Eve offered, sitting down on an ottoman near her husband who kept frowning at Iris.

"I don't think I'm going to keep a scrapbook any longer," he muttered. "But I would like to keep Iris's picture to carry in my wallet."

Eve looked eagerly from one to the other seeking signs of a developing romance. Her husband only frowned deeper, as if Iris were a guard dog and he were waiting for her to pounce. Iris shifted uncomfortably next to Grant, but was secretly pleased by the thought of being a couple with him. "Tell us about the ball," Eve urged, rattling the ice in her glass. "Who was there?"

While Grant embellished the truth with harmless additions that made Eve laugh, Iris tried to picture this willowy woman with straight, dark brown hair as a child growing up with Grant. He had probably told her bedtime fairy tales, making things up to create a better story than the original. She had probably looked upon her big brother in awe, as she was doing now with her fingers laced around her crossed knees.

When Eve had had her fill of tales from the ball, Iris, hoping to warm Bob's icy stare, said, "You have such a wonderful collection of things. There must be a story behind every item." An intricately carved clock hung next to two framed brass rubbings and a collection of pen-and-ink sketches of city scenes. A brass elephant table stood in front of another wall decorated with Japanese fans. Small Oriental throw rugs were scattered over the floor. And wild garden roses stood in unmatched crystal vases. "I especially like those matched swords," she added, hoping to draw Bob into conversation.

"Bob was in the army, and we've traveled all over the world," Eve said when her husband didn't respond to Iris's polite overture. "We picked up at least one thing everywhere we lived to remind us of each place." Eve was near Iris in age, but her husband looked closer to Maggie's age.

Over dark trousers he wore a long, white Mexican shirt with white embroidery. He had a thick neck and square chin. Beneath sparse brows, his gray eyes didn't miss a thing. Iris guessed he would have made a good drill sergeant, but Grant had told her that Bob had been a lieutenant colonel. "The restaurant is my second career," Bob said, running a hand over his cropped hair. "We decided to give it two years and if it didn't work out cut our losses and move on. But the business has been good, so we're still here."

"It's because of Grant," Eve chimed in. "Things really picked up when he moved to New York. He's so creative when it comes to food."

"I learned everything I know from Mrs. O'Connor," Grant said modestly.

"Who was she?" Iris asked.

"Our next-door neighbor," Eve answered. She got up to get a photo album, opened it to the page she wanted and showed Iris. "When mother died, Mrs. O'Connor would check on us every day. She loved to cook and would often prepare dinner parties for her friends. Word started getting around, and she began a catering service, operating out of her home."

"We were her guinea pigs," Grant added. "I used to earn extra money after school by helping her prepare for parties." He patted his stomach. "Leftovers never tasted so good."

Iris looked through the photo album, comparing pictures from Grant and Eve's childhood with the two people today. "The only time we ever had leftovers was on the cook's night out," Iris said.

Bob glanced pointedly at Grant. Finishing his drink, Grant rose to fix another. "Can I get anyone anything else?"

"I think I'll freshen my drink, too," Bob said, rising with Grant.

"I get embarrassed when my sister starts talking about me, so I'm going to leave the room." Grant winked at Eve. "But don't leave out the part about how good I am at the important things in life, like sports."

"Silly," Eve said, shaking her head as the men left the room. "He really has been a lifesaver for us," she told Iris. "He does all the shopping, bargaining with grocers and dealers in markets all over Manhattan and Brooklyn."

Iris smiled and looked beyond Eve to the kitchen where the men had gone. She could see them through the open doorway and wondered what they were talking about.

Grant was opening the refrigerator, searching for a beer when Bob cornered him. "She's out of your league, Grant. Give it up before someone gets hurt."

"That won't happen," Grant said with false bravado, pulling a beer from its case and shutting the door with his hip. He felt as if he had had this conversation before, except last time it had been with his father and the subject had been acting in Hollywood. "I have everything under control."

Bob glanced over his shoulder into the living room where his wife was talking with Iris. Iris caught his eye, which forced him to smile. He lowered his voice, as if she could hear what they were saying. "She has High Society stamped all over her," Bob argued. "What place do you think you can have in her world?"

Grant had asked himself that question the previous night as he had sat across from her in that room filled with the crème de la crème of society. But acting had always given Grant the ability to dream impossible dreams. "Any place I want," Grant said, popping the top of the beer can. "Didn't you see the pictures? I was rubbing elbows with all her friends last night."

"You were acting at that ball," Bob reminded, hands on his hips.

"She likes me," Grant said. He was sure of it after this morning. When the chemistry was right between a man and a woman, anything could happen.

Bob just shook his head. "Nothing good has ever come of your acting, but you seem to forget that. What I want to know is, what happens when the curtain comes down?"

AFTER LUNCH Eve served homemade ice cream in the living room. "I'm glad Grant brought along VCR tapes of movies in which he had had a part," Eve said. "Usually these two make me sit through sports shows on TV."

Iris groaned sympathetically. "I've never been overly athletic and can't stand watching sports. But I love old movies."

"These are pretty old," Eve assured her. "I haven't seen some of them in years." She sat on the floor in front of Bob's recliner so that she would have a good view of the TV screen. "Some of them are so funny."

"Laugh your heart out," Grant said as he inserted the first tape, "because I'm retiring them after this showing." He looked pointedly at his brother-in-law, remembering their talk in the kitchen, and punched the Play button. As he took his place on the couch beside Iris, he added, "You need to know about my other life."

The first movie was *Six Guns to Nowhere*, an attempt at a spoof of Westerns. Iris wasn't certain whether to laugh or not when after ten minutes she admitted she still couldn't figure out the plot. "That's part of its charm," Grant said, placing his hand possessively on her thigh, watching the action scenes closely. "It doesn't have a plot, only a message." He laughed. "It was filmed in Spain, which was the only good thing about it for me." He started fast-forwarding the movie, stopping it long enough for his scenes to play through at normal speed.

"Grant's good, isn't he?" Eve said when the movie finally ended.

Iris merely smiled and gave him the benefit of the doubt. John Wayne would have had trouble looking good in a movie so bad.

"You'll like this next one," Eve said when the title, *Teenage Gigolo*, flashed on the screen. "Grant has some really sexy scenes in it."

On the screen, a much younger Grant played a role that was a variation of what she had watched in action the previous evening when he had been acting as Maggie's lover. The dialogue was thin and predictable, filler for the love scenes. "It reminds me so much of last night's performance," she finally admitted, hoping she hadn't offended him. She tensed, wondering if he was going to take his clothes off in this movie. The story seemed to be leading in that direction.

"Yeah, it does, doesn't it? I used this movie as a reference when I was rehearsing meeting Maggie. An actor draws on his reserves."

Iris felt uncomfortable. Were there other movies he had used as a guide for how he had treated her, too? As much as she disliked watching sports on TV, she began to think it might have been better than these flicks. She was relieved when the movie ended without raising any further questions or any significant clothing coming off.

The movie teased but never delivered. No wonder it had been a flop. "I'm afraid I don't remember any of these movies," Iris said.

"I bet you've heard of this one," Grant said, putting the next one in the machine.

"*Maple Street Nightmare* ? *The* horror movie?" Iris said as the title flashed across the screen and the first gruesome murder took place during the opening credits. "That movie made a lot of money and got a lot of attention. Grant, I'm impressed."

"Don't be," he said, getting up and stopping the movie.

"What did you do that for?" Iris said. "I thought we were going to watch it."

"Didn't you see it when it came out at the movies?" Eve asked.

"Yes, I did, but I don't remember what part Grant could have had. Why don't you play the whole thing?"

He rewound the tape and started it over again. "That's because my part's already over. That was *me* who was killed during the opening credits."

"No!" Iris said, doubling over with laughter. "Play it again, Grant." They watched his movie death three times before Iris could honestly say, "Well, *maybe* it was you."

Bob brought the rest of the homemade ice cream into the living room as Grant put the final tape into the VCR. Bob had remained cordial but distant toward Iris throughout the afternoon.

"This is the one where I made the most money," Grant announced.

Iris sat patiently through the animated credits and then realized, "It's a cartoon!"

"Grant's the voice of the duck," Eve pointed out, giggling. "Do your duck for us, Grant."

Grant had everyone rolling by the time he finished his animated imitations. Tears were streaming down Iris's cheeks. She wasn't certain what to say about his less than illustrious film career, except that he seemed to have a good sense of humor about it all. When Bob and Eve had left them alone to wash the dishes, Iris said, "I'm so glad I didn't know about these films when I asked you to do the role for Maggie. I would have been twice as worried as I was last night."

He took both of her hands in his, knees touching as he faced her. His expression was so serious, Iris wanted to laugh and ask him what role he was playing now. "The other night you said you didn't want me playing games with you. Well, I don't want to play games with myself any longer, either. I'm not good enough to be an actor. These movies say it more clearly than I ever could."

"But, Grant, it's your dream—"

"That's right, my dream. But that's all. Since I came to New York I haven't gotten one job as an actor, except for when your uncle hired me."

She glanced toward the kitchen where she could hear Bob and Eve laughing over the clatter of pots and dishes. "Why are you telling me this, why now?"

"Because I want things to be right between us. I don't want to play games any longer, with you, and most of all with myself. I'm not an actor, Iris. Right now all I am is a short-order cook working in the family business. But I mean to change things."

The room was so quiet she heard the ticktock of the cuckoo clock and a siren wailing in the distance outside. "What are you going to do?"

"I don't know yet. But I wanted to make that clear to you, right up front, so that there won't be any deception between us." He spread his arms and said, "What you see is what you get. I'm through pretending to be someone I'm not."

"Well," Iris said, looking on the bright side, "at least you only have one more performance to make with Maggie for the return interview on *American Scene* with Sheila and her husband."

"Oh, that won't be any problem. Especially since I'll be seeing Maggie a lot between now and then." Iris's quizzical expression made him elaborate. "Didn't your uncle tell you? He wants me to get Maggie out in public as often as possible before the interview. I have a date with her for a performance at Lincoln Center tomorrow evening."

Chapter Seven

Maggie waltzed into the office the morning after her concert date with Grant at Lincoln Center looking brighter than a sunbeam. "Grant is the most endearing man," Maggie announced to her staff, who had lined up outside her office to hear the latest installment of Maggie's romance. "He had a hansom cab waiting for us after the performance with a picnic basket for a midnight feast. It was such a lovely, warm spring night."

Iris stood with her arms full of page proofs for the next issue of the magazine, needing Maggie's approval in order to meet deadlines. Iris halfway listened to the details of the date. She already knew about the picnic right down to the last item in the basket. At her uncle's suggestion, the editors had been the ones to think of the romantic date for Grant to take Maggie on. Iris had shopped for the feast. After Grant had taken Maggie home, he had phoned Iris, and they had talked until two in the morning. The carriage leaving Lincoln Center had made a great photograph that South planned to use in an upcoming photo spread for the magazine. And it was another score for Maggie since Sheila kept the gossip papers supplied with negative information about Maggie's younger man.

Patiently letting Maggie talk until she started to repeat herself, Iris suppressed a yawn from lack of sleep, and tried to get her boss's attention. "These page proofs are due back today, Maggie, in order to meet the deadline. Could you look at these now?"

"Sorry, girls," she said, waving her staff back to work and leading the way into her corner office decorated in peach and gray. "Grant kept me out so late I can't think straight." She feigned a yawn. "That man is attentive and affectionate, and so full of energy, not at all the stick in the mud Bradley Winchester is. Grant just can't keep his hands off of me."

To hear Grant tell it, Maggie was the one who had cornered him in the back seat of the hansom cab. Iris frowned, but refrained from commenting. The work in her arms was long overdue. Maggie sniffed the flowers that the editors had sent in Grant's name the previous week, and ignored the unreturned message slips piling up on her desk. "Why don't you deal with the page proofs, Iris? You've watched me often enough to know my taste if changes are necessary. I have an appointment to get my nails done in an hour. Oh, and I'd like you to go to Tiffany's sometime this afternoon and pick out something special for me to give to Grant."

"What should I get?" Iris asked, annoyed that she again had to take care of Maggie's errands. "Don't you think it would be better if you did that yourself?"

"I really don't have time," Maggie said. "You have such good taste, Iris. And you know how much I hate to shop. I'm sure you'll pick out something appropriate."

Iris decided the easiest thing to do would be to just phone Tiffany's and ask them to select something for Maggie and have them deliver.

She spent the afternoon with the computer technician who worked on laying out the pages of the magazine. In explaining the kind of changes she wanted to make, she learned how to alter the type style of a headline, break up the text of an article into quick and readable boxes of information and select the final photographs from contact sheets. Iris welcomed the extra work and new sense of fulfillment it gave her. She couldn't wait to tell Grant about the increased responsibilities in her career.

"IRIS, GRANT IS DRIVING me mad with desire," Maggie confided the morning after she had gone dancing with Grant. "He kept me up until nearly three this morning, that naughty boy."

Dawn and Tina, who overheard Maggie's remarks as they passed by the office kitchen where Maggie was stirring a cup of tea, exchanged telling glances with Iris, then lingered near the coffee machine to hear more. They were the ones who had engineered Maggie's most recent date, dinner and dancing in Montreal, followed by a return flight home by private jet.

Iris pushed her glasses onto the crown of her head and rubbed her weary eyes. Maggie may have been awake that long by herself, but Grant had again phoned Iris just after one in the morning. They had talked about Iris's new responsibilities at work, and he had listened to her ideas for articles and encouraged her to keep trying new things at the magazine. They discovered they had a mutual love of spy novels, musty bookstores and gourmet coffees.

Tasting the tea and finding it too hot, Maggie asked, "Do you think I should let him make love to me?"

"No!" Iris said, suddenly awake. She put her glasses back in place to focus in on Maggie. "I mean, you hardly know him," she added more calmly. "These things shouldn't be rushed."

"I know. That's what I advocate in the magazine, not to get tangled up in a sexual relationship unless you're willing to accept all the consequences. But he's so young and good-looking, in much better shape than Bradley ever was."

Tina and Dawn had their own opinions, and were eager for the consummation of the romance. Iris wished she could tell them how she felt about Grant, but knew it would interrupt their carefully laid plans for Maggie's romance. As soon as Maggie left that afternoon, Iris sought out her uncle. "Maggie's getting serious about Grant, Uncle Edward," she began, hoping she could reason with him.

"That can't hurt anything," South replied. "In fact, that ought to help our story look more convincing. Croft just won't let up on Maggie and Grant." He sorted through the papers on his desk and slid a society column across to her. "I was at this party with Sheila last night and overheard her telling everyone that Grant is 'the mysterious man who came from nowhere.'"

Iris looked at the picture at the head of the column and passed it back. A smear of black printer's ink stained her hand. "But Grant's not interested in Maggie other than as a job."

"You can't know that," South returned. His eyes narrowed speculatively and he added, "I hope you're not getting involved with him. It's all an act, you know. He's not our kind."

"He's a decent human being," she argued. How could she tell him that she was falling in love with Grant? "It's only going to make it harder for him to get out of this impossible role if we keep this up much longer. Do you plan on paying him forever?"

South began twitching his mustache from side to side in consternation. "What do you propose we do? Tell Maggie we had to pay someone to go out with her?" He tapped his pen against his desk and said, "We have to play this through, at least until she goes on *American Scene* with Croft again. Then we'll deal with it. Anyway, when has a little romance ever hurt anyone?"

THE EVENING that Maggie had plans to meet Grant for an awards banquet at the Grand Hyatt, he had talked Iris into meeting him for a drink at the South Street Seaport. Iris had voiced to herself every argument she could think of against meeting him in public, but the lure of being with Grant was too much to resist.

By the time he arrived, Iris had been waiting for a good fifteen minutes. She was seated at a table hidden by a grouping of potted plants where she could watch the boats on the East River and the traffic crossing the Brooklyn Bridge.

The minute he took his seat she said, "Grant, I'm a little uneasy that someone is going to see us together. And then how will we explain? This meeting is not wise." But the excitement of being with him again made her smile. She readily forgot her uncle's warning.

"I know, don't you love it? It's like having a secret affair." He reached across the table and took her hands. "I think we should always do this, even after Maggie and I publicly break up."

"Have you discussed breaking up?" Iris asked eagerly, scooting her chair closer to the table so that they could speak more intimately. Maggie's latest report on Grant's arousing sensuality had influenced Iris to risk seeing him now. According to Maggie, Grant was breaking down her resistance and it would only be a matter of time before they consummated their love.

"Well, no," he said, tossing his head to the side. "But we all know this can't go on forever."

"Everyone but Maggie knows that," Iris pointed out, not wanting to mention her uncle. She looked down at her hands entwined with his. Hers were ice-cold, but his toasty. She didn't want to let go of him now, or ever. As Grant lit a cigarette, she said, "Do you have to smoke?"

"I'm off duty now," he said.

"Please?"

Grant shrugged and stubbed out the cigarette.

"Grant—" She looked up at him and bit her lower lip. "I think Maggie's falling in love with you."

Grant grinned and adjusted his silk paisley tie. "That's only natural. I'm a lovable kind of guy."

"Grant, be serious a minute—"

"I am being serious," he said. "Otherwise I never would have worn this particular tie with a plaid shirt. But the guy who sold it to me said it's a proper outfit for this informal little function we're attending tonight." He laughed at her pained expression, squeezed her hand and said, "Relax. I don't love *her*."

A waiter carrying a tray laden with soiled dishes stopped by their table long enough to ask if he could take their drink order. As Grant placed the order, Iris watched a group of tourists on the pier outside the side window crossing the gangplank of the *Peking* sailing ship. Behind them she heard the slurping sounds of a capuccino machine and wished she had asked for coffee instead of Chablis. Being with Grant always made her head spin, without the benefit of alcohol.

Once the waiter left, Iris accused, "Grant, I really believe you're enjoying this. You can't have your cake and eat it, too." She had a short fuse lately, with the pressure from the increasing amount of work Maggie had been letting her do, and was confused about the conflicting stories she heard from Grant and Maggie about the direction the relationship was taking. On top of that, Maggie's glowing reports of Grant were being embellished by the staff. Even when Maggie wasn't in the office, someone was telling Iris about Grant as Casanova. It was all Iris could do to bite her cheek and not set the story straight.

Tears misted her eyes. "I'm not doing well being in the middle of this. Maggie's my friend as well as my boss, and I—" She looked down at the table unable to go on. How could she tell this man how jealous it made her feel to hear Maggie talk about wanting to make love with him? Even if Grant wasn't so inclined, Iris knew that Maggie got her way more often than not. After all, she had watched Maggie twirl Bradley Winchester around her little finger. "I think it will be better if you don't see me until all of this is over with."

All the lighthearted replies Grant wanted to make went out of his head. He had looked forward to seeing Iris, spending what little time they could steal together. He couldn't sleep at night for planning ways to romance her on the sly. Talking to her on the phone after his dates with Maggie left him starved for more contact with her. Hearing her say she didn't want to see him now, deflated him. "Iris, the time I spend with Maggie is just a job. She's not my type, and I'm getting tired of pretending otherwise. The prospect of seeing you is the only thing that makes this role bearable."

"Oh, Grant," she said, sadly shaking her head, "why can't we have a normal relationship like everyone else? I hate this game playing and deception. Nothing's fun anymore. I don't even enjoy writing like I thought I would."

"The difference between us and other couples," he said, tightening his grip on her hands to make her see his point, "is *they're* the ones playing games, with each other. We're not doing that. All the games are being played around us. I actually think we're pretty lucky."

"You do?" Her big, green eyes searched his for reassurance. The growing love she felt for him was pulsing in her heart. "But we've hardly had any time together."

"Then let's plan some time away together. Don't you realize how important you've become to me?" His voice caught from the welling passion that clamored for expression. Part of him said to tell her right here and now that he loved her. Another inner voice said to wait for the proper, special moment. Several times he had been tempted to blurt out the truth of his feelings. "I wish all of this was behind us so that we could get on with our lives and start a proper romance of our own."

"Really?"

He reached up and crushed a tress of her hair in his hand. "Don't you realize you're my Cinderella, the kind of woman I want to spend time with? But unfortunately, as Prince Charming, I can't go chasing after you until all of my houseguests have gone home from the ball."

Iris smiled and nuzzled her cheek against his hand.

"I can't put my whole life on hold while I'm playing this grand charade for your uncle and Maggie," Grant said. The gentleness of his hand against her cheek urged her to trust him. "As it is, I can't begin to make plans for my future until this is behind me. What if I went on a job interview and it got back to Sheila Croft? Or what if Maggie found out I was enrolling in night school? How would that look?"

"Not well, I know, but do you have to act like you're having so much fun?"

He rubbed her cheek with the back of his hand, enjoying the spice of jealousy in her voice. "I do enjoy the chance to perform. You knew that when you hired me." He smiled, feeling closer to her. "And I certainly can't deny it isn't nice to have a little extra cash in my pocket in order to afford jackets like this one. And that penthouse is a dream to live in. But I'm just trying to make the best of an awkward situation."

Iris nodded. She was being unreasonable, but she couldn't help envying the time Maggie spent with Grant when she wanted to be the woman in his life. "You're right," she said sensibly as their drinks came, breaking up their hand-holding. "I do feel like the other woman, wondering when you're going to get a divorce."

"It won't be much longer," he assured her. The interview on *American Scene* was coming up. He tapped his glass to hers. "When I first saw you in the bar that night, I knew you'd be an excellent mistress. But I have much more domestic designs on you."

Iris felt her heart jolt as she attempted to read the look in his eyes. What did that mean? Had he thought of the future and marrying her? Did she want to marry *him*? It was too soon to know what her feelings were. But she did want to see more of him, and wanted to know him much better. It was enough for now to know he wanted to be with her, whether Maggie was in the picture or not. "Why does the other woman have to be Maggie? I know how much the breakup with Bradley Winchester hurt her, and I don't want to complicate that pain. But, Grant, when is this going to end?"

Grant forced a smile. "No matter what it may look like, I want you to know, Iris, how much I want to be with you, alone, just the two of us, without worrying what the world will think." As he held Iris's hands in his, knowing he only had a few more minutes before he had to leave her, he wondered not when it would end, but *how*.

"SHUT THE DOOR, Iris," Maggie said, "and set the mail down. I have to talk to you." She wore a lime-green-and-white suit that day with stripes running vertically in the skirt and sleeves of the jacket and horizontally across the back and front. Maggie swiveled her chair to face the bank of windows in the corner office, her back to Iris. There were new flowers on her desk, which the editors had again sent in Grant's name.

Iris was in a hurry to get back to her desk. With all the late-night phone calls and rendezvous with Grant, Iris was behind on her work. There were blank spaces in the page layouts where her columns ran, her copy the last to go in.

Maggie's column could be written quickly, since Iris had been so involved with the magazine's layout that month. And she could pull almost any restaurant from her memory for the Epicurious column. But now that she spent the wee hours of the morning worrying about Grant and Maggie, she had broken her routine of reading late at night, and hadn't finished a book to review.

Iris braced herself for more stories about Grant that Maggie had slightly embellished upon. Maggie had talked about how ardently Grant had kissed her, yet Grant had told Iris he hadn't kissed her at all. Maggie had said things Grant never recalled saying. Although Iris felt confused by the conflicting stories they were each telling her, she knew Grant was telling her the truth.

"Yes, Maggie? Is something wrong?" Iris asked.

"No, nothing's wrong. I was just wondering, how would you go about seducing a man?"

Grant? Iris panicked. "Me?"

"Yes," Maggie said, getting up and stepping to the window where her fortieth-floor office gave her a view of Lower Manhattan and the Hudson River. A haze obscured the more-distant view of the midtown skyscrapers. "How would *you* do it?"

Iris sank onto the chair in front of Maggie's big, white desk, afraid her knees would crumple beneath her. How she had made love was one thing. How she wanted to make love to Grant was another. Telling Maggie how to seduce the man she herself wanted was something else entirely. "You're the one who wrote the book on it, Maggie," she said. "Why ask me?"

Maggie turned, her hands on her hips to reveal the white silk camisole top worn beneath the jacket. "Because everything I've tried, by the book, with Grant just hasn't worked." She paced in front of the windows. "I think I've been too subtle. He's not at all like Bradley."

Iris felt the color drain from her face and was lightheaded. According to Grant, Maggie was about as subtle as an Amazonian. What would he do if she suddenly got aggressive? She gripped the arms of the chair and stammered, "I'm—I'm sure he likes you."

"Then why can't I arouse him?"

Iris looked blankly at Maggie. She should be feeling relieved to know that Grant wasn't tempted to demonstrate his prowess as a man with Maggie. "Maybe he's old-fashioned, or shy."

"Grant?" Maggie laughed and stared out at the Hudson River. "He's the original Renaissance man. No." She shook her head thoughtfully. "It's something else. The man is an absolute dream until we're alone, and then his ardor for me just fades away. What could I do differently?"

Running her thumb over the mail in her lap, Iris said, "I'm sorry I can't help you, Maggie, but I haven't had a real date in more than six months, so I hardly think I'm qualified to tell you what to do." She had to warn Grant. "Could we go over the mail now?"

Maggie thumped her fingernails against the windowpane while she thought. Finally she turned and said, "Just leave the mail. I'll get to it in a little while." She smiled thoughtfully as she picked up a gold pen and began twirling a lock of golden hair around the end. "Thanks, Iris. I think I've got a plan that will melt my Mr. Perfect's armor when I seduce him tonight."

Chapter Eight

"Am I running late, or are you early?" Maggie said as she opened the door to Grant that evening. Her terrier yapped annoyingly at Grant's feet, snapping at his pant leg.

"I think I'm right on time," Grant replied, shaking his leg to discourage the dog. It was wearing a green bow in its hair in a shade to match Maggie's green-and-white outfit. Grant relaxed as he noticed Maggie had every prim button firmly in place. If she had been planning to seduce him as Iris had said, she would have met him at the door half-naked, wouldn't she?

"I'll just tie up my dog in the kitchen," Maggie said.

Grant smiled and remained standing by the door. When Iris had turned up at the penthouse that afternoon to tell him what Maggie planned, Grant had tried to calm her down. Maggie was all talk and no action, at least none that he couldn't handle. Besides, they were meeting friends of hers for a nice, simple, quiet dinner date that evening. What could happen?

"Come in and let's have a drink," Maggie invited, taking him by the wrist and gently tugging him into her apartment. Grant went willingly. He had been inside Maggie's neoclassic apartment before. There was nothing out of the ordinary to be alarmed about. "Have a seat, darling." She led him to the couch and left him there. "Your usual?" She moved to the bar with a slight sway of her hips.

"Yes, fine. How was your day?" he asked politely.

"Rather routine," she replied, plopping ice cubes into a glass. "How about yours?"

For one wild second Grant wondered if she was drugging his drink. But no, she would want him fully awake if she intended to have her way with him. "Why don't you make my drink a straight cola tonight?" he said, adding, "I'm taking some medicine to fight off a cold and I don't want to mix it with alcohol." He crossed his legs and congratulated himself for quick thinking.

"Here you go, dear," she said, settling gracefully beside him like a swan landing after flight. "Cheers." They clinked glasses.

Grant smiled. In another ten minutes or so they would finish their drinks. He would look at his watch, mention the time, and they would be on their way, everything under control.

"There's been a change of plans, Grant, dear," Maggie said, running her azalea-pink fingernail down the side of her glass. "Suzanne and Marty can't meet us for dinner tonight, so I thought we might have an intimate little twosome here. I get so tired of going out every night. Don't you?"

"Uh, no," he replied. "I like going out." Maybe he should have asked for some hard stuff, just enough alcohol to sooth his nerves. "This is great. I know the perfect little Italian restaurant where we can have a cozy, romantic back room to ourselves. I've been wondering when I'd get the opportunity to take you there."

"It sounds marvelous, darling," she said, moving closer and wrapping herself around his arm like a pet boa, "but I had something even cozier in mind for us tonight, here."

Grant lifted his glass to his mouth to block the kiss he saw coming his way. Oh, Lord, why couldn't he have a plane to catch? He looked at his watch. "Well, uh, actually, Maggie, I'm really kind of glad we don't have any commitments tonight."

"You are?" She started kissing his neck, tickling his ears.

Grant wanted to swat her away like a persistent fly, but he couldn't afford to offend her. "Yes, uh, I have a plane to catch tonight. Some unexpected business has come up, and I was hoping we could make an early evening of it."

"Cancel it," Maggie urged, kissing him hard on the lips.

Grant resisted, but she overbalanced him, pressing him against the back of the couch. "I can't," he mumbled against her lips. *Damn,* he thought. *What did women do in situations like this?* He couldn't slap her face and tell her she was too forward. He couldn't threaten to cry rape. Maybe he should lie and tell her he was gay. He grasped her upper arms and pushed her away from him, like a deep-sea diver grappling with an octopus. "Maggie, I'm sorry, but—" He saw the hurt look in her eyes and knew he couldn't be cruel. "Your couch—it's uncomfortable the way the back of it is hitting me."

"Oh," she said, sitting up and away from him as Grant quickly stood. "Well, we could just go straight to bed."

"No, this is fine," he said, giving her a reassuring smile. "I'm okay now." He took a seat in her bentwood rocker and finished his cola.

Her lower lip stuck out in a pout. "We'll just go down to the furniture store tomorrow, Grant, and pick out a new couch."

Grant pulled back his sleeve to check his watch. "I'll still be out of town," he said. He had only been here ten minutes. He couldn't leave yet. "Mind if I have another drink? No, don't get up." *Please stay where you are,* he prayed. "I'll get it myself. Can I freshen yours?"

He kept his back to her while he poured another cola, tensed for anything she might try next. Why hadn't he taken Iris more seriously and come prepared with a string of excuses that would have avoided this situation and let Maggie down gracefully? When he turned from the bar, Maggie was standing in front of the couch, undressing. "Maggie—" he said, his voice pleading for her to stop.

She was a beautiful woman, with creamy clear skin, pretty eyes and an appealing smile. What man could deny she wasn't sexy, especially in that lacy corset thing that pushed her breasts up so invitingly? What man wouldn't want to make love to someone who looked as gorgeous as Maggie?

"Maggie," he tried again, swallowing hard, but his voice cracked. "Don't do this." His pulse raced as she dropped her skirt to reveal the tiniest pair of panties he had ever seen outside of men's magazines. They were worn under a matching garter belt. The sight of her creamy flesh revealed in the gap above the patterned white stockings attached to the garter belt sent his blood pressure sky-high.

She bent to unhook the stockings, her breasts begging for release from the tight garment.

Grant watched her with a mixture of horror and fascination. No man could be expected to perform under such pressure, and yet he found it impossible to look away. "Maggie—" His resistance was weakening. Maybe the easiest way to get out of this situation was to just make love to her and be done with it.

The corset joined the pile of clothing scattered on the floor in front of her.

Grant's eyes traveled from her toes up her long, shapely legs to her full, luscious breasts. The garter belt was the last to go. She looked like Venus rising from the sea of clothing at her feet. "Maggie, you're magnificent," he said, taking a step toward her.

She held out her arms to him. "Come here, darling. Make love to me. I've waited so long for this moment."

Dear Lord, Grant thought. This was any man's dream come true. He was a fool not to take what was so generously being offered. But he couldn't. Aside from the pressure she had put on him, he couldn't do this to Iris. Grant didn't want to admit to Maggie that he wasn't man enough to make love to her. While she was certainly physically arousing, he wasn't emotionally aroused. And he couldn't tell her that he loved someone else, not when that woman was Iris. But he also couldn't just leave her standing here naked as if he didn't notice. He took off his jacket.

Maggie's expression eased into a smile. Her lower lip quivered and she stepped over her clothes toward him.

As she came near, Grant wrapped his jacket around her shoulders and pulled the lapels together in front, holding them tightly as if it were a straight jacket.

"Maggie," he began softly, carefully choosing his words, "it's all wrong this way."

She lifted her big, blue eyes to him, her pretty, chiseled chin quivering. "What have I done wrong, Grant? Why don't you want me?"

"It's not that I don't want you," he said. "You're absolutely beautiful. Every man wants you, including me. But you can't rush things like this. Maybe I'm too much of a traditionalist, but we really don't know each other very well."

Her eyes filled with tears. "I don't understand, Grant."

He put his arms around her, hugging tightly with the barrier of his jacket between them. "It's just not time yet. A man likes to be the one to make these decisions, to take the initiative."

Her cheek was against his chest, and he could tell she was crying now.

How could he make this right? "Maggie," he tried again. "You deserve better than a wham-bam affair. And, uh, I have this plane to catch, you see." He knew it sounded weak, but it was the best he could do. "I don't want to just run off and leave you like that when you deserve to be loved properly."

She looked up at him and gave him the shadow of a smile. "I wouldn't mind, truly I wouldn't."

"But *I* would," he said, putting his hand under her chin and kissing her teary eyes. "The first time should be special, with hours and hours devoted just to you." He held her away from him and smiled. "Tonight just isn't the night. I really should be going, in case the traffic is bad on the way to the airport."

She swiped at her eyes and sniffed. "Let me get dressed and I'll go with you," Maggie said. "It's Friday and I don't have anything planned this weekend. And I've always wanted to watch you in action."

"No," Grant said hastily, his mind racing, "not this time. I'm going to be tied up in boring meetings the whole trip." Was he ever going to get out of here? And if so, what excuse would he use next time?

"Oh, Grant, please?" she said, her voice pleading, her lips pouting, her body tempting.

"Next time," he insisted, which sounded like a promise to her but was a worry to him. "I'd better get going," he said, backing toward the door. "You're such a good woman to be so understanding."

Maggie went with him to the door, still clinging to him. As he opened it, she said, "Grant?"

"Yes, what?"

"Don't forget your coat." She pulled it off and handed it to him, which left her wearing nothing but a small grin.

Grant collapsed against the wall of the elevator the minute the doors closed in front of him. His hand shook as he randomly punched a button on the panel, realized the car was going up instead of down, and quickly corrected his error. No one would believe he had just walked away from making love to the woman who had written the book on romance. He wasn't sure he believed it himself.

IRIS HAD BEEN going crazy imagining Grant with Maggie. When she had gone by the penthouse that afternoon, he had told her she was worrying for nothing, and he had tried to reassure her that he had no personal interest in Maggie. But Iris knew better than to underestimate the power of a woman, particularly when that woman was Maggie Maxwell. It wasn't that she didn't trust her boss, she just knew how irresistible she could be. And Maggie was the only one who didn't realize the perfect man they had found for her was all make-believe.

She had tried to calm down by taking a long bath and reading a book. But she just couldn't concentrate. She flipped on the TV. *Love Boat* was on one channel. An old movie about a love triangle was on another. Championship wrestling only started her thinking again.

She went downstairs to the kitchen to look for an elaborate recipe to prepare in order to keep busy, but quickly lost interest when one of the ingredients called for whipped cream—which reminded her of a letter the magazine had received from a reader who had dressed up in the creamy substance to surprise her husband. Was Maggie that very moment fanning herself with the door of the refrigerator in order not to melt before Grant arrived?

Iris was so tortured by her exaggerated thoughts that she didn't hear the doorbell the first time it rang. It was early, but she wasn't expecting anyone.

"Oh, Grant!" she exclaimed, throwing her arms around his neck and hugging him so tightly he was nearly thrown off balance. His cheek felt smooth against hers. "You're here! Didn't you see Maggie?"

Grant held her, rubbing his cheek against her hair, knowing he had made the right decision in walking away from Maggie. Now that he was with Iris, he couldn't imagine ever thinking any other way. "Yes, I saw her. That's why I'm here now."

Iris embraced his cheeks with her hands, studying his face. "What happened?"

"Nothing happened."

She backed away from him so that he could come inside and shut the door. "Then I was wrong. I guess I owe you an apology, and Maggie, too, for underestimating her."

"Mind if I have a drink?" he asked as he walked into the middle of the living room and stood with his back to the fireplace. "Something strong and straight."

"Sure," Iris said, giving him a worried glance before she left him to fix drinks. When she returned, she handed one to him and sat on the edge of the couch, waiting. "What about your dinner date with the other couple?"

"Canceled," he said, downing half the drink, "if there was such a date. You were right. Maggie did have, uh, other plans."

Iris used both hands to bring her drink to her lips. *I don't want to hear this,* she told herself. *I have to hear it!*

With her big, emerald eyes observing every breath he took, Iris looked like a little girl about to swallow medicine someone had said would be good for her. He finished his drink and repeated, "Nothing happened."

Her eyes were wide, her expression anxious. "She didn't try to make a pass at you?"

"I'd say taking all of her clothes off would constitute making a pass."

"Maggie did that?" She'd read in the magazine about women who did such things, but she had never thought of Maggie as one of them. "Everything?"

He nodded.

Iris pressed her glass against her inflamed cheeks. It was worse than she had imagined. Setting her drink on the coffee table, she sat very quietly with her hands in her lap. It was almost like listening to a lover saying he had just slept with his wife.

"I wouldn't have been in that situation except for you," Grant said angrily.

"But I tried to warn you," she said, getting annoyed. She felt betrayed, yet she couldn't blame him for being upset. *Iris* was the other woman in this situation. Regardless of her feelings for Grant, she had no claim on him. He had made no promises to her.

"I wasn't referring just to what happened tonight."

"You're getting paid," she snapped. "No one had to beg to get you to take the money."

"My understanding was that I was paid to be Maggie's escort, not her prostitute. I do draw the line at certain roles. And anyway, I couldn't go to bed with her."

"Why not?"

Grant raised his hands, then slapped his thighs. "I don't believe this. Did you want me to?"

Iris ran her hand through his hair, rumpling it. "Well, no. Of course not! But how could you not? She's so beautiful, and if she took off all her clothes, I mean—"

"I didn't take her to bed," Grant said, enunciating clearly and slowly, "because *you're* the only one I want to make love to."

As his words sank in, Iris sat absolutely still. Gradually, all of the tensions of the evening washed over her, and she began to cry.

"Don't cry," Grant said, gathering her into his arms. It unmanned him. This was the second woman to cry on his shoulder this evening. "It's supposed to make you happy, not sad."

"I'm just so relieved." She hiccuped, taking deep breaths and locking his waist in a vicelike grip. She looked up at him. "I still can't believe you're here."

"Me, either," he said, resting his forehead against hers, thinking of the nightmare he had been through that evening.

"But how?" she said, drawing away. "What did you do to stop her, I mean, how did you—"

"I told her I had a plane to catch."

Iris looked incredulously at him, then started laughing. "You didn't."

He nodded. "It was all I could think of."

"And she believed you?"

He grinned and lifted his shoulders. "Hey, I'm here, aren't I?" He wasn't about to tell her what had gone through his mind in the process of extricating himself from Maggie's apartment. Now that he was with Iris, he knew Maggie could never have satisfied him when Iris was the one he loved.

"Yes," she said with a sigh, tightening her hold around his waist, "and I'm so glad you are here. If you only knew what I was thinking...."

He rubbed her back and felt the absence of a bra. "Yeah?" He breathed against her neck as he took her earlobe between his lips. "Tell me what you were thinking." He slipped his hand beneath her sweatshirt and moved his fingers up the fine bones of her spine.

The husky sound of his voice aroused her, while his gently caressing hands tantalized. She wanted to be free of the shirt, have the feel of his hands all over her, bringing her body to life. "What would you do," she asked, her lips tickling as they barely brushed the sensitive skin behind his ears, "if *I* took off all of my clothes in front of you?"

Grant moved his hands from her back to her rib cage and gently inched upward to her breasts. Her skin felt soft and smooth and made him impatient to be naked with her, yet the sensation was one he didn't want to rush for the anticipation was heavenly. "I assure you," he murmured, brushing her taut nipples with his thumbs, "I wouldn't have a plane to catch."

Her hand dropped below his belt and she asked, "Does this mean you're going to stay tonight?"

"If you want me."

"Oh, I definitely want you," Iris said, kissing him as she unbuttoned his shirt, her hands impatient to feel his naked chest. "I've wanted you from the first night we met." She pushed his shirt open and ran her hand over the springy dark hairs on his chest. She laid her palm against his heart, which was beating rapidly, and kissed his left breast. Then she pulled her sweatshirt over her head.

Grant uttered an audible sigh and pulled her into his arms. This was where he wanted to be, the woman he wanted to love. Iris's sensuous touch made him feel like soaring in an atmosphere so rarified he wanted to draw more from her. Holding her so intimately after weeks of imagining this moment was like receiving a mountain of gifts. He wanted to open them all at once, yet wanted to savor each sensation, one at a time, to make the moment last forever.

He shrugged out of his jacket and shirt as Iris stood to remove her sweatpants. All that was left were her lacy pink briefs by the time he got his socks and shoes off and stood to unzip his pants.

"Let me do it," Iris said, completing the task of undressing him. She stood, nervously unfastening his slacks, wanting so much to please him and express to him physically how much he had come to mean to her emotionally. As he stepped out of his pants, she kissed his shoulder and whispered, "I want it to be special, Grant. Tell me what you like."

The fact that she cared about his pleasure heightened his arousal. This was what separated the mere sex act from love. "You're so special," he said. "That's all I need."

Chapter Nine

As the first veiled rays of sunlight filtered through the bedroom window, Iris lay watching Grant sleeping beside her. His cheek was dark with the heavy growth of his beard. Curls of hair were ruffled by the sheets wrapped up to his neck. Long, dark lashes fanned his cheeks. Her heart swelled with the memory of the night they had spent together, and she reached out to touch him, reassuring herself that it hadn't been a dream.

He stirred, nuzzling against her hand and opened his eyes. When he saw her, he smiled lazily and murmured, "I love you." Then, gathering her close, he settled back into sleep.

Iris lay in his arms, feeling the rise and fall of his chest, the warmth of his body from the soft breath of his lips to the hard bones of his legs. Even in sleep they fit well together. Their bodies were like two pieces of a puzzle that had been missing from the game and had suddenly found each other. Her back and buttocks cupped perfectly within the crescent formed by his chest, stomach and thighs. His arms arched over her naturally, cuddling her, protecting her. Iris had forgotten how deep and delicious sleep could be pressed against the warmth of a man.

She must have fallen back to sleep, for when she awoke, the room was bright with sunshine. Grant had his head propped on his arm as he watched her. He kissed her and smoothed his hand from her shoulder along her arm, twining his fingers with her own. "I can't believe I'm here," he said. "I feel so happy." He pulled her into his arms, holding her tightly, loving the feel of her as if she were an extension of himself.

"I know," she said, resting her head against his shoulder, letting his hair slip through her fingers. "I kept waking up during the night, amazed that you were here, too. It feels so good." She stared up at the ceiling where shadows from the tree in the patio danced from the breeze. "It's like waking up and finding out you're a whole new person."

"In my case, I am," Grant said as he rubbed the tip of his nose against hers. "The only time I can be myself is when we're alone together." His hands slid beneath her arms, gently stroking the sides of her breasts. Quietly he began telling her how special she was to him.

The soft murmur of his voice heightened the desire within her. She tried to run her hands over his chest to return the warm, glowing pleasure building inside, but he whispered for her to stop. Helplessly she surrendered to his soothing voice and caressing touch. His hands left a trail of quivering desire, tantalizing and promising as he carried her to the brink of fulfillment and then retreated to start the process building higher.

"Just relax and lie still. Let me arouse you."

Iris felt helpless to resist, breathless with anticipation. He knew her so well. From the moment they first embraced, the excitement of discovery had quickly fused into an almost instinctive awareness of each other heightened by the awakening of passion. They had danced together in a wordless craving throughout the night, clinging together in this newfound haven, learning, understanding, bonding.

"I love snuggling with you," he said as he kissed her lips and stroked her back. "I don't think I'll ever get enough of you." His gently ministering hands caused the desire within her to rise until he felt it, too, and joined her in its engulfing caress.

The words he murmured no longer made much sense to him as Grant became ensnared in the trap of passion he had carefully set for Iris. It was as if he had no control over his body. Release rippled through him like bubbles in champagne as the warmth diffused within him. He held Iris tightly, wanting to carry the peace of this moment with him forever.

Her hair lay on the pillow beside him like a soft veil. He took a handful, then opened his palm wide to look at it spread between his fingers. For a moment he regretted spending the night with her, revealing feelings he had kept hidden until now. It should have been Maggie he slept with instead of Iris. Because with Maggie he could walk away with no regrets.

Making love with Iris changed everything. He was no longer able to deny the physical longing that had been building toward this moment. But now in the bright light of morning, he thought he had moved too quickly. He folded her hair tightly in his fist, wanting to hold her to him just this way forever. But how? His future was as clear as the dregs of tea leaves in a fortune-teller's cup. What could he possibly offer Iris?

"What's the matter?" she asked, making a funny face to break up his stony expression.

"Nothing," he replied, stuffing his emotions out of sight. Acting had made him adept at disguising his true feelings. There was nothing he could do at the moment, perhaps nothing he could change until the business with Maggie was finished. He didn't want to expose his dark thoughts about the future to spoil the brightness he saw shining in her eyes. He turned over and began fiddling with her radio until he found a favorite station that played a mixture of country music and top-forty tunes.

Reaching across to the nightstand, Iris put her glasses on. She sat up in bed, tucking the sheets beneath her arms. She sensed his troubled spirit. Like Grant, she chose to pretend there were no obstacles standing between this morning and the day they would be able to be together openly. *What then?* she asked herself. How would he fit into her world?

The doorbell rang and Grant sat up, reaching for his watch, which he had removed last night. "Who could that be?"

The alarm clock said ten. "Probably just the postman," Iris said, tossing back the covers. "Sometimes he has parcels too big to fit through the slot of the door." She pulled a cotton dress off the rack in the closet and fumbling with its buttons, she mumbled, "I'll be right back. Don't go away."

"I can't," he said, folding his arms across his chest as he watched her dress. "You have all my clothes."

Iris grinned at Grant then raced downstairs. "Coming!" she called.

She opened the door to find Maggie standing on the stoop. Iris blinked as if she found the sun suddenly too bright. A man and his dog were passing on the sidewalk behind Maggie. A car horn beeped on Third Avenue. Maggie just stood there, not saying a word.

Iris felt her face flame as she thought of Grant, naked, in her bed upstairs. Her stomach knotted. She clutched the door for support and vowed she would never let herself fall in love with a married man if she ever got out of this triangle. "Maggie," she said numbly, assuming out of guilt that Maggie knew Grant had been with her, "how did you—"

Maggie's carefully made-up face suddenly cracked. She put her hand in front of her ski-tip nose and her shoulders shook as a sob escaped her.

Iris didn't know whether to reach out and comfort her or draw back ready for the onslaught of Maggie's temper. "It's all my fault," she started to say when Maggie's sobbing voice interrupted her.

"Iris, I'm so sorry," Maggie wailed.

Iris looked curiously at Maggie, whom she hadn't seen so upset since the day she learned Bradley Winchester was seeing someone else. "What are you sorry about? I'm the one—"

"I shouldn't be disturbing you. But I didn't know who else to talk to." She opened her purse to search for a handkerchief. "I—can I come inside? I must look like a mess blubbering on your doorstep like this."

"Of course, come in," she said, remembering her manners. If they were going to have a showdown it might as well be without benefit of her neighbors for audience. She closed the door with a click and leaned back against it, braced for Maggie's anger.

Maggie found her handkerchief and dried her eyes. She swallowed and tried to compose herself. "It's Grant," she said.

"I know," Iris said guiltily. She slumped against the door, feeling a strange sense of relief. Maybe it was better this way, letting it all come out before Maggie and

Grant had to face Sheila Croft on the *American Scene* interview.

Maggie teared up again. "Iris, I don't know what's wrong with me." She dabbed at her eyes and tried to stop sobbing.

"Wrong with *you*?" Iris said blankly.

"Yes, me." She twisted her handkerchief as she paced up and down the hallway, heels clicking against the marble floor. "Last night I pulled out all the stops and Grant treated me like week-old Thanksgiving turkey." Gesturing with the handkerchief made her look as if she were surrendering with a lace flag. "I just don't understand," she wailed. "This never happened with Bradley." As Maggie spun around to face Iris, her heel left a black smudge on the polished floor. "Something must be wrong with me. First Bradley leaves me for a woman barely out of college. Then Grant last night—" She couldn't go on. Maggie's chin tilted anxiously in Iris's direction. "Do you think Grant's gay?"

Iris looked beyond Maggie to the stairs, then down at her bare feet. In dressing to answer the door, she had missed a button and fastened her dress crookedly. Her naked body showed through the gap in the dress. She covered the button as if it were an admission of guilt. "I don't think Grant's that way."

"Then it must be me," Maggie said. Her face wrinkled up and the sobs burst out of her again. "Sheila Croft is right. I don't know how to keep a man. I don't even know how to turn one on."

Iris went to Maggie and put her arms around her shoulders. "Maggie, that's not true," she comforted her boss. "Think of all the women who have had lovely romances because you've encouraged them and motivated them and helped them build their confidence about love. You're an inspiration to women everywhere."

"Then why won't it happen for me? The whole damn city of New York can fall in love and I can't," she said angrily.

"Do you really want to fall in love?" Iris asked gently.

Maggie's blond head wagged against Iris's damp shoulder. "Of course. Doesn't every woman?"

Iris took a deep breath, like a swimmer about to dive into chilly waters. "You've gotten so much pleasure out of your work, I thought perhaps you didn't really need a man in your life, except as an occasional escort."

Maggie blotted her handkerchief at Iris's dress, which she realized had gotten soggy from her tears. "I don't need a man to run around and open doors for me, but that doesn't mean I don't want someone to love me." Her lips fused together as if she had bitten into a bitter tart.

Running her fingers through her hair, Iris wondered how to say what she knew Maggie needed to hear. "Come into the living room," she invited, "and let's sit down." The minute she turned, she realized that was a mistake. Grant's clothes and hers were strewn all over the room.

She leaped into action, hastily scooping everything into her arms, hiding Grant's jacket and underwear beneath her own sweats. "The maid doesn't come until Monday," she said as an excuse, shoving everything behind one of the large potted plants. The color in her cheeks was high as she faced Maggie, hoping her boss was too distraught to realize what she had just witnessed.

Maggie sank to the edge of the couch near the fireplace, a distant look on her face.

Iris sat across from her, giving her pulse a chance to return somewhat to normal. "Maggie—" Her voice cracked as she noticed Grant's loafers shoved under the glass table near the toe of Maggie's red shoes. As Maggie's wet, blue eyes lifted to hers, Iris forced herself to go on, hoping she could distract Maggie's attention away from the floor. "You give the impression that because you don't need a man financially, you don't want one around at all. Did you ever think that maybe even the most secure men, like Bradley Winchester, for instance, might like to feel they're needed?"

Maggie crossed her silk-stockinged legs and leaned back on the couch. She placed her fingernail near her lips in thought. "I guess I haven't let Grant think I need him."

Iris tried again. "Men like *Bradley Winchester* don't like being turned down for a date at the last minute any more than we women like it." She spoke rapidly, with desperation in her voice, hoping she could convince Maggie *she* had been the one in the wrong with Winchester. She bit her lower lip and wished anyone other than she was having this conversation with Maggie Maxwell. "Could you have, perhaps, taken him a bit too much for granted?"

"I haven't broken a single date with Grant," Maggie argued.

"I meant with Bradley," Iris stressed. She prayed Grant would stay put upstairs, without making things worse by a sudden, stark-naked appearance. She hoped Maggie wasn't paying attention to the soft sounds of the country music playing on the radio upstairs. Country didn't fit in with Iris's classical tastes.

Maggie looked around the room without really seeing anything and reluctantly shrugged her shoulders as if to say, "Maybe." Iris knew it was the closest Maggie would come to admitting her own failure in that particular love affair.

Iris changed positions to sit on the couch next to Maggie, so that her boss would have less occasion to notice Grant's shoes. She took Maggie's hands and said sincerely, "Maybe Grant isn't the right man for you."

"He seems so perfect, Iris. He's debonair, worldly, can talk at length on any subject." She frowned, remembering a few of their conversations. "In fact, sometimes he talks too much. It's like he's been crammed full of boring facts and he has to tell me every one of them. I guess I just got used to Bradley's quiet ways. We could sometimes read each other's minds." She sighed. "I really do miss Bradley. But it's too late for us."

Iris cleared her throat, resisting the urge to defend Grant. "Everyone said Mitch was the perfect man for me, my uncle, in particular. But they were only looking at him from the surface. Mitch was an entirely different man in public than he was when he was alone with me." She squeezed Maggie's hands. "Don't accidentally get your heart broken with Grant trying to prove something to Sheila Croft."

"I can't let her know she's right," Maggie said. "Just last week one of the tabloid gossip papers quoted her as saying I'm now recruiting men from the cradle because any man older than Grant would know better than to go out with me. No, no, don't pity me," she added, as Iris sighed at Croft's callous tactics. "Grant's exactly the kind of man I asked you to find for me. And I could love Grant if I could get Bradley out of my system. But it isn't easy when he and that orange-haired teenager keep turning up at all the society events Bradley used to take *me* to. She's just using him for her career."

Hope swelled within Iris. If only she could make Maggie see that she was making the same mistake with Grant. "Maggie, maybe you and Grant are simply destined to be friends and nothing more."

"But he looks so good on my arm. Even Edward is delighted with him. He says all the publicity we've been generating will be good for business, like the old days."

Iris frowned. Her uncle was perpetuating the myth of Maggie's romance, pressuring the staff to come up with a host of ideas for the perfect romantic date, hiring a photographer to follow Maggie and Grant as each idea was executed, then blocking out space to feature the results in the magazine. Grant had given them enough material for several future issues, which kept Iris's uncle happy. Never mind who was hurt in the process.

"Maybe the timing was wrong," Maggie said with a sigh. "Perhaps Grant's feeling the pressure of this upcoming interview with Croft more than I realize."

Iris wanted to shake Maggie, get her head down out of the clouds and get her back where she belonged—safely behind her desk at *New Age Woman*. "Maggie, don't you see? Mitch was all wrong for me because I let what other people thought make my decisions for me instead of listening to my heart." She looked up at the ceiling. Grant would be lying in bed somewhere overhead. If only she could openly admit that *she* loved Maggie's "perfect" man and that he loved her, too. "When I married Mitch, I was hurting so much from my parents' death I didn't think about anything. I probably would make the same wrong choices today given the same set of circumstances. But now I know I should have trusted my instincts, which told me Mitch wasn't right for me."

"What has that got to do with Grant being right or wrong for me?" Maggie asked.

"Maggie, I think you still love Bradley." She looked down at their hands, then up again. "No matter what he seems like on the surface, Grant Peters is not the same man. Maybe you want Bradley so much you wish he was."

When Maggie looked at Iris, Iris knew her message had found its mark. Whether Maggie did anything about it was beyond Iris's control. But at least she had looked down from the clouds long enough to see the earth. "Maybe," Maggie conceded in a small voice. Her expression closed up as she opened her purse and removed her compact, inspecting her swollen eyes in the mirror. She wiped the mascara stains with her handkerchief and reapplied eye shadow and blusher. "One thing for sure, Bradley never needed any coaxing when it came to lovemaking. That part of our relationship was always great."

Iris sat quietly beside her, not knowing what else to say.

Snapping her purse shut, Maggie rose in a fluid movement. "You've been a dear to listen to me, Iris. You've always been such a loyal friend."

Would Maggie still feel that way if she knew Grant was upstairs in her bed? Iris wished she could tell Maggie the truth about him, but that would hurt her more. Why had she let her uncle talk her into this? Why had she let herself fall in love with Grant?

"I'd better be going." Maggie said.

Iris wished she could ask Maggie to stay. She hadn't even offered the barest amenity of a drink. She walked to the hall with her. "It'll be okay," she told Maggie, while she wished she could believe that herself.

After Maggie left, Iris felt like a bowl of mush. Moments earlier she had been reveling in the lush awakening of love between her and Grant. But that had been rudely interrupted by her unexpected visitor. Iris couldn't stand betraying Maggie any longer, but she also couldn't accept the thought of losing Grant just as their love was blossoming. Grant had held her and told her he wasn't going anywhere. But no amount of soothing could erase the doubts gnawing at her heart.

It was a warm and breezy summer day, too pretty for them to be cooped up indoors. Grant had convinced Iris they could be together without running into acquaintances or friends by seeing Manhattan as the tourists do, taking a Circle Line boat ride.

"Are you just going to sit there, not saying anything?" Iris asked Grant. The boat had just passed the Convention Center and was coming up on the classic view of Lower Manhattan, but Iris wasn't paying attention.

"You're saying enough for both of us," Grant said, weary of spending his precious time with Iris talking about Maggie, which was all they had done since the woman had left Iris's house that morning. "Isn't the Statue of Liberty inspiring? You know, I've always wanted to do this."

"Grant," she pleaded, physically turning his head away from the view at the railing, "will you listen to me?"

"Okay, I agree," he said, kissing the palm of her hand and removing her hands from his face so he could look at the New York skyline in the opposite direction. "I'm more than ready to see this end myself. But what are we going to do?" He put his arm around Iris's shoulder and pulled her to his side, needing the feeling of her close to him to remind himself he was giving up the fancy clothes and penthouse apartment for her. He had known all along it was only temporary, but he had gotten used to the flashy life-style.

"I don't know," Iris said, searching his eyes for an answer. His hair was blowing in the breeze.

"After the stunt she pulled last night, I'm afraid to be alone with Maggie again. How do you say no politely without crushing the woman's ego?"

Iris pulled away from Grant, too restless to enjoy the activity in the harbor. The air smelled of fish and diesel fuel. Cold flecks of spray kept stinging her face. Her face was damp, as if from tears. "I'm going to talk to Uncle Edward and tell him just to call the whole thing off."

"Fine with me," Grant said, "but he's enjoying this romance more than Maggie is." Grant wondered if Iris knew how active South had been lately, making certain they got the most prominent table in fine restaurants, keeping tabs on Sheila Croft with a private investigator, coaching Grant on how to pose when the photographers caught them together. Grant didn't mind a little direction, but he resented dictatorial orders. Lately South had become downright obsessive, demanding daily reports from Grant on where they went, who saw them and what was said. South didn't want Grant to speak to reporters, believing that a strong, silent, mysteriousness would add more machismo to his image. Grant didn't like anyone stealing his lines, particularly when it was Maggie whose chatter with reporters very often put him on the spot. But South loved it. "I'm not so sure he's going to let me out of my contract too easily."

"Contracts were made to be broken," Iris quipped. "But maybe we'd both better talk to him." She worked it out in her head. They would have a meeting with him on Monday and the three of them would figure out how to release Grant from this false romance without hurting Maggie.

Grant kept staring straight ahead, intent on some flotsam off the port side of the boat.

"Grant?" The twitch of his eyebrows was the only sign that he had heard her. "When Maggie took off her clothes last night—" Iris pushed her hair off her face to keep the wind from whipping it into her eyes "—what did you do?"

"I told you. I didn't do anything."

"But—I mean, well—" Iris stammered as unwanted images flashed through her mind. She let go of her hair, letting it fly in her face, and gripped the railing with both hands. She had believed him last night, and she had no reason to disbelieve him now, especially after Maggie had been so upset over the failure of her seduction plan. She faced him now, jealousy tempered with curiosity. "Does this happen often to men?"

"Not to me," Grant assured her, bending down so that he could rest his elbows on the railing and squint into the distant haze at the Verrazano-Narrows Bridge. "You know, it's funny, but men fantasize about what happened to me last night. I've had the same fantasy lots of times myself. But in a dream, it's just you. The woman isn't real. You can't hurt her feelings or make her cry. I was praying a 747 would collide with the building to get me out of there."

Iris stared at him intently, looking for the slightest hint of a lie in his eyes.

"I admit I considered making love to her as the gentlemanly thing to do, but that would have just made a bad situation worse. When you kiss a woman in a movie, she knows it's because it's in the script, not because you really love her. What I, *we*, are doing to Maggie is despicable, because she thinks the lines I'm speaking in public are real."

The truth of Grant's words suddenly struck Iris. She visualized a naked Maggie offering herself to Grant and then being rejected. Maggie must have felt total humiliation, yet she was willing to try again. Iris would have crawled under a rock for months if the same thing had happened to her. She suddenly felt sorry for her boss and sick to her stomach. "You've always been such a loyal friend," Maggie had said that morning.

"Oh, Grant, what am I doing in the middle of all of this? How could we have forgotten that Maggie is a woman with real feelings? We created a perfect man, except that he can't, won't, love her back. How cruel and unthinking."

Grant stepped forward and enveloped her with his massive arms. Iris realized that she had helped create a situation that had gotten out of hand.

"Look," Grant suggested, "let's get out of town and forget about Maggie for the rest of the weekend. We could take the train and be in Connecticut in no time. I have a friend who has a really great French restaurant and we could stay in one of those bed-and-breakfast inns."

Iris lifted her face to Grant and smiled. "That sounds romantic."

"Trust me, it will be," he said, giving her a conspiratorial look that warmed her memories of their previous evening together.

When they returned to Iris's home, she went upstairs to pack while Grant phoned for train schedules. She had barely filled her cosmetics bag when Grant said, "The next train leaves in forty-five minutes. I'm going down to the corner to get a taxi."

"But I haven't packed yet," Iris said, glancing frantically at her closet.

"Can't you wear that again tomorrow?" he asked, admiring her yellow-and-white pullover and designer jeans. "If we hurry, we can pretend we're eloping."

Iris liked the sound of that coupled with Grant's spontaneity. She pulled a sweater out of the closet and tied the arms over her shoulders. "Ready when you are," she said, feeling like a child who had suddenly been given a ticket for an amusement park ride.

Hand in hand they ran down the sidewalk to the corner and cavorted in the street until a taxi stopped to pick them up. By the time Grant bought the tickets and they found the correct track number, they had ten minutes to spare before the train left the station.

"I love trains," Iris said as they sat by the window watching the congestion of the city recede as they entered the countryside of Connecticut. "I used to ride them when I went home from boarding school." She rested her head against the back of the seat. "There's something very comforting and rhythmic about the clackity clack of the wheels. And people tend to talk more to you on trains when they rarely do on airplanes or buses."

"I'd much rather kiss than talk." When he had her attention, Grant smiled and slipped his hand around the back of her neck so that he could gently nudge her closer.

Resting her head against his shoulder, Iris looked lazily out of the window and imagined spending another night in bed with Grant. She wouldn't even mind if they skipped dinner altogether.

The innkeeper, a friendly giant of a man who faintly reminded Iris of a butler her family had once employed, didn't seem particularly surprised at the absence of luggage. He handed them a skeleton key with a fuzzy fuchsia ball attached and gave them directions to their third-story room. "The bath's a little crowded up under the slope of the roof in that room, but it's the only one left with a private facility."

Grant thanked him and led the way upstairs, wishing he had thought of this sooner so that he could have gotten the best room in the inn for Iris. He opened the door with a bit of trepidation until Iris's response reassured him.

"Oh, Grant. It's lovely," she said, clasping her hands together at the sight of the brass canopied double bed. There was an antique dresser and sideboard with marble tops and a cozy chintz-covered love seat.

Grant thought it looked a bit too frilly, but if Iris was happy, he could live with ruffles and bows for one night. He put his arms around her and backed her toward the bed. "Good thing we didn't bring suitcases," he said as the back of her legs encountered the mattress. "There's not much room for luggage."

"Grant," she said as she fell back on the bed, her weight pulling him with her, "you're overdressed as it is."

THE RESTAURANT that belonged to Grant's friend had been converted from an old two-story house where the front two rooms served as the dining area. There couldn't have been more than twenty tables in all.

Iris followed Grant to a square table covered with a pink linen tablecloth in the corner of the front room. They had a brief exchange over who would sit where before Iris decided she wanted to sit in the back where she had a view of the cozy room. "This is such a good idea, Grant."

He looked around the room where one other couple was seated. "I was hoping you'd like it. It's one of my favorite places." He hadn't shaved that morning, and his cheeks were dark with the heavy growth of his beard. His hair was ruffled and carefree in its natural, all-American style, the way Iris liked it. He picked up the menu the waiter had left.

"Grant!"

Grant turned and stood as the chef came toward him with open arms.

"Josef told me he thought it was you out here." He gave Grant a healthy hug and slap on the back. "How have you been?" he asked, speaking with a thick, guttural accent.

"Couldn't be better," Grant answered, and stepped aside to introduce Iris. "This is Oscar Esterhazy, Iris, an old friend of mine."

"Not that old," Oscar replied with a hearty laugh. "But he'd like to make you think that. She's pretty, Grant." The top of his balding head came just up to Grant's shoulder. His face was dark, as if he had spent years working outdoors. His features were thick but expressive. The bushy thicket of dark eyebrows twitched when he talked, carrying on a conversation of their own.

"Oscar and I met at a tasting fair at one of the big hotels not long after I started working for Eve and Bob. I learned a lot of tricks from him."

"And not all of them about food," Oscar said, laughing at his own joke. "This man can cook circles around me. We were in a little competition, and all the judges voted Grant the winner." He kissed his fingers to his lips. "Remember that caviar-and-mushroom soufflé? Superb." He put his hands on his hips and said, "The offer still stands, Grant, if you ever want to leave your sister's place I'll hire you in a minute."

Iris tried to place the accent. French? Dutch? She had never been a linguist.

"Thanks, Oscar," Grant said, shifting uncomfortably as he was reminded of his lowly position. "I'll keep that in mind."

Oscar looked at Iris as if she would give him more details about the two of them. "How did you meet this guy?"

"It's a long story," Iris said, picking up the menu as if to say, "please don't ask."

"Someday," Grant promised his friend, "you can get me drunk and I'll tell you all about it."

"It was that way between you?" he said, hovering closer, waiting to hear more. When neither one answered, he gave up. "This is a special occasion, having you here, Grant." He plucked the menu from Iris's hands and offered, "Why don't I prepare a special meal, a sampling of small portions, so you can see what I've been up to lately? It will be my treat. In return, you can give me some of your trade secrets."

Grant laughed, "Be glad to, Oscar, but you're getting the short end of this deal."

"Oh, I don't think so," Oscar said pleasantly, patting his friend on the back like a favorite son-in-law as Grant took his seat across from Iris. "Let me tell your waiter, Josef, what to bring you."

The minute he was out of sight, Iris leaned across the table and whispered, "Grant, do you think he's read any of those gossip pages about you lately?"

"Oscar is Hungarian. The only English he reads is recipes." Grant exaggerated, but he hoped it would calm Iris's fears. "That's why I wanted to take you here, because he's my friend. And if he has been reading those papers, he wouldn't say anything."

As the waiter brought the aperitif of the house made with Scotch and fruit, Iris spread her napkin across her lap and hoped Grant was right. When the appetizer of *fruits de mer* arrived, Iris started to relax, tasting the sampling of oyster, shrimp, halibut, sardine and mussel, each morsel served with a unique, flavorful sauce.

Oscar came out of the kitchen to ask for their opinion and Iris said, "I'm in love." Oscar beamed and returned to prepare the next course, a quail egg with caviar served in a tiny capped dish set on a doily decorating a saucer. The saucer rested on an artfully folded napkin beneath which another saucer sat on top of the main plate.

"He's good, isn't he?" Grant said when Iris commented on the elaborate presentation of each course.

"This restaurant should be five-star," Iris raved. "It would be jammed every night if some of my friends knew about this place." The portions remained small, enough to tempt the appetite and leave Iris eager for the next offering.

A claret soup was set in front of her, served on a plate graced by a rose. The bowl of a silver spoon held a rich liver pâté with chicory. Oscar appeared to ask for their opinion. Grant spoke knowledgeably about each dish, identifying subtle flavors and spices that had gone into the preparation. Iris was impressed by his expertise.

Josef decanted a second bottle of wine. When Iris saw the half partridge served with grape leaves, toast and potato chips cut like waffles, she said, "If I hadn't woken up with you this morning, I would think you were trying to seduce me with this meal." Grant smiled to know he had pleased her and she added, "And it could still work for later on tonight." His grin widened as he topped off her wineglass.

When they turned down the offer of cheese, Oscar reappeared to ask what they preferred and what they didn't like. "The freshness of the food as well as how it is prepared makes all the difference," he told Iris. "Nothing comes out of a refrigerator. If it isn't used by the end of the night, it's thrown away."

When Oscar told her dessert was still to be served, she protested, but found herself unable to resist three frozen soufflés flavored in chocolate, strawberry and Grand Marnier.

As they left the restaurant and walked back to the inn, Iris said, "You have such a talent for knowing good food, where to find it and how to prepare it. Oscar seems very impressed by you. If he can create such a gastronomic feast, imagine what you can do." He had looked as proud as if he had prepared each thing himself. Iris had no doubt he could have done so with equal expertise.

"Oscar is a friend," Grant said. "He's being kind."

"Have you ever thought of owning your own restaurant one day?"

"I don't have the money," he said.

"No, but I do," Iris returned. She halted him in the middle of the sidewalk and lifted her face for a kiss. Suddenly she longed for the feel of their bodies together. She wanted him badly enough to fight for him, even if that meant spoiling her uncle's game. She only hoped they could find a way to spare Maggie's feelings. "Oscar is a genius. But *you* are the star chef of my life, Mr. Peters. Shall we go back to the inn and create something delicious in bed?"

Chapter Ten

Knowing that Maggie would be at the photographer's studio on Monday morning to select the model for the next month's cover, Iris and Grant arranged a meeting with her uncle. Facing Edward had always been unnerving for Iris, like a summons to the headmistress's office in prep school. She reminded herself that the last time she had confronted him something good had come out of it. He had given her a job at the magazine.

"What do you mean we should stop this role we created for Grant?" he demanded, his dark eyes flashing. "We've got such a good thing going here. This could ruin everything for Maggie."

"That's why we came to you," Iris said, pleading with her uncle. "Maggie's already been hurt by what we've done. We have to put a stop to it."

South threw up his hands. "How has Maggie been hurt? She's constantly in the news. This romance has given *New Age Woman* a badly needed shot in the arm, just like the old days when we were so controversial going against Croft. Back then, even bad publicity was good for us. Maggie loves all the attention, and frankly, so do I."

As Iris started to protest, Grant interrupted her. "Mr. South, I don't think you understand what's involved. When you created the perfect man for Maggie, you overlooked one thing."

"The entire staff pulled together to create the perfect romance." South began pinching the ends of his mustache in thoughtful agitation. "What could we possibly have missed?"

"I can't love Maggie back."

South's worried expression eased into a smile. He shrugged as if what Grant had said was inconsequential. "All you have to do is give the *illusion* of—"

"No," Grant said firmly, interrupting South. "We're toying with Maggie's emotions. If this was a play and she knew what her role was supposed to be, it would be easy. But I can't pretend something I don't feel for Maggie when it's Iris I love."

"What?" South groaned and fixed Iris with an angry stare. It reminded her of the way he had looked when she told him she and Mitch were getting a divorce. Grant squeezed Iris's hand, reminding her they were in this together. "You signed a contract," South reminded.

Continuing to hold her hand, Grant looked at Iris. She had warned him that her uncle would bring that up. "I'm willing to keep up the role a little longer for appearance' sake. But we have to figure out a way to end it, soon, before Maggie gets hurt further."

South spread his hands. His voice softened. "Even if the two of you do have some misguided notions about each other, I don't see why that should affect our plans. What has happened that I don't know about? Things were going so well—" Before he allowed Grant to explain, he said, "Iris, would you mind if I spoke to Grant alone a moment?"

"Yes, I would," she said. "This concerns me as much as it does Grant."

"It's okay," Grant said, his intense expression telling her he'd like to tell her uncle a few things himself.

Iris didn't want to leave Grant alone, but his eyes encouraged her to do as he said. In all her twenty-eight years she had never understood her uncle. Maybe Grant would have a better chance if they had a little man talk between them. She couldn't put her uneasiness into words or know what to warn Grant about. After all, her uncle had always helped her when she had come to him with problems. "I'll go get a cup of coffee," she said. "But then I'm coming back."

The minute Iris was gone, South's dark eyes bore down on Grant. He slammed his fists on his desk. "What the hell do you think you're doing with Iris? The two of you in love, ha!" he barked. "If she's in love, and I have my doubts knowing that niece of mine, it can only be with this fantasy man we've created for Maggie."

Grant had expected South to be displeased, but he hadn't been prepared for such an outburst. "Iris has known from the beginning who I really am," Grant insisted. "And she wants to end this as much as I do."

South pushed back his chair and stood up to gain the power advantage. He stepped around his desk, looming in front of Grant. "You think so? Well, you just go back to living in that pigsty where we found you, and get your old job back at that hamburger joint, and see how long she stays with you."

Gripping the arms of his chair, Grant called up all the reserves of his acting skills and tucked his true emotions out of sight. He thought of the day Iris had found him in Eve's Garden and he had asked her, "If I had told you I was a short-order cook, would you have given me two minutes of your time?" When all the smoke screen of this deception was cleared away, nothing had changed between them, except one thing. "Iris loves me," he said with more conviction than he felt. "And I love her."

"You think that's enough to get you by in this world?" South laughed cynically. "Iris comes from the same mold as Maggie." South jabbed a fleshy finger at Grant's face. "She's never worked a day in her life. What she's doing here is just recreation, something to tell her friends about. She could just as easily take up needlepoint and it would be less of a headache to me. She's used to men with money, status and a career." South folded his arms across his chest and leaned against his desk. "She wouldn't last a month in your world."

"Iris is stronger than you give her credit," Grant said, his eyes steely as he looked for a chink in South's armor. He couldn't defend his own position, but he could stand up for the woman he loved.

South shrugged nonchalantly. "You think so? Then prove me wrong," he challenged, adding, "The only hope you have of winning Iris is to keep up this role we've designed for you. Play it through to its natural conclusion, no matter what it takes to keep Maggie happy." He thumped the first two fingers of his right hand against his left palm as he watched Grant. "And enjoy Iris as much as you can in the meantime, because the minute you are no longer Mr. Perfect, Iris will leave you quicker than sailors jumping off a sinking ship."

South's insinuations made him sick, but Grant said calmly, "Your emotional blackmail won't work on me. You can't manipulate human beings like chess pawns." Hadn't Bob said the same thing about Iris the day Grant had brought her home to dinner? "She's not one of us. How will you fit in her world?" Grant felt ill as he remembered his reply to Bob. "I'm an actor." But how would she feel when the act ended?

"You're the one who's going to come out on the short end if the truth comes out." South's words were like hammering nails in Grant's coffin. "Think about it." When Grant didn't reply, he stepped over to the window. With his back to Grant he said, "You play your part well, and I'll see that you're rewarded handsomely."

"I don't want your money any longer," Grant stated.

"I never did think you were worth what I'm paying you. But I'm a reasonable man. I can see about setting you up in some sort of respectable business after this is all over. I have a lot of connections in this town, and believe me, I can make or break anybody." South glanced over his shoulder at Grant and smiled. "Especially someone who's pretty near broke to begin with." The door of his office opened and Iris walked in, looking anxiously at both men.

South smiled pleasantly. "Well, here's Iris, Grant." His eyes were on Grant as he said, "I think we've managed to clear the air on several matters."

Grant nodded slowly. It was clear that South was in this for his own personal gains, regardless of anyone's feelings. In order to put an end to the perfect role, he and Iris would have to think of something without South's help.

"But what—how?" Iris demanded, looking from one to the other. "Will someone please tell me what's going on?" She pushed her glasses to the top of her head.

"I think Grant understands how important the upcoming *American Scene* interview is," South said, his eyes daring Grant to defy him. "It's crucial to go ahead with it." He paused, looking sadly at both of them, adding, "That is, if we don't want to hurt Maggie further. Remember last time when Winchester dumped her shortly before the interview?" He spread his hands helplessly. "And look what happened."

Iris glanced from her uncle to Grant. "We don't want to make things worse," Iris agreed. "But Uncle Edward—"

Grant stood and put his hands on Iris's shoulders, steering her toward the door despite her protests. "Come on, Iris. There's nothing we can do about anything here."

Iris tried to protest, but Grant urged her out of her uncle's office and steered her down the maze of hallways of South Publications. They stopped by the bank of elevators.

"I guess Uncle Edward's right," Iris said. "Everyone is expecting you to be on *American Scene* with Maggie. She would be hurt terribly if you backed out now."

Grant kept a smile on his face for the benefit of the receptionist who was watching them through the glass doors of South Publications. He punched the Down button. "Your uncle doesn't give a damn about anyone's feelings. All he cares about is money. It almost makes me glad I'm nothing but a cook. At least that's an honest living that doesn't damage people's lives." He jabbed the button again.

"Grant," Iris implored, "he's only thinking of Maggie. If you just didn't show up, imagine what it would do to her. We can't tell her the truth."

Grant's eyes narrowed as he looked at Iris. If she could be duped by that uncle of hers, maybe she *was* only in love with the role he was playing. "His sole concern is himself and his precious magazines. He doesn't care about Maggie, or you, or me."

She glanced toward the offices of South Publications and said, "Maybe I should talk to him alone."

"It won't do any good," Grant stated, impatiently pushing the elevator button again. "If anything's going to be done, we're going to have to do it ourselves, without your uncle's help."

"Then you'll do the interview?" Iris asked.

The number of their floor lighted up above the elevator. A bell rang. "Right now I don't know what I'm going to do. But contract or no, I'm not letting your uncle control me anymore."

Iris put her hand on Grant's as the elevator doors opened. "Grant, you can't just leave me hanging like this. We have to figure something out."

Grant braced his arm across the elevator doorway to hold the car. "I need some time alone to think."

Iris dropped her hand and stood helplessly in front of the elevator as he stepped inside. She felt as if he were leaving her and going much farther than the lobby floor.

Seeing the constricted look on her face, he reached out and snared her wrist, tugging her into the elevator with him just before the doors closed, sealing them inside. Grant pulled her into his arms and held her tightly.

"I don't want to hurt Maggie," Iris said, raising her chin and seeing the concern in his eyes.

"It'll be all right," he assured her. "We'll find a way out of this, together." He kissed her and held her until the car stopped and the doors opened on another floor. They were no longer alone. "I'll call you tonight," he said with a squeeze of her hand as the elevator opened onto the lobby and he stepped out.

When Iris returned to her desk, Maggie had returned and was beaming at her staff, who were waiting for their usual romance update. Iris wondered what she was so happy about. "Will you look at this?" Maggie said, opening the newspaper she had carried under her arm. Iris recognized it as one of Croft's favorite forums for gossip. Maggie spread the paper on her desk so that her women editors could see. Iris didn't think she could stand seeing another picture of Maggie wrapped around Grant. She hung behind the others.

A front-page photograph showed Bradley Winchester trying to hide his face as his young girlfriend, Liv Germaine, did a cancan kick on a tabletop. "Isn't it wonderful?" Maggie said, beaming. "The bimbo got up there and actually stripped in front of everyone. Poor Bradley, he was too much of a gentleman to run out of there, like any other man would have done, and got his picture in the paper, too." She sat behind her desk and turned the paper where she could look at the photo again. Maggie seemed on the verge of a smile. "Maybe this means there is still hope that Bradley will return to his senses, after all."

"Have you talked to Grant about *your* feelings for Bradley?" Iris asked, thinking this might be a way out for them. "I mean, it wouldn't be fair to lead Grant on if you still love Bradley."

"It doesn't matter how I feel about Bradley," Maggie snapped, her chilling professional tone and demeanor suddenly returning. "He left me." She folded the newspaper so that the photo was prominently displayed. "It's almost poetic justice. The woman is half Bradley's age. It had to end sooner or later. But I will enjoy turning him down if he comes running back to me."

Dawn asked Maggie for details about her date on Friday evening with Grant. Maggie blushed and said, "I don't want to talk about it now. Don't all of you have work to do?" Dawn raised her eyebrows in Iris's direction and led the staff out of Maggie's office.

When everyone but Iris had left, Maggie paced restlessly around her office and finally confided, "I think Grant is seeing someone else. What do you think I should do about it?"

Guilt, joy and trepidation filled Iris at once. "Are you sure?"

"I have no proof," Maggie answered, "but he's been acting strangely. I tried calling him all weekend but he was never home. I know he said he was going to be out of town, but if it was only business, wouldn't he have left a number where I could reach him?" She fingered a delicate blossom in another of the flower arrangements that the girls in the office kept sending in Grant's name. "Doesn't that sound like signs of infidelity to you?"

Everything felt like a dream to Iris. Maggie's voice sounded magnified. She seemed to be moving in slow motion. And all attention was directed at her. She knew this was the perfect chance to tell the truth, but she hesitated, imagining how Maggie would react. She thought of how wan and listless her boss had been right after Bradley Winchester had started seeing his new girlfriend. Maggie had put up a brave front for her staff, but Iris had caught her off guard and found her crying in quiet moments. But then she thought of how topsy-turvy her life had been since meeting Grant. And instead of enjoying his company and shouting her feelings to the world, she had to walk on eggshells around everyone because of Maggie. It wasn't fair.

Maggie pulled a rose from the bouquet and sniffed it as she walked around her desk to peer out of the corner windows. Iris knew that Maggie was myopic around men. That was part of the reason she had lost Bradley. She hadn't paid enough attention to him because of her self-interests. If she hadn't been so image conscious in the first place, Iris wouldn't have had to recruit Grant for this grand dating scheme. And if she ignored this opportunity to speak the truth, Maggie would get more deeply involved with Grant. Iris cleared her voice. "Maggie, there are some things you need to know about Grant."

"Yes, I'm sure there are," Maggie said, absent-mindedly running her finger along her lower lip as she stared out the window. "I wonder if Bradley's missing me now."

"Maggie, I'm trying to tell you about Grant," Iris said.

Her boss turned from the window, her eyes refocusing on Iris as if she had forgotten she was there. She waved her hand dismissively and said, "Oh, he'll probably explain everything when I see him tonight. Men like to keep women guessing their whereabouts. They think it somehow makes them more macho and mysterious." She glanced at her watch. "If you don't mind, Iris, can we have this chat later? I have several phone calls I'd like to make."

Iris stood her ground, weighing her options. It was obvious that Maggie wasn't in a mood to talk. Her mind was geared in what Iris termed her "one-track mode." Until she switched out of her self-centered dream-world, nothing anyone said about anything would have much impact. If she was going to tell Maggie the truth, she needed to pick a better time. Maybe she should just let sleeping dogs lie, as her uncle had urged.

Tina Powers stopped by Iris's desk later that morning. Iris made a show of going through Maggie's mail to avoid talking to Tina. She was supposed to start work on a new article about work pressures in women's lives, but her heart wasn't in it. She pushed the letters aside and hugged her stomach while Tina probed and prodded to find out what was wrong with Iris. "Are you sick?" she asked. "Can I get you something to drink?"

Needing to talk to someone, Iris realized Tina had been in on the charade from the beginning. It had been Tina who had first recognized Grant's potential as Mr. Perfect. Lifting worried eyes to her friend, Iris told her what had happened, how she and Grant had fallen in love and how Maggie was being hurt by the deception as much as they were.

"Wow," Tina said, her shoulders slumping as Iris filled her in on some of the details. "We've all been so busy playing with the perfect romance, I didn't even see this coming. I should have just kept my mouth shut when I saw him that night in the bar and none of this would have happened."

Iris wondered if things would have been worse if Grant had never come into their lives. She thought of him as he had been that morning, so close yet so far. It was as if a thick glass wall were keeping them apart. She felt a headache starting behind her eyes and pushed her glasses onto the crown of her head, massaging her temples.

Tina put her hands on her thighs and said, "What are you doing to do?"

Shaking her head, Iris murmured, "I don't know, but we've got do to something soon. Maggie's worrying about her womanhood because she can't get Grant to make love to her. Grant's uncomfortable around her because she's obsessed with the idea of seducing him. It makes me cringe just to think of the two of them alone together in a limousine, much less her apartment. I feel as if the world is spinning out of control around us." She laid her glasses on her desk and put her face in her hands. "Maybe Uncle Edward's right. What choice do we have but to see it through to its natural conclusion?"

Tina rested her hand on Iris's shoulder. "We can fight back."

"How?" Iris mumbled into her hands.

Tina chewed her lower lip in thought. "Well, we were the ones who created the perfect man that day in the photographer's studio. We can destroy him the same way."

Iris looked up at Tina, a flicker of hope in her eyes. "But I can't convene all the editors. Uncle Edward would fire everyone if he knew we were conspiring against him. He thinks this is great publicity for the magazine. He wants Grant to keep encouraging Maggie."

"We don't need everyone in on this. You and I can figure out something." Tina chewed her fingernails in thought. "I know," she squealed with delight. "We could fake Grant's death! The FBI and the CIA do it all the time. I don't know how you'd go about it, getting a new identity for him and all, but I'm sure we could find out."

"That's what got us into this mess in the first place," Iris reminded. Her headache felt worse. "We'd just be creating more lies and getting in deeper than we already are." She chewed her fingernail as they both thought in silence. "But since we publicly created Grant as a hero, let's publicly make him a rat." Her expression brightened as she thought of how to accomplish that. "We could get him to dance on some tabletops, or something, like Winchester's bimbo girlfriend."

"That's good," Tina agreed. "If he embarrasses Maggie badly enough she'll look like a fool if she *doesn't* dump him."

Iris put her chin in her hands and stared at a chip of plaster on the wall near the light switch. Before Grant had come into her life, she had lived a nice, predictable routine. Now her life was a complicated mess that she didn't know how to untangle. "If only Maggie would go back to Bradley."

"That would solve everyone's problems," Tina agreed. "But you heard her—she would love nothing better than turning Bradley down as revenge."

Iris ran her hands through her hair, then blew her nose with a tissue. "Why does love have to be so complicated?"

Tina put her hand on Iris's shoulder. "If it was easy, it wouldn't be so special." She sat in the chair beside Iris and said, "I really envy you."

"Me?" Iris rubbed her forehead. "Why?"

"You and Grant must really love each other to put up with this. Any other couple would have split the minute the going got rough. He must be a special guy, and loyal, too, if he turned down the chance to make love to Maggie."

"How can I get him out of this? What do we have to do to be free to love each other?"

Tina put her chin in her palm and was silent while thinking. "All Grant has to do is revert to type, be himself, do all the little things that annoy Maggie, all the things that annoy all women about men."

Iris listened attentively. It might work. "He could start smoking again," Iris suggested tentatively. She thought of his scratchy beard. "And quit shaving."

"Take Maggie to a Knicks game."

"And spend all day watching the sports channel on TV while listening to country music." It was an ideal solution since Maggie was in love with the image they had created for Grant, not the real man Iris knew who had a few annoying flaws.

"What's going on here?" Dawn asked as she passed Iris's desk and saw Iris and Tina huddled together.

"Nothing," Tina answered, swinging her leg. "We're just trying to think of ways to kill a romance. Don't you think it would make a good article?" She swiveled around and asked Dawn, "What turns you off about men?"

Dawn thought for a minute. "I hate it when they won't talk to you, when they say they're open but they're not. Oh, and it really gets me when a man expects me to pay for the date, or go Dutch. It's okay once in a while, but he should have told me that up front instead of when we were standing in front of the cash register."

"Let me write this down," Iris said, opening her desk drawer to remove paper. She adjusted her glasses in place and picked up a pen to make a list.

"I hate it when Harry starts taking off his clothes at the front door and leaves a little trail of laundry all over the apartment." Iris looked up to see that Dawn's assistant had overheard their discussion. Iris made a note, but the objective was to save Grant before he had to shed any clothing.

"After they take you to bed the romance wears off. No more flowers. No more little notes. They stop holding your hand, opening your door and eventually the sex stops, too," Tina said with a sigh. "But then you get to start the process all over again with a new man."

As other staff members overheard them and joined in to voice their gripes, Iris wrote as fast as she could. Tina's idea had unleashed a fury of pent-up complaints.

"Don't you just hate it when men have to have their night out with the boys?" Dawn asked.

"The only thing worse than a night with guys is a night spent with another woman. Men who think they have to date every woman in sight are not attractive," Tina said, smiling knowingly in Iris's direction.

Iris wrote "infidelity" in big letters. Maybe it was time she and Grant were open about their relationship.

GRANT ENTERED the penthouse apartment and remembered the day Iris had first brought him there. He had been so innocent then, filled with high hopes of renewing his dream of becoming an actor. He had wanted to impress Iris the same way he used to impress Eve when she was a little girl, by making her think of him as a hero. Acting was the only way he knew how.

He stepped over to the bank of windows and looked down on Central Park. There were people sitting on park benches, jogging, walking along the wooded pathways, all living normal lives. Grant longed to join them, to be as carefree as they appeared to be. But he couldn't because everyone, including Iris, thought he was someone other than who he truly was. He wished he could just run away from everything, the way he had done as a teenager, leaving school to become an actor.

He went into the master bedroom where he had stashed a pack of cigarettes and looked at all the fine clothes that South's money had bought. The clothes suited him. And he had enjoyed strutting around in them like a rich, European businessman, getting envious looks from women, being recognized on the street, having his picture in all the society pages, living with all the public trappings of wealth. Grant couldn't blame Iris if she had fallen in love with the role he had been playing for Maggie. Grant had fallen in love with the flashy character himself.

He pushed hangers around in the closet until he found a favorite pair of faded jeans. He tossed the Dior shirt he had been wearing onto the bed and pulled on a yellow T-shirt with the logo of the Pittsburgh Little Theater. He found the cigarettes and lit one with a match from a Grand Hyatt hotel folder. Who was he trying to fool? The penthouse, the expensive clothes, all came attached with very short strings to South's fingers. All actors were just puppets who couldn't do a thing without a writer and a director deciding which string to pull. No matter how glamorous a role they created, the actor reverted to a wooden-headed puppet at quitting time.

The old life wasn't so bad. He was as good a chef as his friend Oscar. People came into Eve's Garden because of *him*. Some liked to watch his shenanigans at the grill, but most kept coming back because of his gourmet specialties. Bob and Eve were making a profit. With the money he had saved from this stint with South he could become a full partner with them, as Bob had been urging him for months.

But what about Iris? Where did she fit into that scenario? More importantly, would she want to be part of that kind of middle-class world? He thought of the night he had first cooked for her, when he had asked the criteria for *her* Mr. Perfect. She hadn't given him any clues. She had merely asked him to be himself. Grant felt as if he had even failed in that. How could she know who the real Grant Peters was when he was just now coming to terms with that himself?

Grant had been sitting on the terrace chain-smoking for hours when Iris turned up unexpectedly at the penthouse. The stereo in the living room was playing country music tunes full blast. Iris noticed several cans of beer on the wrought-iron table next to his chair. She waited while he flipped off the stereo before she asked, "Grant, are you okay?"

He looked at her and wondered if she would still be with him when he went back to the work he knew best. "Oh, sure, I'm fine," he said.

Seeing him dressed in that ghastly T-shirt made her realize that while he looked terrific in a tuxedo or dinner jacket, he was most at ease like this. Iris smiled shakily and gave him a quick hug. He was probably still upset after their meeting with her uncle. "Grant, I have good news," she said. "We've figured out how to change you from Mr. Perfect into Mr. Perfectly Awful."

"Who's 'we'?"

"Tina and the other girls who created you. We're going to destroy the romance the same way we built it up. All you have to do is act out all the things that turn woman off about men. We've made a list."

Was South right? Did Iris have her own private agenda of ways to keep him looking like Mr. Perfect forever? He drew on the cigarette and didn't say anything.

Iris stopped babbling when she realized Grant wasn't listening too closely. She watched him curiously, wondering why he didn't seem more excited by her solution. Going to him, she took the cigarette from his hand and crushed it out, then twined her fingers with his and said, "Grant, don't you understand? We've figured a way out."

His eyes narrowed. "Before talking to South this morning, I was willing to stick it out a little longer, but now I'm not so sure it wouldn't be better to tell Maggie everything and just say to hell with this role."

"I almost told Maggie myself this morning," Iris admitted, her voice slow and solemn. "But the truth of what we've done would devastate her if it ever came out publicly. Now I'm glad she didn't really give me a chance to explain." She tightened the grip on his hand. "Grant, it'll just be a little bit longer, then we'll be free to see each other in public." When he continued to stare at her without saying a word, she added, "That is, if you still want me."

Want her. Lord, if only it was that simple. He didn't resist as she put her arms around him. Grant stroked her hair and wished he could voice his doubts. But South's words kept echoing in his mind, and he couldn't bring himself to ask Iris if they weren't true, because Grant was just as guilty in loving the pretense of being a successful man she could look up to. "I'm so damned afraid of losing you," he admitted, "I can't think straight."

She ran her hands over his chest, loving the feel of him, enjoying this moment alone. "I'm not going anywhere," Iris reassured. "And I don't want to share you with anyone." She smiled at him and said, "There are so many things I want to do with you—introduce you to some of my special friends who live on the Cape, and take you to some of my favorite art galleries, especially the one where I found most of my Aztec and Mayan artifacts. And I can't wait until you impress everyone by cooking a meal for them some night. My dinner parties will be the envy of everyone."

He felt the fine bones of Iris's shoulders and the softness of her breasts. He ran his fingers down the firmness of her rib cage and held her more tightly, wanting to memorize every detail of her for the time when he couldn't hold her. Grant crushed her more tightly to his chest, wanting to imprint his body on hers, to be joined with her in more than memory.

"Grant, aren't you listening?" she asked when he didn't say anything. "Don't you want to do those things with me? I don't mean to imply that we won't do what you enjoy also. But—"

"It's okay, Iris," he said, managing a smile so that she wouldn't guess the depth of his gloomy mood. He put his hand in her hair, cradling her close to him. "Everything you're suggesting sounds wonderful. Are you sure it's what *you* really want?"

"Grant," she whispered, "I love you." She felt the hardness of his thighs and the firm muscles of his chest. For an instant she resisted the flash of desire she felt at being in his arms. She had come here to talk. But she wanted to make love with him, here and now. She slid her hands beneath his T-shirt, loving the rough cushion of hair on his chest. She didn't think she could ever get enough of him. "We belong together," she said firmly. "I want everyone to know it."

Grant offered no resistance as she began to undress him. The seductive playfulness of her hands aroused him further. Grant took her hand and led her to the couch. Stripped of their clothing, all pretension was absent, the raw need for each other exposed. And it felt right. Grant sought solace in her body, embracing the look and feel and smell of Iris, loving the sight of her, marveling in the way they fit together. They belonged together, but could they be so well matched in public?

Caressing her with his hands and lips brought quivering delight to her skin and a heady, trusting look to her eyes. Grant felt his heart swell. He had to believe in what he saw now, the truth of their coming together. He wanted to brand her with his love, so that no matter what happened between them, she would always feel bound to him.

Lost in Grant's intimate touch, his lovemaking cut through the superficialities of the outside world and bared her vulnerabilities. His gentle caresses fired her senses, made her feel warm and accepted, free to express her most hidden desires.

Granted wanted to lead, but he also wanted to follow as he kneaded her muscles, wanting the moment to last forever, knowing it would end all too soon. As her own emotions matched his, he began murmuring senselessly as unsated love carried him over the brink and broke in a warm pool of longing for more.

It had never been like this before, so intense, consuming. Yet in the heat of their passion, they were still teaching and learning from each other, the desire to please making each caress a touch of pure love. Iris lay holding him tightly, whispering his name softly, over and over. She felt a bittersweet mixture of emotions, as if this were the last time they would be together. But that was silly. They were just beginning their relationship.

Grant eased his weight off of her and cuddled her closer, weaving his fingers into the lushness of her hair, kissing her lips and her cheeks. He drew back and traced the contours of her face. He could tell by the way she avoided his eyes that she was uncomfortable. He didn't need to ask what was wrong. He knew. He couldn't offer comfort and tell her everything would be all right. Because, as he held her in his arms and kissed her, he wasn't sure himself that he would ever come closer to living with a dream.

As tenderness replaced the passion, an ache filled his heart, and South's words echoed in his mind. "She won't stay with you." Reluctantly he sat up and picked up her clothes. "You'd better get dressed," he said. "I need a cigarette."

Iris held her clothes in her lap and watched his naked body as he moved across the room. His abruptness made her feel abandoned. "Grant," she said softly, "I love you."

Do you? his eyes asked, but he couldn't bring himself to say the words out loud. Only time would give him the answer. Right then he felt as if their time was running out. "I love you, too," he responded, pulling on his jeans. "But right now that doesn't change anything."

Iris started dressing, wondering why there was an undertone of anger in his voice. Hoping a lighthearted chatter would dispel his darkening mood, she said,

"Why don't we do something downright domestically disgusting tonight, like making homemade pasta together? I could run out and get some wine and we could make a big mess in the kitchen. We could play some Italian classical music to create a romantic mood instead of that country music you were playing earlier. Afterward, we could take a bubble bath together with scented candles, although it would probably take some in the industrial-strength size to get rid of the cigarette smell in here."

"So far you've named two things *you* don't like about me," he pointed out, zipping up the jeans. "Why don't you admit that you don't think I'm good enough the way I was before you 'created' me?"

"What are you talking about?" Iris said, surprised by his unexpected outburst. It took her a minute to realize what she had said that had upset him. "You knew all along I didn't like your smoking. If you didn't smoke you'd think it was an unpleasant smell, too. And as far as your taste in music goes, I've never held it against you. You don't care for my classical tapes, and I haven't made a big deal about that. If you don't like Italian we'll find something else."

Grant lit a cigarette. "Our differences go much deeper than personal habits and musical selections," he said, "or are you the only one who doesn't see that?"

"I don't understand what's gotten into you," she said. "We just made love together. What more do I have to do to show you I love you?"

He pulled the T-shirt over his head, then held out the hem so that she could read the logo. "Look at this, Iris. This stands for the man I really am, not the rich, international financier everyone wants me to be. When I go back to being a chef, can you tell me you're still going to love me without wishing I was that other person?"

Iris stared blankly at Grant, confused by her own uncertainties. What he was saying hurt, but she couldn't deny that the doubts were real. "Are you telling me you've been pretending with me?" she asked. "I told you a long time ago not to play games with me."

"Damn it, Iris!" he stormed. "I haven't been playing games with you, not in the way you mean. All I'm saying is maybe we've all been playing games with ourselves."

Her heart jolted in fear of losing him. She thought of all the tenderness he had shown her and the encouragement he had given her to pursue her dream of being a writer. He had made her feel important as someone other than Edward South's niece. "It isn't fair," she pleaded. "We haven't had a chance to find out who we are as a couple yet. We're just getting ready to start our life together."

"I don't know," Grant said, lighting a cigarette as he paced in front of her. "I just don't know anymore." He ran his hand through his hair, ruffling it askew, and looked at Iris. Sitting on the edge of the couch in front of him, she even had the same aristocratic carriage as her uncle. Were they really any different? "I'd like to believe it's that easy, but right now I just don't see any daylight at the end of the tunnel for us because of our backgrounds. We come from two different worlds."

Iris was still buttoning her blouse when the front door opened suddenly. She turned to find the doorman with his key still in the lock. Maggie stood in the hallway behind him. Iris felt her face blanch as Maggie strode past the uniformed doorman and stopped in the middle of the penthouse living room. Iris looked down at her blouse and hastily put her hand over the unfastened buttons.

"Sorry, sir," the doorman said when he saw Grant, "but Ms Maxwell, here, thought you weren't home. She said you were expecting her." Grant said something to the doorman, who quickly withdrew, leaving the three of them locked in a stony silence.

Chapter Eleven

"Have I come at a bad time?" Maggie said, her eyes overly bright and expectant, doing her best to hide her surprise at finding Iris here with Grant. Except for the rise and fall of her breasts from her rapid breathing, she stood as still as a statue, waiting for someone to say something.

The room was so quiet, Iris heard a clock ticking. "Maggie, I—you—we—" Iris knew she and Grant had to tell Maggie the truth now, but she didn't know how or where to begin. Her troubled eyes flew to Grant for help.

"Maggie," Grant said, stubbing out his cigarette, "I think you'd better sit down." How did he tell a woman who thought she loved him that he loved someone else? No one had written *this* scene into the script.

Maggie ignored his suggestion and frowned distastefully at the cigarette. "When did you start smoking, Grant? It's not like you."

"There's a lot you don't know about me," Grant said and repeated, "please sit down, Maggie." He made a move toward her, but Maggie sidestepped away. She looked at Iris. Her eyes took in the unbuttoned blouse and Iris's tousled hair. Her eyes flashed angrily, and then softened with a glaze of unshed tears. She folded her arms beneath her breasts and walked around the room as if she were an interior decorator about to make changes. Iris and Grant exchanged glances behind her back. Finally, she faced the view of Central Park, her shoulders shaking.

Giving Maggie time to compose herself, Iris finished buttoning her blouse and searched near the couch for her shoes. "Maggie," Iris said gently, "we didn't plan for this to happen." She looked directly at Grant. "But I love Grant." Iris wanted to go to Maggie, but she tried to put herself in Maggie's place. Would *she* want to be comforted by the woman who had betrayed her? "Maggie, I'm so sorry." She felt overwhelmed by guilt, knowing that her love for Grant was only part of the truth they had kept hidden.

When Maggie turned, her face was flushed with color, her eyes sparkling, but she was laughing instead of crying. Iris didn't know whether to feel relieved or alarmed.

"I suppose I should be grateful," she said as she laughed harder. Her hands shook, but she tried not to show it. "At least now I know there's nothing wrong with me as a woman." She looked at Grant. "The other night when—"

Grant finished for her. "I couldn't make love to you. It wasn't because I didn't find you attractive, but because I was thinking of Iris. That's the only reason, Maggie."

"Well," Maggie said, crossing the room to settle graciously in one of the overstuffed leather chairs. She held out her hand and studied her pink nails. "I suppose that's understandable. After all, Iris, you did come to know Grant through all the things I told you about him. And you were the one to select my gifts for him. And we were together the night of the charity ball." She combed her fingers through her blond hair and twirled a tendril thoughtfully.

Iris was wary of Maggie's calmness. It was like waiting for the eye of a hurricane to pass. When Sheila Croft had attacked her on TV, Maggie had invented Mr. Perfect. When Edward had pointed out that Maggie didn't have a man, Iris was sent in search of the impossible. Maggie had a talent for viewing life through rose-colored glasses. Should they tell her everything, shattering the last of her illusions now that she knew about their affair? "Maggie," she said tentatively, "are you okay?"

"This hasn't come as any great surprise," Maggie replied, her eyes glittering dangerously, "although I didn't expect it to be you, Iris."

"I wanted to say something this morning," Iris said helplessly, "but I didn't know how—"

"Maggie," Grant interrupted. He wouldn't let Iris take the blame for the lie they had all concocted. "Iris didn't want to hurt you. If anyone's at fault, it's me."

Maggie acted as if she hadn't heard a thing Grant or Iris had said. "What is that awful shirt you're wearing, Grant? You look terrible, darling." She fanned her face at the smoke in the room and crinkled her nose. Then very calmly she said, "This does change things a bit, doesn't it? I know there's a shortage of men and sharing is not an uncommon practice today. In fact, we have an article scheduled on that very topic for the next month's issue of the magazine. But I never thought it would happen to me."

"Maggie, I've been unfaithful to you," Grant said. The web of lies they had so innocently spun was spinning out of control, wrapping all of them in a tight, nasty, suffocating cocoon. "I don't intend to stop seeing Iris."

When Maggie's eyes met Grant, they were icy and distant. "Far be it from me to try and fight the call of the wild. All I ask is that you please be discreet, Grant."

"Maggie!" Iris gasped, thinking of how crazy it made her to think of Grant with Maggie. "How can you say that? I love Grant. And *he* loves *me*. We're not just playing around behind your back. We're serious about each other. And I'm not going to share Grant, even if you think you could."

Maggie wiggled her shoulders as if she had a sudden chill. "Iris, I don't think you understand. I need Grant. He's the only thing keeping Sheila Croft off my back."

"I don't believe this," Grant said, throwing his hands up in the air. "You're both acting like two old dogs with no teeth fighting over a bone. This has gone far enough. I can't pretend any longer. It just makes everything worse." Grant realized he had reached the point of no return. By killing the romance with Maggie, would he also be condemning his relationship with Iris to death?

"Pretend what?" Maggie said, curiosity outweighing her wounded pride.

Grant stood in front of Maggie. "I'm not the man you think I am," he confessed, speaking rapidly, as if he might change his mind if he didn't get it all out at once. "I'm an actor who Iris met in a bar one night. Edward South hired me to play the role of leading man for you."

Maggie's lower lip quivered. Her blue eyes seemed bigger. "He *paid* you to go out with me?" Her voice cracked, reflecting the anger building within her. "Like some tawdry gigolo?"

"It was the only thing we could think of to save face with Sheila Croft," Iris added hastily, wanting to acknowledge her role in the deception. "I couldn't find anyone who lived up to all of your expectations for the ideal man. But frankly, you've always asked too much of men, Maggie."

Maggie sat quietly, her hands calmly folded in her lap, as if she were listening to the reading of someone's last will and testament.

Grant felt the need to stand up for Iris. He had wanted the role more than anything and had left a good job to chase a stupid dream. "It seemed a sensible idea at the time. No one was going to get hurt by us making a few appearances together. We didn't count on it lasting this long, or having this result. We just didn't think it all through."

Iris kept waiting for Maggie to say something, to get angry or to cry. Her stillness was frightening. "Maggie, we know we've hurt you. Can you ever forgive us? We meant well, it just turned out so twisted."

Maggie lifted her shoulders nonchalantly, but her eyes reflected her pain. "Well," she said on a long sigh. "I'll just have to learn to live with it, then, because I'd rather have a slightly imperfect man than no man at all on *American Scene*."

"Maggie, it's over," Grant said wearily. "Give it up. I'm not anything like the man you think I am."

"So what?" Maggie said, turning her angry gaze on Grant. Tears of rage made her eyes bright. "I won't let Sheila Croft get the best of me. I'm sure Edward realized that when he hired you. And I'm not through with you, Grant Peters, whoever you are. You owe me. And you'd better believe me when I tell you I'm a woman who gets her money's worth."

IRIS SAT nervously on the edge of her chair as she and her uncle watched Maggie and Grant on TV. She would be so glad when this interview was over and Grant could stop the charade. Iris had convinced him that he had to make this final appearance. Because he loved Iris, Grant had agreed to play along. After all, now that Maggie knew the truth, they would be able to give a more convincing performance together.

For the greater part of an hour he had adequately fended questions with a suave performance that had enchanted the studio audience and kept Maggie smiling for the TV cameras. Sheila, who everyone had been so worried about, had sat pleasantly beside her husband, Sir Ashley Croft, looking like a pussycat. Iris kept waiting for her to sharpen her claws on something Grant or Maggie said.

"Sheila Croft must be having an off day," Iris commented to her uncle as they watched from his living room. "I've never seen her so reserved."

South kept his eyes glued to the TV screen, but his nervousness was revealed by his habit of pinching the ends of his mustache. "I took out a little insurance policy to make sure she'd mind her p's and q's this time," he mumbled.

Iris looked curiously at her uncle, who had been relieved to know that Maggie knew the truth about Grant and still wanted to continue their act. "What do you mean?"

He reached for his martini, found the glass empty and rose to pour another. "I hired a private investigator to take a hard look at the background of her husband, Sir Ashley. Information is power, you know."

On the TV screen, Grant was explaining how he had met Maggie, incorporating all three versions of the stories Croft had heard. Iris tensed, expecting her to take advantage of Grant's narrative, but she didn't say anything. "She's actually being *nice*," Iris said incredulously. "What did you find out about him?"

South smiled craftily. "Sir Ashley Croft is from New England, rather than merry old England. Boston, to be precise. His English accent is as phony as Grant's German. Sheila actually *bought* him his English title just to make him sound as if he's the landed gentry. It appears that Sheila had as much trouble finding Mr. Perfect as we did." He laughed at his own cleverness. "I let her know I'd make a few such facts publicly known if she gives Maggie any more trouble."

"Then our problems are over," Iris said with a relieved sigh. "If Croft backs off of Maggie, Grant can go back to leading a normal life."

"Oh no, it's far too late for that," South said, coming back to the couch with another drink. "Sheila may no longer be looking for loopholes in this romance of the century, but the rest of America is. I'm afraid this little role will have to be played out to a satisfactory conclusion."

Iris stared at her uncle. "You're acting as if Grant doesn't have a will of his own," Iris said. "He only agreed to go on *American Scene* because I convinced him he should. He doesn't want to play Mr. Perfect any longer."

"Grant's still under contract with me," South reminded gleefully. "And Maggie's not ready to let him go, either."

Iris looked at her uncle and saw him in his true colors for the first time. He loved playing God with other people's lives. No wonder he had remained single. No woman in her right mind would put up with him. Yet all this time, she had looked upon him as a benefactor. He had tricked her into thinking he really cared about her. Grant was right. Edward South only cared when his money was involved. "You're wrong about Grant," Iris said. "You'll see."

On the screen, the host of *American Scene*, Martin Langley, asked Grant, "What's in your future?"

Iris watched Grant as he said, "Since meeting Maggie, my life has totally turned around." That was certainly true, Iris thought, especially with all her help. "I'm thinking of spending more time in the States, going into the restaurant business, maybe opening a place of my own." Good for him, Iris thought. If that didn't prove her uncle's impotency, she didn't know what did.

Langley chuckled with the studio audience at Grant's reply and said, "No, I meant what's the future hold for you and Maggie? When's the wedding date?"

Before Grant could reply, Maggie answered, "We haven't set a firm date yet, but I've always loved summer weddings."

"What—what she means is that I haven't actually proposed," Grant stammered on TV. "We don't want to rush into things."

Iris turned accusing eyes on her uncle. "Did you put her up to this?"

South couldn't contain his amusement. "That would have been a little extreme, even for me. Maggie has a mind of her own," he said as he listened to Maggie expound on big church weddings and bridesmaids dressed in blue. "But it's not a bad idea. And it's certainly what everyone expects after all the times they've been seen together. It would get wonderful press."

"That's all you care about," Iris said, standing up as the host wrapped up the show. Unless Maggie took a gun and shot Grant, she didn't think anything worse could happen in the remaining minutes. "I was wrong about you, Uncle Edward. You don't play God. You're the Devil himself."

He looked as if it were a compliment. "Maybe so, but this devil wields a lot of power. Peters was an unknown actor before I hired him. And look where I've gotten him, on national TV. He knows a good thing when he sees it."

"Your interference has gotten him virtually engaged to Maggie on national TV. A woman whom he doesn't love, and who doesn't love him. I do!"

"Loveless marriages aren't anything new. You think Sheila and Sir Ashley of Boston really rip up the bed sheets together?" South asked. "Maggie and Grant look good together. You could even cover the wedding, Iris, under your new byline."

Iris snatched up her purse, ready to leave and said, "I don't want to write that story, or any story for you. You've intimidated Grant and me long enough. You never really cared about my writing, whether I had any talent or not. You were just pandering to me when you gave me that job."

"It seemed to make you so happy. I'm sorry you feel that way," he said, not denying the accusation.

As much as it hurt to give up the opportunity to have her own byline, Iris realized her uncle had manipulated her into being dependent on him long enough. By doing so he had kept her the same way he was trying to keep Grant—under his thumb. "Well, I don't want your job anymore, and I'm sure Grant will tell you the same thing." She headed for the door. She should have listened to Grant when he said he wanted to end it all before the interview. "And I won't come running to you for favors again, Uncle Edward. Your kind of help only hurts people."

"No," he said, making no move to stop her, "I suppose you'll go running to Grant. The two of you are so alike. You both have big dreams and hopes, but no way to make them come true." He paused with his drink halfway to this lips. "Just remember, Grant's not really the man he seems." He started laughing as Iris wrenched open the door. "The man you fell in love with only exists as long as I keep picking up the tab. Money may not buy love, but I've just proved it can buy a pretty good illusion of it."

Iris was seething with anger by the time she reached the sidewalk outside of her uncle's apartment building and hailed a cab. She couldn't get his taunts out of her mind. Like it or not, there was a lot of truth in what he had said. Grant's future without her uncle's help didn't appear to offer much. But then, neither did hers. Iris didn't mind a few imperfections, but she was afraid of living with another Mitch, a man who wouldn't take responsibility for his own actions, or his future. And she *did* care what her friends thought.

A boxy Yellow Cab pulled up to the curb. Iris opened the door and got in. "Where to?" the driver asked.

For a minute, Iris sat staring at the man. She didn't know where she was going, everything had happened so fast. She wanted to be with Grant, but he would still be at the TV studio, or with Maggie. When he asked her again, Iris gave him her own address.

The driver whistled. "Nice neighborhood. That where you live?"

Iris ignored him. Without her blue-blood standing and her family's money, she didn't have much to boast about. Grant may not have finished college, but all that Iris's fancy girls' schools had taught her were social graces. Grant at least had a goal to give his life direction. It wasn't his fault if his desire to be an actor had outweighed his talent. He had put his heart and soul into it, as he would do with anything he set his mind to, because he was a passionate person. Iris had merely decided that she wanted to be a writer and asked her uncle to wave his moneyed wand to make it happen for her. It was the easy way out.

And she had taken the easy way out marrying Mitch, because she had been afraid of being alone, and her uncle had said they would make a good match. She had even taken the easy route by hiring Grant rather than admitting to Maggie she couldn't find a man to meet her expectations. If she went home now, without letting Grant know how much she supported him, then she would be taking the coward's way out. She was ready to go after what she wanted—and that was the man she loved.

THE BARTENDER SLID another draft in front of Grant and removed the empty glass. "I hope you're not driving tonight," he said.

"Nope," Grant assured him. The chauffeured limousine was parked prominently out front awaiting his instructions. He picked up the glass and briefly stroked the chilled side against his cheek. This is where it had all started, where his life had started to go wrong the night he met Iris. He had been playing games that night, with her and with himself, pretending he had a bright future. Now, he didn't have a future or a past. Sheila

Croft had been right. It was as if Grant Peters didn't exist. He was nothing but an image created by Maggie's fantasies.

Grant took another swallow of beer and tried to forget the argument he had had with Maggie in the limo after the interview. "What do I have to do to get my life back? You made it sound like we were going to get married," he had demanded of her.

"I didn't plan this little scheme we find ourselves caught in the middle of," Maggie had reminded with frosted politeness. "But it has served the magazine well. And according to Edward, your contract is open-ended and can only be terminated by us. Do I need to remind you that you are being extremely well paid for your services?"

"Maybe so," Grant had admitted, "but I think you need reminding that your selfishness started all of this. I don't blame Bradley Winchester for finding someone else. You're too self-centered to notice anyone who doesn't polish your sphere of stylish vanity." Grant had watched Maggie's beautiful face flinch from the callousness of his statement, but at the time he had been so angry, he hadn't cared whether he hurt her or not. "If you would act more like a woman and less like a bureaucrat, none of us would have had to go through this ridiculous drama."

Grant didn't know who he was anymore. One more beer and maybe he wouldn't care. As he lifted his hand to signal the bartender for another round, he noticed his brother-in-law, Bob, enter the bar. Grant had phoned him from the limousine and asked him to meet him at Dream On. He knew that Bob and Eve had been watching the show from home. He had even asked them to tape his final performance. Grant had assured them it would be all over after that. Now, what he thought would be the final curtain had suddenly become only the end to act 1.

Grant signaled to let Bob know where he was. While Bob threaded his way through the bar, Grant shook another cigarette out of the pack, realized it was the last one and crushed the package. He left his empty glass behind and headed somewhat unsteadily for a vacant table where Bob joined him.

One thing about his brother-in-law, he had never been one to say "I told you so." Bob pulled his chair closer to the cocktail table and waited for Grant to speak first. The waitress stopped by their table to take their order.

"What are you drinking?" Bob asked.

"Beer," Grant mumbled. "They don't have hemlock."

"Guess I'll have the same," Bob said as the girl left to fill their order. He picked up a book of matches and twiddled it between his fingers. "Eve's pretty upset." He glowered at Grant. "What's all this business about marrying Maggie Maxwell?"

"That wasn't in the rehearsed dialogue. She just started ad-libbing, and I had to cover for her." He ran his hand over his face. "I tried to make it sound like it was something that had just come up in conversation, not anything definite between us."

"It didn't come off that way," Bob said. He kept flipping the match folder lid open and closed.

"Yeah, I know," Grant said miserably. "If she had just kept her mouth shut— Croft wasn't giving her a bit of trouble. Just a few minutes more and we would have been free of this whole mess. But no—"

The waitress returned with their drinks. Grant dug in his pocket and asked Bob, "Do you have any change for some cigarettes?" Bob laid a five-dollar bill on the waitress's tray while Grant told her which brand he'd like to have.

When she left, Grant laid his palms on the table and leaned closer to Bob. "Even when everyone follows the script, actors have no control over their personal lives. They're always pacing, waiting for someone to give them an audition. Or if they get the part, waiting for some writer to change their lines. And worst of all, when they're out of work, they're waiting for someone to give them another job. I'm tired of always waiting to live my life."

Bob tipped his glass to Grant's. "I wondered how long it would take you to realize that."

The waitress returned with the cigarettes. Grant opened the pack and quickly lit one up. "I told you the other night I was ready to quit when Maggie learned the truth. I didn't think things could get worse."

"Give it up, Grant, and come back to the restaurant with us."

"Believe me, I'd like nothing better," Grant assured him. "But how is it going to look for you having Grant Peters, well-known international financier, cooking for the Manhattan lunch crowd? And besides, I've got a contract to honor."

"Abraham Lincoln freed the slaves a long time ago, Grant. And who the hell cares what people think?" Bob said. "You're good at what you do. You've a hell of a talent as a chef that's just begging to be tapped. If you think I'm buttering your ego, I'll show you the books. The business has suffered since you left. Eve and I want you back. That's all that matters, what *we* think."

Grant gave his brother-in-law a half smile. Bob had never been one to mince words. Even when Grant had first come into the business, he had made it clear he was only giving Grant a job because Eve was his sister. Eve had always looked up to her big brother, thinking he could do no wrong. But Bob had also been the first to give Grant's innovative menus credit when the business started picking up. And Bob had been the one to make Grant believe he had talent as a chef. "I wish I could just walk out and put an end to this nightmare."

"So walk," Bob encouraged him. "They wouldn't dare sue you. The whole story would come out and then they would look as stupid as you feel." When Grant was silent, Bob read his mind. "You're thinking of Iris." He let out a weary sigh and sadly shook his head. "Grant, she's not one of us. She'll never be happy with your lifestyle."

Grant didn't need his brother-in-law stirring up the fears he had wrestled with since the meeting with South. "It's not just that," Grant said, running his hands up and down his glass of beer, pretending Iris wasn't his main concern. Grant wanted to disappear so that Iris would remember him as her Mr. Perfect, the same way his sister, Eve, always thought of Grant as her hero. "It's the whole notoriety that goes with being in the public eye. What are people going to say if I suddenly turn up as a chef tomorrow morning? There will have to be so many explanations."

"If that's all that's bothering *you*," Bob said, "then take a vacation for a while. Go visit your father. Go to a cooking school. Just disappear. People forget a lot quicker than you give them credit for."

Grant thought of his father and how he had reacted when Grant had left school to seek an acting career. "Be a man," his father had urged, "and stop running the minute life gets difficult. This acting is just playing at life. When are you going to get real, Grant?'' If he suddenly dropped out of character now, he'd be copping out again, just as he had done before. ''People don't forget,'' Grant said, thinking of how he had hurt his father. Iris, Maggie and a host of other people would be hurt if he admitted the fraud. ''I'm like a cornered animal. If I can't run, then I've got to fight.''

Chapter Twelve

The doorman at Grant's temporary Fifth Avenue apartment building stopped him on his way to the elevator when he returned home late that night. "Sir, I hope you don't mind, but you have a visitor waiting in your apartment. She assured me it was okay with you."

Grant ran a hand through his hair, wishing he hadn't drunk quite so much beer. Confronting Maggie again was more than he thought he could handle right then. "It's okay," Grant said wearily. Somehow he would have to put her off, unless she was up there with a minister or justice of the peace. And if that was the case, he could take advantage of the penthouse terrace to jump off the roof.

The apartment seemed empty when he first went inside. Grant tensed, wondering what surprises Maggie had in store for him. She wasn't in the kitchen or on the terrace. That left the bedroom. He prayed that his befuddled reflexes would be quick enough to slip out of her next contrivance. Grant went slowly down the hall, the plush carpeting cushioning his footfalls. When he reached the bedroom and saw Iris, he sagged in relief. "Thank God," he said, "it's you."

Iris jumped from the sound of his voice. She had been so busy with what she was doing, she hadn't heard

Grant come in. "Oh, Grant, you're here," she said, running to him and putting her arms around him. His clothes smelled of cigarettes and his breath of alcohol. She hugged him tightly, reassured to have his arms around her again. "I was beginning to think you were never coming back."

"Believe me, I considered it," he said, running his hands up and down her back, holding on to her as if he needed her for his strength. "I thought you were Maggie just now."

She looked up at him. "No, I—it's just me." In his absence her imagination had been running wild, thinking of him eloping with Maggie, spending the night with her.

He saw the question in her eyes and explained, "Maggie and I had an argument after the show. I guess you know she practically proposed to me."

Iris nodded and caught her lower lip between he teeth. "What did you tell her?" she asked.

"What do you think I told her?" he said in exasperation, dropping his hands as if she had accused him of adultery. "I'm not going to marry her. But I was so angry with her I didn't make much sense about anything else. After I dropped her off, I met Bob at Dream On." He looked beyond her to the bed where his new wardrobe was spread out. "What are you doing?"

Iris closed her eyes. Thank God her fears had been groundless. There was still time to help Grant. "I've been packing your clothes," she said, "so that we can go away together for a while until things calm down around here. It'd be like eloping. It would be the perfect time to meet my friends at the Cape and just take a vacation from life for a while."

"No," he said, putting some distance between them. He ran a hand over his hair and wished his head wasn't so foggy from all the drink. He shook his head and paced in front of the bed. Until now, seeing them stacked on the bed, Grant hadn't realized how many clothes he had accumulated from this role. He fingered one of the Christian Dior ties. This time the costumes wouldn't go back to the wardrobe mistress. "I can't go anywhere yet."

"But Grant," Iris said, cocking her head and looking at him curiously, "you have to."

He shook his head. "No, South was right about one thing." Grant took out some of the clothes she had folded into a laundry bag. "I have to play this out to its natural conclusion. I don't want a lot of untied shoelaces to trip over the rest of my life."

"Grant, the longer you keep pretending, the worse it's going to get." Iris put her hands on her hips and squinted at him. "We have to just walk away from it cold and let Maggie and Edward deal with the consequences the best way they can. You owe this to us."

"A few days ago you were begging me to keep acting," he reminded.

Iris went to him and wrapped her arms around his arm to stop him from unpacking everything she had just folded. "I was wrong to ask you to stay with Maggie until the interview was over. Maggie's as selfish as Uncle Edward. I should have listened to you when you said you wanted to get out of it then."

Gently he removed her arms from his. "Iris, I have to do this my way. I'm not playing by South's rules any longer. This time *I'm* writing the script. Listen to me. I have a plan."

"No. You won't listen to *me*!" she accused, feeling the panic rising, constricting her chest. "It's gotten out of control. I had a plan, too, remember, and it didn't work. Grant, this is bigger than both of us. You have to get out now." When he continued unpacking, her voice rose. "I told you a long time ago not to play games with me. If you see Maggie again, that's just what you'll be doing. Don't you see? They're never going to let it end."

He threw down the shirt in his hands and grasped her upper arms, forcing her to look at him. "I'm going to end it," he promised her, "but I have to end it as Mr. Perfect." He shook her gently, angry at Maggie, himself and all that his acting was doing to his love for Iris.

Iris jerked away from him, breathing rapidly. "You actually love this, don't you?" she accused, backing away from him so that she could see him more clearly. "The audience, the full house, having all of America waiting to hear what your next move as Mr. Romance is going to be. I don't think you want to end it at all." Images of Mitch flashed through her mind. He had played childish games, too. "Grant, when are you going to grow up?"

Grant felt a sense of déjà vu wash over him, as if he had had this same argument before. But last time it had been with his father. "That's what I'm trying to do now, if you'll just trust me to do it my way," he said angrily. "Iris, I'm doing this for us."

She stared unbelievingly at him. "No, you're doing this for you, Grant, and you're going to have to do it all by yourself." How could she fight for him if he could be so content to stay with Maggie and live the life Uncle Edward had arranged for him? "Well, I guess there's nothing else to say then, is there?" she said angrily. *Tell me you love me!* she wanted to scream, but when he continued to stare at her, she spun around and left him standing in the middle of the bedroom.

"My uncle was right," she yelled when she reached the front door and realized he hadn't followed her, hadn't even tried to stop her. "You're just a big pretender. You've been acting all along for Maggie *and* me." She wrenched open the door, wishing he would deny her accusation. But he didn't, so she stepped into the hall and forced herself to slam the door on him, hoping it would be as easy to shut the love out of her heart.

BRADLEY WINCHESTER SAT in the conference room of his theatrical agency reviewing tapes that had been sent to him by aspiring actors and actresses. As usual, he was rejecting far more than he was setting aside for follow-up with personal interviews. His thoughts were on Maggie and how beautiful she had looked the night of the charity ball. He had kept the newspaper clipping from the night on his desk, along with a stack of clippings in which she had been linked in recent weeks with that Peters kid.

Off to one side was the newspaper that had run Bradley's photo with Liv Germaine. His secretary had brought it to him, setting it quietly on his desk without a word. Winchester hadn't bothered to cut that one out. But he also hadn't brought himself to throw the newspaper away. He had kept it as a reminder of how miserable life had been with that outlandish artist.

His secretary, Mary, knocked softly at the door before entering his office. "This just came by special messenger," she said, handing him a package. "I thought you should see it right away."

Winchester nodded dispassionately and dismissed her, then punched the Rewind button on the VCR, needing a distraction. The package was attached to an envelope marked urgent, which he ignored. As he set about unwrapping the package, his thoughts again flew to Maggie, and his eyes strayed to the photograph he kept framed on his desk. It showed the two of them in one of their happier moments on Bradley's yacht. Maggie's hair was pulled back in a ponytail to keep it from getting tangled in the wind, and her nose was streaked with a generous dab of sunscreen. If Bradley hadn't been the one hugging her in the photo, he wouldn't have recognized her as the same glamorous woman depicted in the recent society pages.

"Damn it!" he muttered to himself, "I still love Maggie." He forced his attention away from the mementos of Maggie that surrounded him in his office and tried to concentrate on his work. The VCR clicked, signaling that the tape had come to the end. He ejected the rewound tape, set it on the Not Interested stack, and fed the tape from the special delivery package into the machine.

"Face it, Winchester," he scolded himself. "Your plan to incite Maggie's jealousy by having a little fling backfired. What woman wouldn't want Mr. Romance?" Someone like the Lothario on the screen in front of him. *Teenage Gigolo* Winchester rolled his eyes at the title, thinking of the lengths some actors went to to get his attention. He could close his eyes and tell the acting in this tape wasn't worth his time. He pushed the Fast Forward button, giving the actor the benefit of the doubt. In his present mood he would probably brand Robert Redford a two-bit player.

Winchester was just about to stop the tape when suddenly he realized what he was seeing. He sat straight and looked closely at the screen, playing the previous scene over, then advancing to other scenes on the tape. Maggie and Peters had been so heavily on his mind, at first he couldn't trust his eyes. He stopped the tape and ejected it from the VCR. The label confirmed his suspicions. The actor on the tape was Grant Peters. Frantically Winchester searched the desk for the package the tape had come in. He ripped open the envelope, which had been taped to the front, and read the short note. "Grant Peters will be at the bar Dream On this evening at seven. Maggie needs you." The address followed. He turned it over, back and front, but that was all there was.

Winchester fed the tape into the machine again and replayed the movie. But the acting was so bad he couldn't sit through its entirety. He picked up the note and reread it, then looked at his watch.

"GRANT, DARLING, that's the third time in less than five minutes that you've looked at your watch," Maggie said, crossing her elegant, silk-clad legs as she sat across the tiny cocktail table from him. "If you were concerned about being late for dinner, we didn't need to stop for a drink first." She looked around the room, as if searching for something to admire about the decor.

"I needed a drink," Grant said, motioning for the waitress to bring another round. If Winchester showed up, as Grant hoped he would after seeing his résumé tape, Grant would need more than a stiff drink for the ensuing encounter. "And we're not going to dinner together," he added. "I told you, we're here to talk. That's all."

"Then let's talk, dear," she said. "I have all night. And there's no one else I'd rather be seen with than you."

Grant glanced at his watch again. What if Winchester hadn't viewed the tape? It wouldn't be the first time a New York theatrical agent had ignored him. Surely the letter he had included with the delivery would get Winchester's attention. But what if he had been out of town? What if Grant had alerted all of the society photographers about their whereabouts in Dream On for nothing? He was nervous and miserable, wishing he could make amends with Iris, or at least explain. But he was also worried his plan might not work, which would prove Iris had been right. What if he was trapped in this soap opera nightmare forever?

He looked across at Maggie and felt sorry for what they had done to her. She wasn't a bad sort, basically shy beneath that hard, career edge. But he was also angry at her for making things worse. As he watched her beautiful eyes roaming listlessly around the room, he saw her expression suddenly change. Her big, blue eyes came to life, the same as when she had seen Winchester at the charity ball. Grant's back stiffened and his breathing became rapid and shallow. Winchester was here. That had to mean he still cared about Maggie. Grant prayed he cared enough.

"Why, hello, Bradley," Maggie said pleasantly as Winchester came up to their table and stopped beside Grant. "Where's your cute little artist friend? On a tour of nudist colonies?"

Twisting in his chair, Grant met Bradley Winchester's eyes, as dark as the devil's. Winchester's cheeks were gaunt, deeply sunken. His hair looked grayer than Grant remembered. His thin upper lip formed an uncompromising slash across his face. "You're a fraud, Peters," Winchester said, his voice low and threatening. "I'm here to see that you leave Maggie alone."

"Bradley?" Maggie said curiously, her face flushing, wondering how he had learned the truth. Had she been the last to know that Grant was an actor? "Leave Grant alone." She put her hand on his arm, goading him, "He's my Mr. Perfect."

"No, he's a fraud. Just a two-bit actor—a very bad one," Winchester informed her, pushing Maggie's hand aside. Grant made a show of protecting Maggie and started to rise from his chair. In his haste, his chair pivoted over into the couple at the table behind him. The woman screamed. Suddenly everyone's eyes were focused on the commotion at Grant's table.

Winchester grabbed Grant by the tie and pulled him up tight. His right arm was cocked back and his hand was rolled into a fist. "Maggie's my woman. You hurt her and I'll kill you," Winchester snarled.

Grant wished Winchester would hit him and get this scene over with. "If she's your woman," he said defying Winchester as the tie tightened around his neck like a hangman's noose, "why did you walk out on her? She told me you turned her in for a flashy new model."

"That's none of your business," Winchester growled, his nostrils flaring like a bull backed into a corner.

"I'd say it is," Grant reminded, "since Maggie has decided she's going to marry me. Women can trade in old lovers on new models, too." Grant didn't see Winchester's fist coming. All of a sudden there were lights, cameras and action. The next thing he knew someone was helping him up off the floor of the bar and Winchester was being physically restrained by the bar's bouncer. His mouth tasted disgusting from the blood streaming from his split lip.

"You leave Maggie alone," Winchester warned, "or that's just a taste of what you'll get from me. I'm not going to let her be played for a fool the way I was." He grasped Maggie's wrist, reeling her in close to his side. "Maggie, you're coming with me."

GRANT STARED at his lip in the mirror. The swelling had gone down and it didn't look too bad anymore. If he had had a mustache it wouldn't be the least bit noticeable. The bedroom of the penthouse apartment was reflected in the mirror. Grant peered at the room behind him where all of his clothes were spread out on the bed ready for packing as they had been the last time he had seen Iris. Now that his role as Maggie's Mr. Perfect had ended, it looked as if his own romance had ended with it. He had hoped Iris might call, at least to say she had seen the photograph of Winchester's macho return to Maggie.

Grant picked up a clipping from the society section and stared at the fuzzy newspaper photo, the last for his acting scrapbook. Winchester was standing over Grant, who lay sprawled on the floor. The only thing Grant recognized was his shoes. The caption read, "Bradley Winchester, theatrical agent, and Grant Peters, international businessman, duke it out over the queen of romance, Maggie Maxwell."

He rubbed his sore lip and returned to the business of packing in order to vacate the penthouse. Unlike the movies where fistfights were done by stuntmen, Winchester's blow had packed the full power of a man trying to protect the woman he loved. Grant was lucky he hadn't lost his front teeth. At least Maggie had loved Winchester's Errol Flynn style. The two of them had made the society pages every day since the bar brawl. Grant was publicly off the hook and could resume his life again. "Everything is coming up roses," Grant said sarcastically as he tossed things into boxes and suitcases. He'd rather have his Iris.

He tried to tell himself it was best to let it end this way, with Iris still thinking of him as Mr. Perfect. South was probably right, she wouldn't like living in his world. And that was obviously the reason he hadn't heard from her. The more things he packed, the angrier he became. They had been too good together to just throw it all away without a backward glance. Grant wasn't ready to give up so easily. If Iris didn't call him, he would go see her just as soon as he got settled into his new place. If their relationship had to end, he didn't want it to finish with bad feelings between them.

Grant had packed up everything from the bedroom and was just starting to collect his personal items from the kitchen when the doorbell rang. He set a carton of gourmet coffee items aside and went to answer the door.

Edward South invited himself into the room. Affronted, Grant remained beside the front door, keeping it open for his exit. "Did you come to collect the key?" Grant asked. His jaw clenched as he poised to tell South he could take the key and everything else and shove it.

After surveying the room, satisfied with signs of Grant's packing, South turned and faced him. "No, actually, I came to tell you how impressed I was with the way you managed to get Maggie and Winchester together again. Frankly Peters, I didn't think you could be that creative."

Grant stepped away from the door, but left it open. South had never been known for confrontations, and Grant wasn't going to encourage him. "It wasn't all that creative," he said cautiously, not certain he trusted Winchester's magnanimity. "It was more a sensitivity to other people's feelings."

"Whatever," South said, lifting his shoulders diffidently, "it did the trick." He glanced around the room. "You here alone?" When Grant nodded he said, "I half expected Iris to be here, but I guess I was right. The minute your 'perfect' world ended, she left you. That's my Iris."

Grant wished he could prove South wrong. "If you didn't come for the key, what are you doing here?"

South smiled. "To show you I'm a man of my word, I came to give you the bonus I promised."

Grant frowned as South reached into the vest pocket of his camel hair suit and pulled out a check. He held it out to Grant as if it were feeding time at the zoo. "Well, come and get it Peters, it's yours. You earned it."

Hesitantly Grant accepted the check and stared at the five figures.

"What's the matter?" South asked, grinning diabolically. "Isn't ten thousand dollars enough for you?"

"That's generous of you, Mr. South," he said, casually reaching in the T-shirt pocket for his cigarette lighter. "And I want to thank you for having given me this job. It taught me a lot about myself and what was really important to me. One of the things I learned was that dancing at the end of someone's strings isn't worth any amount of money."

"Money is everything in this world, Peters. Iris would still be here if you had learned that lesson."

"Well, let me show you what some people think about your money and power, Mr. South." Grant flicked his lighter and set the check on fire as if it were no more significant than a cigarette.

South frowned angrily, flashing dark eyes at Grant. "You're a fool, Peters."

"You're entitled to your opinions," Grant said, setting the burning check in an ashtray. "And I honestly don't care what you think anymore. I've fulfilled the contract, so our business together is finished."

"Do you need any help finding your way out, Uncle Edward?" Iris said icily.

Both men turned to find her standing in the open doorway. South glared angrily at Grant and said, "You two deserve each other." He brushed past Iris and slammed the door as he left the apartment.

Iris stood smiling at Grant, hoping he would forgive her for staying away so long, wishing he would take her in his arms and forget they had ever been apart. "Grant, you were wonderful," Iris said when she found her voice again. "I could never have stood up to my uncle that way." She pushed her glasses up the bridge of her nose.

At the sight of her, Grant broke into a wide smile, then winced as it gave his sore lip a twinge. "I didn't realize you were standing there," he admitted. She was wearing a white skirt and a yellow-and-white shirt over a sea-green tank top, which made her look like a breath of springtime to Grant.

"I wasn't certain you'd still be here," Iris said, running her hand up and down the narrow leather strap of her shoulder purse. She could hear her favorite classical music station playing softly in the background.

"I'm just packing up," he explained. And then before she could move, he went to her and took her in his arms. Iris sighed against him, her body molding to his, and he knew it would be all right between them. She had come back to him on her own. Somehow they would work through all the obstacles his role as Mr. Perfect had created for them. "I missed you," he whispered, nuzzling his face against her hair, loving the fresh scent of her perfume.

Iris held him tightly, resting her cheek against his chest. "I wanted to say I'm sorry about the other night," Iris murmured. "I kept thinking you might call. But I really can't blame you that you didn't."

"I was hoping *you* would," Grant admitted, "after you saw the paper."

"What paper?" she asked, nervously tossing her hair back from her face and peering up at him.

"All of the society columns from the past couple of days," Grant explained, "and especially the one that I arranged where Bradley Winchester punched me out. He and Maggie are back together again."

Iris shook her head. "No, I didn't see any of that. I didn't want to read those gossip pages because I couldn't bear the thought of seeing you with Maggie." A frown creased her forehead. "When did Bradley hit you? Did he hurt you?"

Grant felt his heart hammering and his confidence rising. "I can't say I didn't have it coming," Grant said, "but it wasn't as easy to take as a fight scene in a movie." He rubbed his jaw and explained how he had sent his résumé tape to Winchester's office and arranged to be in Dream On where Winchester could find him.

So that was his plan, she thought, staring at him with admiration, wishing she hadn't been so upset that she had refused to hear him out.

"Iris," he said softly, "we have to talk."

She nodded and pushed her hair out of her eyes. When she looked up at him, she was squinting, the way she did when she was standing too close to him without her glasses.

Grant swallowed. "You have to ask yourself if you really love me, a man who's not wealthy, who's just a chef—and a damned good one—but still struggling to build a career for himself. I want the truth. No games between us, remember?"

She looked down. Her heart caught in her throat. "What you're asking is can I love you as you are? Can we blend our two very different worlds together?"

"Yes," he said. All the doubts were hammering at his breast. At least now he was facing his fears instead of pretending they would go away by not bringing them in the open. But echoes of South's voice and Bob's warning seemed no less strident.

"Grant, I can't give you an absolute answer. And to be fair, you can't for me, either." She took a deep breath. "We've had so little time together aside from the stress of this whole affair with Maggie. You've brought such joyous dimension to my life. Before you everything seems flat. But all I can say to your question is I very much would like the chance to know you better, in every way possible. I do love you."

"Oh, baby," he said, hugging her closer to him. Together they would work it out, in their own way, regardless of how it looked to outsiders. They held each other, savoring the warmth of another's love, which they had missed in their days apart. The soft, romantic strains of a Chopin waltz lightly filled the room from the radio.

"When did your taste change for classical music?" Iris asked with a smile as they drew apart.

"The day I met you," he said, pushing a strand of hair out of her eyes. Then he shrugged and confessed, "At least I'm trying to get used to it."

Iris laughed and slipped out of his grasp to change the station, searching for the country tunes she knew he loved. "I can make a few compromises, too, you know." She hugged him tighter. "Grant, I was drifting, just like you," she said, clinging to him as if they had been apart for years instead of days. "But I didn't realize just how much I had allowed my uncle to chart my course. I'm through with that now. I want to make something of myself so that you'll be proud of me."

"I'm already proud of you," he said. The expression on his face made him look like a child on Christmas morning. He felt as if his heart were lodged somewhere between his chest and his mouth. "You're so sensitive to everyone's feelings, so loving and caring. I couldn't stand the thought of losing you, but I was so afraid you were in love with Mr. Perfect, not Grant Peters."

"Part of me is," she admitted, smiling up at him, "but I won't hold that against you as long as you can fall in love with a secretary for the IRS." When he laughed softly against her ear she told him, "I want to try to get a job on a newspaper or magazine, somewhere that Edward South doesn't have an ounce of influence."

"You're a good writer," he said. "I'm sure you won't have a bit of trouble getting a job. Or you could always write menus for me. I'm going to become a full partner in Eve's Garden."

Iris drew away from him, pleased by his decision. "You know, I once offered to set you up in your own restaurant. The offer still stands if you're interested. I'd like for us to be partners in everything, Grant."

"That's generous of you, Iris," he answered. "But I don't want to take any more shortcuts in my life. I want to do things myself, for both of us." He ran his fingers through her silky hair. "At least now I know what I want to do with the rest of my life."

"And what about the rest of your day," she said throatily, running her hands over the muscles of his back, loving the feel of her man, "now that we're together again?"

"Well," he said, taking her hand and leading her toward the bedroom, "we could always cook."

Epilogue

Iris watched the steam curl up from the coffee cup that Grant had just brought her. It was sitting in the midst of a wide variety of his cookbooks, which he had used to plan the new menu at Eve's Garden. Iris had spread out the cookbooks over one of the tabletops in a corner of the restaurant in an effort to organize her project. She wanted to create an eye-catching new menu to complement the recently remodeled restaurant.

Iris had been delighted to contribute her talents to the family business. It made her feel even closer to Grant, who had told her from the beginning that he needed her support and encouragement, but he didn't want her money to influence his career as the restaurant's gourmet chef. But she was having difficulty concentrating this morning because, as usual, her thoughts were filled with Grant and the conversation they had had the previous evening.

"It's still good, isn't it?" Grant had asked as they lay in bed reading, rubbing toes together and snuggling cozily every time one of them turned a page on a chapter or reached for a different magazine from the stack that had been accumulating. "I mean, here it is nearly a year since we got married, and it feels just as exciting to me as that weekend we spent in Connecticut."

"It's better," Iris agreed, giving him a hug and readjusting her reading glasses as they went askew from kissing him. She gave him an intimate squeeze. "I love moments like this."

"Me, too." He tossed his magazine to the floor and rolled over to gather her into his arms. "You're still as sexy to me as you were back then when all I could do was dream about being with you because we couldn't be together."

Iris giggled as his kisses behind her ear started to tickle. "Stop that. Be serious." She laughed.

"I am being serious," he said, slipping his hand beneath the bodice of her lacy gown and kissing her neck. "We're so good together, I sometimes can't imagine how it could be any better."

"I know," Iris agreed, stroking his hair and rubbing his back. "I can't, either, unless we were to have a baby."

"Umm," he murmured, his lips against her shoulder. "I've been thinking that, too."

"You have?" Gently Iris pushed him away from her so that she could read his eyes. "Really?" With the remodeling project at the restaurant occupying so much of Grant's time and her own work on the staff of a small neighborhood newspaper keeping her busy, Iris hadn't wanted to bring up such an important personal subject. But the thought of a baby had been constantly on her mind.

Grant nodded, and his lips spread into a grin. He knew how much that would please Iris. And he couldn't think of anything more wonderful than creating a new life between them, watching a baby grow and knowing it was theirs. "As good as business has been since Bob and I became partners, I figure we're going to need some good, cheap child labor in a couple of years.

Where else can you get good help but from your own family?''

''I never realized you were such a schemer,'' Iris said, laughing. As lighthearted as his reasoning was, she knew that Grant wanted children, too. He had told her that the first evening he had come to her house.

''Two or three busboys would be an asset to the business, don't you think?''

''What if they're busgirls?''

''I could live with that,'' he assured her, ''very nicely.'' He kissed her. ''Don't you think we should get started on this plan now?''

Iris tightened her arms around him in a loving hug. ''You really are perfect, Mr. Peters, for me.''

''How's it going?'' Eve asked, startling Iris out of her deep thoughts. She pulled back a chair and sat next to her sister-in-law.

Smiling, Iris said, ''I'm having trouble concentrating on food this morning.'' She thumbed through one of the cookbooks in front of her and made a face at the others.

Eve looked at the room that she had helped redecorate. Workmen had knocked out a wall in order to add more dining space. They had boarded up the picture windows in front and expanded into the rear to create an intimate garden area. Bob was hammering near the redesigned entrance in order to hang some of the personal treasures from their travels that he and Eve had kept stored in boxes until now. The effect gave the room a homey atmosphere with a more-sophisticated face-lift. ''I'll be so glad when we reopen on Monday. All of the construction work has given me a headache. Bob,'' she yelled, ''can't you find somewhere else to work for a while? Iris is trying to write.''

"No, no," Iris protested when he stopped hammering and glanced apologetically over his shoulder at the two women. She scooted her chair back to face him. "It's okay, Bob. You're not disturbing me." Workmen who were installing the new sign had been coming in and out of the restaurant all morning, but Iris had barely paid attention to them.

"You sure?" he asked. "I'm almost finished here anyway."

She waved for Bob to continue with his work. Iris smiled at Eve's husband. He had been a little slow to accept her into the family. But once he realized how much Iris loved Grant and that she wasn't the snob he had prejudged her to be, he had relaxed around her. Now, Iris felt closer to him than she had ever felt to her uncle, and they treated each other with respect. "I can't concentrate," Iris told Eve, "because of Grant. Last night we decided it's time to start a family."

"That's terrific," Eve said. "I wondered how long you'd wait, especially since you won't have to hire any baby-sitters with Bob and me so close. But what about your writing?"

Iris's grin widened. She played with her pen. "The only reservation Grant had about our having a baby now was over that point. He wasn't sure I should give up my work."

"He is your number one fan," Eve agreed.

"Oh, I know," Iris said. "I couldn't ask for a more supportive husband."

"Having a baby doesn't mean the rest of your life has to go into mothballs."

"I know." Iris picked up her coffee cup and stared dreamily at the wall. "It's meant so much to me to see my stories in print and to know it's because my new editor recognizes my talent. I don't want to give that up.

It's wonderful to know that Grant thinks it's important, too."

A month after Iris had quit her job at *New Age Woman*, she had found a job on *Our Place*, a neighborhood newspaper that had a small staff but was the ideal place to showcase her work. She had been assigned the arts and entertainment columns, which was what she knew and loved best. Occasionally she wrote how-to articles from her personal experiences, which the editor was always happy to use in his continual hunger for new material. Her most recent article had been "How to Cope When Your Spouse Stops Smoking."

Setting her coffee cup down, Iris said, "I was thinking of asking my editor if I can work part-time." She looked at Eve as a sounding board. "Since Grant and I don't need the money from my job, I don't have to work eight hour days to prove I'm a writer. As long as I keep my hand in, I'll be happy."

Bob stopped hammering, adjusted the cuckoo clock on the nail and asked, "Is this thing up there straight?"

"It looks fine," Eve answered.

"I wonder if that guy's finished with the new sign," he said, and went outside to check on the progress.

"From what you've told me about your boss," Eve said, turning back to Iris, "he'd probably agree to anything just so that he wouldn't lose you." Eve smiled and patted her sister-in-law's hand. "I know that's how we feel about you. You've been so good for Grant. Even Dad said so the other night when I called him. By the way, he's coming out next week to see all the changes we've made in the restaurant."

Some of the strain between Grant and his father had eased when Grant married Iris and when Alex Peters realized that his son had finally put thoughts of an acting career behind him. A baby would surely bring them closer. "He's been so indulgent with me, I hate to think how he'll be with a grandchild."

"You'll keep him in line," Eve assured her, "the same way you keep my brother on track."

"Talking about me again?" Grant said as he came into the room wiping wet hands down his jeans. They were stained with potting soil from his work in the garden room.

"Your father's coming for a visit next week, Grant," Iris said.

"Oh?" He stopped at the table behind Iris and put his hands on her shoulders. "Is he staying with us?"

"No. He's staying with us," Eve answered. As Grant affectionately nuzzled Iris's cheek, she feigned a shocked expression. "Please, not in public. Save your energy for when you're alone and can concentrate on making a baby."

Grant chuckled and wrapped his arms around Iris from behind. He rested his chin against the top of her head. "We've been practicing that for months." When Eve laughed at his cockiness, he kissed Iris again and straightened, keeping his hands on her shoulders. "I just finished repotting that Norfolk pine the Winchesters gave us for a Christmas present. But I can't figure out where it would look best. Since you two are so good at rearranging furniture, why don't you advise me on the plant?"

Eve rolled her eyes as if to say all men were helpless without women, but her smile said she loved that particular imbalance. She shoved back her chair and rose.

Grant politely helped Iris with her chair and kept his arm around her shoulders as the three of them walked to the rear of the restaurant. There was a trail of potting soil across the brick flooring, which Eve and Iris exchanged glances over but remained silent about.

Neatness had never been Grant's strong suit. "What do you think?" he asked, standing beside the tree, which he had left in the middle of the room.

"You could have at least put it somewhere out of the way," Eve commented, "so that we'd have an idea of where it should go."

"Knowing that you would probably make me roll it all around the room anyway," Grant told his sister, "I left it in this convenient, central location." He put his hands on his hips. "Well? Where do you want it first?"

Iris folded her arms and smiled at the two of them arguing over the tree. She was glad that they were keeping it in the restaurant since the tree was a symbol of how she and Grant had met. When Bradley and Maggie had brought it to them at Christmas, Iris knew all hard feelings had been healed between them. Bradley had even taken Grant aside and thanked him for making Maggie realize that she belonged with him. Iris wished it had only been that simple at the time.

Since then, Bradley had gotten in the habit of taking prospective acting clients to the restaurant for business lunches. Iris had felt a bit uneasy about that, thinking that it would make Grant nostalgic for the life he had given up in order to be a chef. But Grant had said he had no regrets. If anything, he felt sorry sometimes for those aspiring actors and the uncertainties of that lifestyle.

Even Uncle Edward had come to accept Grant with grudging respect. Iris stayed in touch with him because he was family. But she let him know that she was happy in her life with Grant, and didn't need her uncle to lean on any longer.

"I like the tree there," Iris agreed after Grant rolled it into the far corner of the room. "It puts this table in a romantic sort of niche." She moved to stand beside Grant, slipping her arm around his waist.

"Perfect for hiding behind for kisses," Eve decided, and realized Grant and Iris had forgotten she was there.

PAMELA BROWNING

. . . is fireworks on the green at the Fourth of July and prayers said around the Thanksgiving table. It is the dream of freedom realized in thousands of small towns across this great nation.

But mostly, the Heartland is its people. People who care about and help one another. People who cherish traditional values and give to their children the greatest gift, the gift of love.

American Romance presents HEARTLAND, an emotional trilogy about people whose memories, hopes and dreams are bound up in the acres they farm.

HEARTLAND . . . the story of America.

Don't miss these heartfelt stories: American Romance #237 SIMPLE GIFTS (March), #241 FLY AWAY (April), and #245 HARVEST HOME (May).

Harlequin American Romance

COMING NEXT MONTH

#249 MATCHED SET by Karen Toller Whittenburg

There was plenty of room in Lesley's Texas home for her and her son, as well as her aunt and uncle, but she had no intention of taking in boarders. But Aunt Bentley had other ideas and, on her own, struck a deal with Adam Frazier and his young daughter. Suddenly the sprawling house seemed stifling. Could Lesley keep her distance from the handsome stranger?

#250 WE GIVE THANKS by Linda Randall Wisdom

Sara Murdock had been ostracized from the small North Carolina town of her birth ever since she had returned fifteen years ago with her infant son—and no husband. But she'd struggled to make a home in the only place she had roots. Then the new preacher arrived. The appearance of Jess Larkin meant one thing: the truth about her son's parentage was about to explode all over town.

#251 HONEYMOON HOTEL by Barbara Bretton

Pocono Mountain honeymoon hotels meant waterbeds and heart-shaped tubs to John. But to Maggie they meant adventure. Ringed by barbed wire, surrounded by security guards, her little inn had been commandeered by PAX, the secret organization that was about to plunge Maggie and John into an exciting and dangerous world where fantasy and reality become one.

#252 A COLONEL FOR JENNY by Anne Henry

Researching the history of an old mansion introduced Jenny Bishop to Colonel Stephen Carmichael. But too quickly Stephen became more than a client, and too late Jenny found out he was not a free man. She'd heard the lies, now she wanted the truth. What was the real story about his wife and daughter?